COLD PLATE SPECIAL

COLD PLATE SPECIAL

ROB WIDDICOMBE

SALTIMBANQUE BOOKS

NEW YORK

Dedicated to the memory of
Mike "Cinderblock" Holtzman

COLD PLATE SPECIAL

1

KILLING MOTORCAR WAS something I had not thought about in a long time. A good long time. Maybe a year. Ten solid months at least. I was done with all that. Completely done. Sure, he would still cross my mind every now and then in a fleeting way, like anyone from your past will pop into your head for no special reason—a teacher or a neighbor or a distant uncle. But it had been a while since I last fantasized about putting Motorcar's lights out, an act I used to visualize constantly and in glorious variety and detail. When things started getting better, the fantasies stopped. I thought I was cured.

I thought it was over.

The cheap walls of my cubicle were covered with a pale charcoal blue fabric. A kind of glorified burlap. Lately I had been spending a lot of time staring into their blue charcoal depths. I drew a weird comfort from losing myself in the cool span of blue-gray fibers, the rough and fuzzy texture. My eyes zoomed out, zoomed in. Lately the boredom had been gripping me by the back of the neck. The documents, the e-mails, the computer screen, the technical difference between paper clips and binder clips. The minutiae of every blah detail. The nervous buzzing from the overhead fluorescent lights. How the broken copier vibrated and knocked like a washing machine with a lopsided load. The sick waves of fake butter smell from Renada's microwave popcorn that roamed the cubicle paths like a toxic industrial gas. And there was Jeff Teeler down in Trusts & Estates with his air whistling. He knew that full-on whistling was unacceptable in a professional law office, so he whistled silently. Teeler's peppy birdsong was so muted that all you could hear was the air blowing through his lips. Whatever the tune was, only he knew. I kept meaning to call him out on it, but I could never find the right words. Something like: *What's that hit song you're not whistling there, eh Teeler?* But by the time I had thought of something good to zing him with, he had already blown on by.

The office walls and carpet were beige like a flooding river of bad milk, swallowing everything. The bathroom was beige. The filing cabinets were beige. The people I worked with, beige. My enthusiasm for the job, even beiger. At home in my tiny suburban Maryland cookie-cutter apartment, the tan carpet and the eggshell white walls joined forces to create an overall theme of quietly muted beige. And according to my lease, I wasn't allowed to paint. I couldn't get away from it—the safest, least offensive, most neutrally dull color ever invented.

But beige did seem to perfectly match my milquetoast existence at Reinhaus, Thompkins & Watts LLP. The job was cheese-grater-to-the-brain times a million. At my interview, they made the whole paralegal thing sound like I'd be privy to all these hot cases. A "key team player," they said. Somewhere along the way they forgot to mention the illustrious title of Glorified Copy Clerk. Or the ever-exciting Kid Fetch-a-File. Wait until I'm a lawyer, I told myself, then I'll be the one who makes the paralegals and secretaries run around like headless chickens on a mad scavenger hunt. Hail Mr. Jarvis T. Henders, Esquire, they shall chant unto me. And of course, I will constantly be smoking everyone's ass with ice-hot verbal zingers. *Those documents aren't going to redact themselves, Colonel Bozo. Chop chop!* I couldn't wait. I was just paying the proverbial dues. And these dues had to be paid because without the paralegal tag on my résumé and some bitchin' LSAT scores, no half-decent law school would even glance at me sideways. My college grades were nearly toast after my second trip to rehab in three semesters. Or was it three trips in two? Did the one I skip out on after four days even count? Now I was sober and awesome, and with the paralegal cred, I'd be able to form myself into prime lawyer material. It was all part of my Master Plan (the "MP") to become the stellar legal genius who saves the world, while unceremoniously crushing my adversaries under a brutal iron foot. Also included in the MP was the mega-mansion. The killer speed-boat. State-of-the-art satellite home theater system with triple quadraphonic sound, if they have that. And of course the Italian marble Jacuzzi with high-intensity jets capable of Swedish deep tissue massage—something I could really appreciate after a long hard day of suing people.

Until then, I would have to wade through the beige like a one-eyed robot with a dimming battery pack. I was sick of everything in the world and wanted to die, but overall somehow I actually felt pretty good. Maybe even great. Yeah, definitely real great. Then after lunch I found myself sitting there, zoning out in the cube again. I started thinking about how a vodka tonic sure would cut the boredom. Just one, a little one, to slice through the sterile medicine fog. Just a little teeny tiny one. But as I knew all too well—one becomes five and it doubles from there. Then the army of flying electric space robots comes swarming back in and that was it. Toastville. Some people drink too much and crash their car. I black-out and see flying space robots kickboxing with Zeus at the epicenter of a galaxy-wide nuclear accident hoe-down. Stuff like that. Meanwhile, back in reality, my ass would be getting tossed out of the bar for throwing a wild flurry of random air punches or yakking on a waitress. I was amazed they ever let me back into Cogbill's.

So I focused my attentions on coffee. Coffee was wholesome. Coffee was real. And what could be more real than its rich dark roasted glory, steaming and eager in the cup, with seven teaspoons of sugar and its promise of unconditional caffeine? Or my beloved instant iced tea, stirred to blackness, keeping me alive, keeping me going.

Keeping me sane.

Keeping the flying space robots out in space where they belong.

I tapped my fingers on the desk and scratched the back of my neck, even though it didn't itch. I listened for Teeler's silent whistling but didn't hear anything. I looked at the clock. Everything is great, I told myself. Really, really great. Soon this general lameness will pass and my world will explode into a stunning electric blossom of awesomeness. Yet the longer this went on, the more it felt like something underneath it all was wrong. Something was off. Something major. I could feel it sloshing around in the raw nerves at the bottom of my stomach like a cluster of evil swamp worms.

And I knew exactly what it was.

Motorcar.

He'd been creeping back into my consciousness lately. Maybe the work tedium had made me vulnerable. I had this nervous stomach condition going back years, and the grotesque thought of Motorcar was like a cinder block slowly dropping to the bottom of a gurgling death lagoon, otherwise known as my guts. Then it spread out from there like a cloud of nuclear hell waste, all the way from my stomach to my fingernails. There was nothing I could do about it. The only thing that ever helped was getting blitzed.

Motorcar.

Damn him.

Before long I was flirting with the ideas again. The things I could do to him with a shovel. With an axe. A 55-gallon barrel of cyanide. Everything would be fixed if I could have just closed my eyes and died. Unfortunately, that was impossible. So I just swallowed it down and went and got another cup of coffee. And then another cup.

And then another.

2

CARLY LOVED STEAK. She knew all the cuts. Knew that a New York strip was better than a rib-eye, but nothing could touch an aged, grass-fed, center-cut filet. She was very particular about done-ness, too. In her opinion, anyone who wanted it cooked medium to well-done was an unredeemable pussy. She wanted it as bloody as possible. And washing down each bite with a fine red wine was absolutely mandatory. But I had to skip that part, to her infinite disgust. When she and I were first going out, the steak thing impressed me. Here was a girl who knew what she wanted, and she wanted only the finest in meats. But after about a hundred dates at Eddie's House of Prime, I wasn't as impressed. Eddie's was the most expensive steakhouse in a thirty-mile radius and I was so full of excellent steak I was starting to get puffy cheeks and a spare tire. One time I suggested we go to Outback or J.J.'s Bar-B-Que and you'd have thought I was promoting Cheez-Whiz on Saltines as the featured hors d'oeuvres at her wedding gala.

"Are you kidding me?" she said. "Outback? Skank meat."

"But Eddie. He's killing my bank account."

"What bank account?" She laughed at her own hilarity. Then she got all serious. "If you're gonna be a rich lawyer and treat me to the good life one day, you'd better get used to it now."

"Yeah. The good life. I'm getting there."

I ran my finger up and down the non-steak choices. Carly didn't even need to look at the menu.

"What are you getting?" she asked.

"Oh, I dunno. Chicken fingers?"

"That's an appetizer."

"I had a pineapple bacon burger for lunch."

She rolled her eyes. "Uh…weirdo?"

"What?"

"No, it's just a little strange that you would eat such a big lunch when you knew we were going out to eat."

"We always go out to eat."

She gave me a death look.

"Sorry—I was hungry."

"But you're not hungry now are you, dork-wad?" Carly would have smoked me as a lawyer. She was always ready with a holster full of barn-burning zingers. I just sat there and stared at a blank spot on the menu and wished I was someone else.

Carly started tapping a fingernail against her water glass, so I knew she was about to say something. "Aren't you going to ask me what I'm getting?" She smiled like it was going to be this earth-shifting, royal surprise.

"What?"

"Guess."

"I don't want to guess."

"Guess anyway."

"Okay," I said. "A twelve-ounce strip, bloody."

"Nope. The filet. Mooing."

"Right. Still mooing."

For all Carly's massive intake of partially cooked beef, she was actually skinny. She was also kill-me-now gorgeous, with these smoky cat eyes that had this way of narrowing and hypnotizing me into giving up ninety-eight percent of all arguments. Her parents had named her for Carly Simon. Whenever she met anyone, she made sure to let them know this, as though she held a claim to some small portion of Ms. Simon's fame. One time I suggested she have Carly Simon Jr. tattooed on her forehead but she didn't seem to think that was too funny. And it wasn't funny because I'd missed my comic timing and it came out sounding mean. She iced over pretty fast and then believe me the booty doorbell was not answered that night. But it's not like my comic timing was winning any awards in the first place. One of the main reasons I wanted to be a lawyer was so I could master the cutting art of the verbal zinger. Law just seemed like the perfect format within which to master this craft. To be *The Zing Master.* To be able to completely and totally burn someone with my words. To an unrecognizable crisp. Yeah. Now *that* was a goal.

We sat there. I was overwhelmed by a strong desire to not speak. I limped through my chicken fingers. My stomach felt like a condemned Soviet-era sewage treatment plant. It wasn't easy to sit there and watch Carly chew her steak and make "mmm" sounds. She had this whole theory about the art of chewing and how if you chewed a certain way you could peel back secret layers of magical steak flavor. She could've written a book on how to chew up meats.

As a big-time caffeine addict, I took long morning coffee breaks, sometimes downing seven or eight cups before noon. And afternoon coffee breaks. Sometimes I had two cups going at once. The coffee at work was low-grade crap, but it was free. I drank higher quality coffee at home. And instant iced tea. These were habits I had picked up in rehab. The road to sobriety for me was navigated on the back of a coffee plantation pack mule. I was also developing a weakness for the pineapple bacon burgers down at Nurgle's. Anything to color in the beige. I would flirt with secretaries who were old enough to be my mom. Have endless pro sports recaps in the break room with the other guys. They had Facebook blocked but I could play all the video pool or Smoke the Rabbit I wanted. Spend an hour cleaning my fingernails with a toothpick. I even caught myself silently whistling a couple times. Mostly I dreamed of 5:30 and prayed that none of the lawyers would give me an assignment that would put me into overtime.

I was staring into my computer screen one day, formatting this Excel chart I made called Phone Calls by Plaintiff to Langdon Gastrointestinal. There were twenty-seven. I examined one of the entries, wherein the plaintiff guy had called the clinic on a Sunday. Mmm—Sunday, eh? That's odd—no one calls a clinic on a Sunday unless they're up to something. There's the smoking gun right there, yessir, this one's gonna be a slam dunker. The judge will laugh this trial right out of the courtroom and into the municipal parking lot. Yeppers. But not before I've blown them all away with a series of perfectly executed triple ballistic hell zingers, of course. I actually didn't know anything about the case, but I was practicing for the day when I would be in charge of such things and heroically discovering such smoking guns. I'd be large and in charge, soaring on the silver-tipped wings of kick-ass lawyer glory, burning people left and right, forward and aft. When those thoughts inevitably turned beige, I imagined an even more exhilarating way of making a living, like being one of those guys who travels around the world collecting meteorites and then selling them to rich people on the Internet. The Meteorite Hunter. I'll install custom display cabinets in the walls of my stylish beach bungalow to display my way sweet collection of space rocks. But after sitting and thinking about being a meteorite hunter ten, twenty, forty times, that idea became a cartoon parody of itself like everything else. I kinda just wanted to be the lucky victim of a fatal train accident. Was that really so much to ask? Probably. So things would come full circle and I'd again take comfort in my dream of becoming a beloved and soul crushing litigation superstar.

One late afternoon when the tedium was about to fully liquefy my brain, I decided to check out the powers of Citizen Search, this cool-ass database we used to track people down, get their real name and any aliases, run background checks, find out if they owned a house, boats, how many cars. It was so awesome. The lawyers used the information against people in civil court to make sure they coughed up all their wealth if they lost the case. Citizen Search had my imagination completely stoked— the whole idea of tracking someone down to exact a cold justice on them. It made me feel like I was this top-secret cyber private eye type dude. I just needed someone to hunt down. But months had gone by and the attorneys hadn't giving me anyone to look up. Instead they'd give a four-inch thick stack of papers to stamp CONFIDENTIAL on every page.

And I'd say: "Speaking of confidential, anybody to track down on the old Citizen Search today?"

"Jarvis, I'll need those documents stamped, scanned and back on my desk no later than four-thirty."

Gee, thanks.

So I decided to just log on and go for it. First it was ex-girlfriends. Renee, Debbie Danger, Katherine Mosley. Then all the old friends I could think of. Then family members like Uncle Harold, whose secret nickname was Uncle Pie-rold because he used to sit by himself at family gatherings and eat entire pies. He was dead but I still found info on him. Citizen Search nailed all of them. Turns out that Debbie Danger wasn't so dangerous anymore—married with two kids in Iowa, two cars and a house worth $102,000. Now she was just Mrs. Deborah Huddleston. Wasn't long before I started running out of people, so I looked up ex-girlfriends' family members, local news anchors, my landlord. Anyone whose name I could remember. I looked up that lady I got into a car wreck with in '08. My old boss at Palisades Paintball. Kevin Nobles from high school who got busted for running a crystal meth lab in his grandparents' garage and was still in jail. And he never even managed to successfully manufacture any meth. When I ran out of real people, I started on movie stars, famous mobsters, dead politicians. I also looked up Dr. Leifer, my old physics professor with the loud, wheezing asthma. Hated that guy. How dare he fail me for showing up to the mid-term wasted on bourbon—didn't he realize I had a problem? And that Nazi science nerd owned a boat, too.

At some point I really ran out of people. Everybody except one. The one person I was *not* going to look up on Citizen Search was Motorcar. Or whatever his real name was. It sounded like "Motorcar." That's what we called him, anyway. No way I was going to look him up. I wanted to enjoy daydreams of torturing him to death with a weed eater, not learn anything about his actual existence. That would've made him too real.

I heard the silent whistling and looked up. Sure enough, Teeler was walking by. For the first time I noticed that Teeler kind of looked like Motorcar. He *did* look like him! Now I hated Teeler's guts. I might have to do something bad to Teeler. I went to get a cup of joe to shake it off. I made it double strength and chugged it. But it didn't help at all.

3

CARLY SANG OUT of key with her headphones on while putting together a marinated pork tenderloin. On the rare night that she cooked, it was always some major meat, of course. She tenderized. She chopped. She basted. She bought fine meats. The pork smelled good as it started to roast, the scent of fresh garlic and basil wafting through the apartment. But sitting there on her couch watching the Red Sox whip the Orioles in HD, my stomach started twisting up. In one split second the fine aroma turned into the stench of rotten sewage.

"Smells great, doesn't it?" she yelled out from under her headphones.

"Yeah. Smells great."

"What?"

"Smells great!"

By the time the meat was coming out of the oven it was really hitting me. A mixture of nausea and a nervous, uncomfortable bubbling. I wanted to die and then puke.

Carly had also made asparagus, but she cooked it in the bottom of the meat pan so it was pork-flavored asparagus. Who does that? We made our plates in the kitchen, mine with the smallest portions I could hope to get away with, and took them into the living room.

"Can we watch something else?" she said.

"Can't we just see if they catch up next inning?" I heard her fork hit the plate a little too hard. Now I really didn't want to eat. My intestines were in full clench. I got down about three bites and I was done.

"This is great," I said. "Really delicious." I took a couple more tiny bites for show and chewed them dramatically. "Mmm…" I set my plate down on the coffee table and put my hand on my stomach.

She was pissed. I could smell it through the marinade.

"You've got to be kidding me," she said.

"What?"

She looked at my plate.

"I'm not done yet," I said. "Just taking a break."

"Yeah, right."

"What's that supposed to mean?"

"What's that supposed to mean," she mocked me.

"I didn't do anything!" I yelled.

Carly slammed her plate down on the coffee table.

"No, Jarvis, you didn't do anything. You never do anything."

"Yes I do! Sorry. Jesus. What do you want to watch? Whatever you want."

"*Law & Order.*"

"Okay, *Law & Order.* Fine. Jesus."

I flipped the remote to *Law & Order*, resumed with my plate and tried to take another bite of pork. She watched me force it into my mouth.

"Don't even bother," she said.

Now I clanked my fork on the plate. What a psycho beeyotch. I mean, it's not my fault I have an iffy stomach and I like baseball. I uncarefully set the plate back on the coffee table and exhaled through my teeth. I focused on a spot near the stereo. Then I unfocused on it. *Law & Order* was on TV, but the room felt more like *Chaos & Destruction.*

After the show, Carly broke out some chocolate ice cream, which helped the mood and my stomach. We both tried not to clank our spoons, at least. Later on as we were getting ready for bed, she said sorry when she bumped into me by the bathroom, so I guess things were better. Still, we slept as far apart as possible in the bed. No snuggling, no kiss goodnight, no nothing. I didn't even know what was wrong. Fine, I thought. I didn't want to have sex anyway. I felt like crap. Carly seemed to fall asleep right away while I lay there with my eyes bald open, picturing a cement truck dumping its suffocating load on Motorcar as he slept in his camp counselor tent.

Goodnight, Motorcar.

At work I continued to drone on in amber waves of beige. I guess I was getting used to it. And now that I had my perpetual daydreams of killing Motorcar back, I was really in my comfort zone. It was getting close to 5:30 and I called my main homie Ben. He was also my only old friend left in the area. Seemed like most of the others from our high school crew had gone out into the Great Beyond, far away from suburban Maryland. The only ones who stayed behind were Ben, myself, a few random dudes and some weirdo goths who I never got along with. But at least I didn't live in my parents' basement like Ben. And the random dudes. Pretty sure most of them were still kicking it in their parents' basements, too. Not sure where the goths lived. Caves maybe?

When I said let's get a beer after work, Ben knew it meant non-alcoholic beer for me. Or just tons of coffee or iced tea. The near-beers tasted like crap, but if you downed enough of them you could fool yourself into thinking you had a buzz. If you drank like, fourteen. Get a beer after work also meant meeting at Cogbill's, a sports bar in the old strip mall next to Krispy Kreme. It was the only place we ever went. *My name is Jarvis Henders and I am twenty-six years old and I hang out at a shopping center.* I said this to myself as I waited for an old lady to clear her Buick out of a prime parking spot I had my eye on.

"Howdy," Ben said, walking up as I got out of my piece-of-shit red '96 Hyundai.

"Yo. Whuttup."

"Yer looking at it."

Ben had been going through a cowboy thing, wearing cowboy boots and jeans and a plaid Western shirt. And he was also growing a moustache, but it was still in the wispy stage. He stopped short of wearing a cowboy hat, but I think he had one at his house. I wondered if he wore it at home and made cowboy talk to himself in the mirror. Whoa little doggie and Giddyup thar, pardner, etc.

We went inside and up to the bar and ordered our respective beers. Cogbill's was this giant faux-rustic type place with rough wood paneling and these big, comfortable bar stools designed for patrons to sit on their asses for hours and watch sports on the wide-screen TVs hanging from above. The big bowl of complimentary popcorn appeared before us, dry and salty, to make you drink more.

"How's work going?" Ben asked.

"Soooo fuckin' boring."

"I thought you liked it."

"I did for the first few weeks."

Ben shook his head, slowly and deliberately like a thoughtful cowboy. A campfire philosopher.

"How about your gig?" I asked him.

"Same, I guess." He shrugged. Ben was the assistant manager at a call center for a credit card company. One of the select few still left in the actual United States. His job wasn't anywhere near as boring as mine. I had Teeler's silent whistling and the omnipresent beige. Ben oversaw employees who would smoke pot in the parking lot at lunch and come back to their cubicle singing and laughing like eighth graders. There were frequent ice cube fights in the break room until Ben threatened to disconnect the ice machine. He managed slackers who would call in with excuses like: "My girlfriend caught on fire. I'll be in around two-thirty." Ben even had two guys break into a fistfight in the cubicles once. Over this redhead who worked in Processing. Seemed like there was always some wacky shit going down in that place.

"Y'wanna order some cheese sticks?" Ben said.

"Sure thing, pardner."

So we ordered our cheese sticks and we ate them. My fake beer was warm, so I finished it and ordered an iced tea and a cup of coffee.

"You know what, dude?" Ben said after a while. "I might have to kill my boss."

"That guy Maurice?"

"No, that's Manuel. But not him. My regional supervisor. Brenda."

"What did she do? Is she hot?"

"No. She looks like a tree. Talks to me like I'm a fourth grader. Totally fucking condescending."

"That sucks."

Something about his mentioning "fourth grader" made me think of Motorcar. I pictured him walking into the bar. I force him to eat an entire bar stool and then shoot him. In the face.

"What's the matter?" Ben asked.

"What? Nothing."

"You look like you're freaking out."

"Yeah, no. I mean, no worries."

Ben was the only person I had ever told about Motorcar. We were sixteen and getting drunk on a Saturday night and decided to play *What's Your Biggest Secret*. Mine was Motorcar. Ben's was that he accidentally saw his mom naked one time when he was thirteen and it gave him a boner. It had filled him with such a feeling of catastrophic horror that he made immediate plans to kill himself. Pretty sure we never would have told each other these secrets if we hadn't been taking challenge shots from his dad's fifth of Beefeater.

"If we were living in another time, like in Medieval times? I'd kill Brenda."

"Murder wasn't exactly legal in Medieval times, dude," I said.

"Yeah, well, they didn't have CSI and shit back then."

"Just lynch mobs."

"Good point."

"You know who I'd like to kill?"

"Who?"

"Motorcar."

"A what?"

17

"The guy from summer camp. Remember?"

"Um…no."

"You know—the camp counselor I had?"

Ben shook his head. With force.

"Motorcar? I told you about that. Back in high school."

Ben squirmed. I could feel the temperature going up in the room. The mental temperature.

"I know you remember. The counselor at summer camp who—"

"All right, all right. Sort of, I guess."

"Sometimes, I think I could—I'd go and pop that motherfucker." I pulled the trigger on an imaginary gun and looked at my hand, nodding.

Ben looked like the proverbial deer-in-the-headlights.

"Hell yeah," he said. "You should definitely, um…cap him for sure."

"Believe me—I think about it all the time."

"Shit, I would. I'd torture him first, though. With razor blades or something. Slowly."

"Yeah."

"Or you could mail him a pipe bomb and watch from across the street when he opens it. Ka-*blam*!"

"Okay, okay." Ben was getting a little too into it. Motorcar was my person to have kill fantasies about. So I changed the subject to pro football draft picks, a safe topic. What wasn't safe was the mound of cheese sticks sinking to the bottom of my swamp waters. By the time I got home, I felt like I was pregnant with a cheese baby.

I watched TV for a while and called Carly. She didn't answer, so I left a message: "Hey. It's me. Bye." I went to bed and tried to beat off, but I couldn't get a boner. I felt like I was just a temporary visitor in my own body. Like everything in life was on hold and I was really supposed to be somewhere else. Some*one* else. It felt like there was this giant shit-storm moving in. A bad one, with big purple-black death clouds and poison rain. A real nuclear winter.

I stared at the ceiling. Then I squeezed my eyes shut and saw the flashing aluminum of my magical bat. I saw Motorcar's head. I saw a screaming Medieval mob swinging his detached limbs through a bloodthirsty crowd. That's how they would have done it back then. Back when there was such a thing as justice. Back when revenge was healthy.

4

I WAS SITTING in my cubicle working on another Excel spreadsheet, typing dates into cells in a column called *Dates*. I had been fighting the jumpy swamp nerves all day and they were winning, crawling up my neck disguised as heartburn. It scared the crap out of me when a secretary popped her head in.

"Jarvis?"

"Wha—! Oh. Hey."

"Mr. Reinhaus wants to see you in his office right away."

Something was up. Normally she would have just said: *Steve wants to see you.*

"Um...right-o," I said.

Steve Reinhaus had this way of being intently focused on something and not really there at the same time. He gave me a hard look when I first stepped into his office. When I sat down he stared out the window like he was contemplating the sublime poetry of the astronauts on their tethered space walks or some shit. He snapped to it, though.

"Jarvis."

"How's it going?"

"I have these invoices here from this vendor. Citizen Search."

"Invoices?"

"Been using the program quite a bit, I see." He looked down at the invoices and then back at me with a dead stare.

"Yeah, um, it's a great website. Very effective. Definitely one of the firm's better resource tools for all aspects of—"

"Do you realize that you ran up over two thousand dollars running searches on this?

"Seriously?"

"Seriously, yes."

"No." I shook my head. "I thought the searches were free, like, we pay a flat subscription rate, y'know?"

"No, I don't know." He started tapping his finger on his desk, loud. "The searches were free for a two-week trial so you can learn the program, Jarvis. After that, we get charged. A lot."

"Oh. Shit."

"And you don't remember this from your training session." He said it like an accusation rather than a question, using his lawyer tricks on me.

"Wow. I mean, seriously, Steve—I will pay it all back. Every cent. I'm really sorry."

"Yes, you will be paying it all back, Jarvis." Then he started gazing in the direction of his wall of diplomas, which were geometrically arranged on his oaken walls. A sort of angled pyramid of success, glinting in the sunlight.

"This is the problem I have now," he said. "There are a few days you spent two, three, even four hours running searches on people. This was time you were supposed to be working."

"But I was working."

"Not according to these invoices."

"Well, that was lunch, too. My lunch hour in there?"

"What on earth were you looking up Marilyn Monroe for? Richard Nixon? These people are dead."

"Actually, you'd be surprised by just how many people across the country have those same names."

"Perry Mason isn't even a real person—he's a fictional character."

"There's actually a slew of Perry Masons in the Indianapolis area. A whole clan of them. I'm not sure if they're related to the real one or not. I mean the fictional one."

Reinhaus looked at me like I was an idiot. Then he started to drift off again. I was in deep trouble and the walls of my stomach were straight melting. I could see the shit storm really gathering above and I was completely umbrella-less.

"You can take the payments right out of my paycheck,

Steve. Or I tell you what, I can put the whole amount on my credit card? How about that?"

"Jarvis." He wasn't listening to me at all. "Our clients' trust is the life blood of this firm."

Oh no, I thought. I swallowed. Pretty sure he heard the gulp sound.

"When you bill the client for paralegal work, and you don't bother to do that work, when you play video games instead, or engage in some other form of fucking off, do you know what that is?"

"No, sir."

"When you engage in the type of behavior that you've been engaging in here, you are not only misrepresenting this firm, but you are in effect stealing from that client."

"Right," I said, but I knew it was all bullshit. Ripping off the clients through over-billing was how the place stayed in business. But it wouldn't do any good to argue. The guy was a professional arguer.

"We simply cannot risk our credibility by employing someone who's an ethical liability."

I wanted to puke. His expression was half sympathetic and half damning. Then he shook his head for effect. "Jarvis, you've really given me no other choice than to terminate your employment here, effective immediately."

I couldn't think of anything good to say. Just sat there frozen.

"You've got one hour to remove your belongings and yourself from firm property," he said. "Leave your working files as they are. We'll go through those later."

Remove myself. Like I was a potted plant. I got up from the chair.

"And I'll take you up on your offer to put your Citizen Search charges on your credit card. Please see Janice Moran on your way out and she'll take your card information. Does that make sense?"

"I understand."

"And if you don't pay for it now, I'll take you to court."

23

"I…um…"

"Is that clear?"

"Yessir. Clear as…crystal clear." My voice was shivering.

Steve was already looking back down at the crap he was working on when I'd come in. Why was I being such a mega-pussy? I even closed his office door quietly on the way out. I totally should have slammed it shut with a cold blaze of righteous fury. Or at least said something sarcastic.

There were already some empty boxes sitting outside my cubicle. They were really ganging up on me. Was it Teeler? That pervert!

The only stuff to clean out was a picture of me and Carly snowboarding and a magnifying glass I bought one Saturday on a forced antiquing trip. It was pretty anti-climactic, when they tell you to clean out your things in the next sixty minutes and all you have is a picture and a knick-knack. And some peanut butter cheese crackers. I almost threw the magnifying glass into the trash, but I figured I might as well take it to my next job and never use it there either. Maybe I could use it to get some better focus on why my life was so fucked up. One day I felt awesome and mighty, the next like a giant stupid loser. What was up with that? But this was not the time for analysis. This was the time for panic.

I looked at the snowboarding picture of me and Carly through the scratchy lens of the magnifying glass. I could see Carly's eyeballs from behind the blue lenses of her sunglasses. She was looking away from the camera, probably at some ski instructor's ass. I pulled out my shirt tail to wipe the dust off the picture. I should have come up with something to burn Reinhaus with in there. Something like: *Steve, I used to think you were a benevolent master, but you're really a malevolent bastard.* Always, always too late with the best zingers. I had to work on that. Screw being on the zinger receiving end. I was so done with always being the zingee.

I filled the boxes up with my working files and grabbed a rolling cart from the mailroom. I rolled the files, three boxes' worth, back to the freight elevator area and dumped them out into a super-can that was sitting there. Let them sort it all out, if they even find the crap before the trash gets dumped. I was surprised no one had been assigned to watch me or escort me out of the place. I left without making eye contact with anyone. Screw them. I wasn't going to pay for jack. They could keep my last paycheck for the Citizen Search bill and round out the rest from Reinhaus' millions. I was gonna need my credit card for living expenses. Damn.

I threw the magnifying glass and picture into the back seat of my car. I left the cheese crackers behind for the next sucker. I started up the engine and thought about what a lying slimeball Reinhaus was. I hope he remembers what he did to me when he and his secretary were roasting in the molten pits of hell. I was pretty sure she was the one who put the boxes by my cube. Like she was being all helpful, but she was actually rubbing it in. I hope she realized she was going down to the hot place for that.

Holy shit—I can't believe I just got fucking fired!

Fuck!

I headed out of the beige corporate office park forever and peeled out onto the service road. I pictured Reinhaus' flesh melting off his bones in one of Satan's high-tech torture ovens. He and Motorcar could sit there holding hands while they burned. I pulled out onto the main road really, really wanting a beer.

Or three.

Or fifty.

There was a nice hot wind blowing through the car, enough to dry any sweat before it started. Some cool a/c would have been nice, but I had the stripped down version of the '96 Hyundai. Aside from the bottom of my stomach being twisted up into wet knots and the nuclear winter rolling in over my head, I actually felt kind of relieved. I was finally free of that beige hole.

To get beer or not to get beer, that was my dilemma. I tried to smell the big blue sky. I just needed some caffeine. I got fired right before my mid-after-lunch coffee break. Life is so effing unfair. A fired, recovering alcoholic and I couldn't even have one final afternoon jolt of free coffee. That coffee sucked anyway. I'll never have to drink that swill again, I said to myself. Never. I was so much better off now. Much, much better off.

5

I STOPPED AT the Zoom Thru on the way home and something pulled me toward the beer cooler. A powerful electromagnetic force commonly known as the ripping desire to get wasted. It was hard-wired into my nervous system. I walked by the cool glass doors and visualized myself picking out a few six-packs. It was too damn hot for coffee anyway, *right?* And getting fired was a special occasion, *right?* But I knew if I did it the lights would come down again. And I'd be breaking another chain of sobriety I'd built: twenty-two months, three weeks and five days since my last drink. It would make the day a double doomsday that I would never forget—the day I got fired and my legal career took a hard kick to the nuts and I couldn't handle it. It would have been so common. So obvious. So I kept on going.

I poured myself a nasty cup of overcooked gas station coffee. That's about when it started repeating in my head: *I can't believe I got fucking fired.* Over a dumb website. What a lame-ass thing to get fired for. I should have gone out in flames of wild glory, busting all the crooked lawyers there. Gotten some smoking hot dirt on them and then run a complex blackmailing scam or something. But getting fired for going on Citizen Search? Okay, so Debbie Danniger is now Debbie Huddleston. That's great for her—she doesn't have to put up with people calling her Debbie Danger anymore, but was it worth my future? I'll always think of her as Debbie Danger anyway, so what difference does it make if she's Mrs. Huddleston now? Who gives a fuck!

I can't believe I got fired.

The reality was really hitting me. I felt the white hot panic of disaster pressing against my chest like a steel weight. *Fuck, shit, damn!* Yeah, that job was painfully boring, but what did I have now, the thrill of unemployment? *I just can't believe I just got fired. Oh my god! Give me boring back! I love beige!*

The coffee went straight to my stomach like a bad oil spill infecting a landscape of rotting wetlands. Cup was drained by the time I got halfway home, though. I really wanted to just die. My teeth were vibrating. The only other time I'd ever gotten myself fired from a job was for drinking, sort of. I showed up for work at a summer landscaping job with liquor on my breath from the night before. The boss was this ball-busting religious dude who accused me of drinking before work. I don't deny that I'm an alcoholic, but that didn't mean I got up at the butt-crack of dawn and started doing shots. Of course, it didn't help that I backed the truck up over two brand new, three-hundred dollar professional-grade weed eaters. Anyway, that was just a summer job when I was in college. This shit now was real. The paralegal gig was supposed to be my ticket to the big time, William & Mary, UVA or Tulane. I aspired to the lifestyle of the Southern lawyer. I loved the idea of the South with its tranquil pace and lush trees and humid summer afternoons. I was going to be a modern-day Atticus Finch, kicking back on my wrap-around porch, issuing toxically witty barbs over non-alcoholic mint juleps. Now I was fucked. I needed at least a year at a good firm to put on my law school application, and one that would give me a stellar reference. I only made it five months at Reinhaus, Thompkins and Watts.

I can't believe I got fucking fired.

I could feel the tattoo forming on my forehead in bright red letters: *LOOZER.*

I pulled into my parking lot. I wished I'd had another cup of that boiling sludge coffee to throw in Reinhaus's face. I could shoot it through a fire hose and burn his whole family. No, not his family, they didn't do anything. Just him, but I would use like three fire hoses of boiling hot coffee at once.

My apartment was oddly bright inside. Wasn't used to being home so early in the afternoon. It reminded me that I had just gotten fired. Sharp sunbeams were shooting in through the living room window, illuminating gazillions of suspended dust particles. I threw my keys down on the table and put my sunglasses back on. I felt like an imaginary version of myself, suspended in mid-air like one of the dust particles.

I just can't believe I got fucking fired.

I made a super strong instant iced tea and chugged it down and made another one. Even stronger. It was almost black. I put on some Billy Joel and started smoking one of Carly's menthol cigarettes. Menthols to me were just cough medicine sticks, but Carly had left them lying around and I was feeling zany, really flirting with the edge here. I blew the smoke out into the sunbeam and watched the dust particles go crazy. Free entertainment. God, was I screwed.

I tried not to think about getting fired. I took a shower and put on some almost-clean cut-off sweat pants and an old tee-shirt. I went into the kitchen and opened the freezer door and stuck my head in and took a few deep breaths. This always made me feel better. I started doing it the first time I quit drinking. When I was jonesing for a vodka tonic or a sudsy brew, I'd go and stick my head in the freezer and take a few deep breaths. Like someone smacking you in the face but it didn't hurt as bad.

The afternoon dwindled away in a swirl of Billy Joel albums and lethal instant iced teas. I commemorated the passing of five o'clock by sticking my head in the freezer again. Not too long after that, Carly came over. She let herself in right while I was doing this warped dance to *Movin' Out*. She scared me and I screamed for a second. Her mouth was moving but I couldn't hear over the music, so I went to turn it down.

"Hold on," I said.

"What is *with* you?"

Carly was on her way home from work. She popped in like that every once in a while. I suspected it was so she could catch me beating off or something. She was wearing one of her receptionist's outfits—high skirt, low-cut top. She had her powers and she used them.

"You scared the shit out of me." I forced a chuckle. Then I went over to kiss her but she stuck out her cheek with a cold formality. I stepped back and looked at her. She didn't know I'd been fired yet and she already looked mad, the skin on her forehead creasing up.

"What?" she said.

"Nothing. What?"

She sniffed the air. "What are you doing *smoking*?"

"Nothing. I mean...I guess I'm kind of celebrating."

"Celebrating what?"

I smacked my thigh and said: "Well, I quit my job today. Yeah. And let me tell you—"

"What!"

"—it feels good."

"Jarvis, you did *not*! Why!" She threw her purse down on the couch, hard. It made a slapping sound. "Oh my god."

"I don't have to take that shit off of anybody," I said, waving my hand when I said 'anybody' like I was swatting at gnats.

"And you're celebrating this?"

"Well, not really, I mean...kind of. I guess."

"What happened?" she demanded.

"I got into it with one of the partners about this whole stupid...I just...dude, he is such an asshole."

"What did he do to be such an asshole?"

"Well, for starters, he got all uptight just because I went...I spent too much time on this program, and—"

"What program?"

"This subscription database thing. All I did was...it accidentally ran their bill up a little. And when I offered to pay it all back, I mean, completely *all* the fuck back, he was like, *hello—I am Captain Psycho Boy now.* So I mean, I'm not taking that bullshit off any-bod-y, right? I know who I am." I swatted at the squadron of imaginary gnats again.

"Are you fucking kidding me? You quit over that?"

"Yeah, no. I mean..." I shook my head. "It's hard to explain."

She read me. Not like a book but like a cocktail napkin with some notes scribbled on it. I was a terrible liar. I needed to work on that.

"Jarvis. Did you quit or get fired?"

"Not exactly."

"That wasn't a 'not-exactly' question."

"Okay," I said. "It was kind of...I dunno...mutual, I guess? You should be the damn lawyer."

"I'm not the one trying to get into fucking law school, you idiot!"

"I know, I know."

"God—you suck!"

All the energy drained out of my body in a millisecond.

Carly lit a cigarette and blew the smoke out real hard. Everything in her world was pretty much divisible into one of two extreme categories: "great" or "sucks." Didn't matter if it was a bagel or a ballet. She did have a lesser-used, third category: "weird," that she saved for things she didn't understand, like the cowboy phase Ben was going through or art. So at least she didn't think I was weird. But once she decided that something or someone sucked, it was really hard to convince her otherwise.

"I can't believe it," she said.

"I know. Me either."

"Were you looking at porn?"

"No, baby, of course not. It's called Citizen Search. You look people up on it."

"What people?"

"Just...people. I was bored. On my lunch hour and stuff."

"Who were you looking up?"

"I don't know. People from high school. Old girlfriends, that one professor who—"

"Old girlfriends! You just lost job because you're obsessed with old girlfriends?" Now she was really pissed.

"No, no. I'm sorry. I was just bored. Come on."

"Come on, what? Bored? I guess you're going to be really fucking bored with no job, huh?"

I felt like a little kid getting yelled at by my mom for breaking a crystal vase. I shrugged my shoulders and then dropped into a sulk.

"If I wanted to date a loser," she said, "I would have stayed with Ron."

"I thought he owned his own marketing company."

"Well, he's doing a lot better than you are at this point, that's for sure." She looked me over and shook her head. "You are so weird."

That was it. The silence was heavier than a corpse swinging from a low-rent ceiling fixture. I had no idea what to say. I sucked *and* I was weird. I had just gotten the double death sentence. She grabbed her purse from the couch.

"Where are you going?" I said.

"Don't worry about it."

"Come on, Carly—"

"Jarvis, I can't do this. You're just going to…how can you do something so stupid? Stupid enough to get fired for, ruin your future and all your goals—and then sit around here like you're celebrating? What is *wrong* with you?"

"Well, it's a…I was trying to put a positive spin on it. I don't know."

"That's all you can say—*I don't know?*"

"I guess. I mean…"

She put out her cigarette and put her fingers on her temples. "Oh my God—you *suck!*"

"I know."

She slammed the door with perfect timing. For a second I thought I should go after her and say *please-baby-no-wait-I'm-sorry* and all that stuff, but I didn't. I just stood there. I felt like I was falling through the floor. I'll text her later, I decided. Or I'll call her and talk her into loving me again. She'll realize that I'm great and don't suck. She just needs some time to cool down. We'll work it out. Everything will work itself out. No problem. I am not suck-weird. I'm amazing and awesome. Her vision is just clouded right now. Yeah—her vision is clouded.

God, I wanted a drink.

I started pacing the apartment thinking: *this isn't happening.* It felt like anvils were being launched into my guts from all sides. I was pacing faster and faster, caffeine screaming through my veins. I decided to go after her. I ran outside with no shoes on, but her car was already gone. I went back in and stuck my head in the freezer for a minute, but it didn't make me feel better. I fidgeted and paced and sat down and turned on the TV but then turned it off right away. I stuck my head in the freezer again and took a deep breath, but it didn't do anything again.

This isn't the fuck happening.

I sat on the couch for a while with my head in my hands, telling myself how much none of this was happening. Then I called Ben.

"Dude," I said. "I am having the official worst day of my life."

"Can't be worse than the one I had. Another run-in with Frank. Bitch has it out for me."

"Well, check this out—I got fired today and I'm pretty sure Carly just broke up with me."

"Yeah, *right.*"

"I'm totally serious."

"You need an injury in there too, like a broken arm or something." He laughed.

"Dude," I said as darkly as possible.

"Are you for real?"

I didn't say anything.

"What's wrong?" Ben asked.

"I just *told* you. Jesus."

"Damn."

"Cogbill's later? I gotta get out of here for a while."

We made plans to meet at eight. I tried to shake the feeling that my best friend was a clueless moron. I had bigger problems than that. I spread out on the couch and wished a meteorite would come crashing through the ceiling and put my lights out for good. No such luck. Then I called Carly.

She didn't answer. At first I left simple messages: "It's me. Call me back."

I texted her. I called her. On the third or fourth voicemail I got apologetic: "I'm sorry for what happened, baby. Please call me back. We can't just end it like this. Please. I'll buy you a steak?"

How was I going to afford steaks now, though? I went to go stick my head in the freezer, but I punched the refrigerator door instead. Some of the magnets came flying off. Guess I was getting a little emotional. Carly was the only girlfriend I'd been able to hold onto for more than five months. And with her high-polish ceramic skin and slinky bedroom eyelashes, and oh lord—that tight swimmer's body—she was someone I was proud to have as my girlfriend. Someone I could go into Cogbill's with and people would say: *Damn, Jarvis sure has a hot girlfriend. He is not a faggot by any reasonable estimation.* Now it was gonna be me and Ben going in there and everybody'd go back to thinking I was just some corporate douche in a puce polo shirt. And now an unemployed one. The loss was really starting to bite. Carly was the one pushing me to do all these great things: become a kick-ass attorney and purchase a fleet of personal sailboats. Each perfect baby of ours was going to get its own perfect custom fucking sailboat. I had it all planned out!

This isn't happening.

I can't believe I got fired.

I can't believe Carly just dumped my ass.

I called her again. She didn't answer so I texted her. My neck was getting hot and itchy. I scratched but it just made it hotter. I left another message. I figured I'd try the assertive approach on this one: "If you don't call me back soon, I don't know what I'm gonna do. Call me back. Okay, bye."

Soon her phone was just making a busy signal. And so was my brain. Or rather the hysterical train wreck that had become my brain.

This really, really isn't anywhere near really happening.

I realized I was pacing after I started pacing again. All over the tan-beige carpet. My stomach felt like pure toxic rot and my head like some kind of broken free-twirling death gyro. A broken bobble-head doll on PCP. And the hot neck thing— what was up with that? But I kept on scratching and rubbing it. With all my other problems, I really didn't need a case of hot neck. Now I *really* wanted a drink. I made some iced tea instead, with five tablespoons of instant tea, then six, then seven, until it was as black as my outlook. I chugged it down. It burned my throat. Time to go to the bar.

On the drive over, my thoughts went between Reinhaus and Carly, from disaster to catastrophe. My life was a full-on disastrophe. At about the fifth traffic light before Cogbill's, I had a flash of: *screw that job,* followed by: *and who-needs-her-anyway?* This was great—I was free now. Free to do whatever. Free to date whoever I wanted. That job blew chunks anyway. I *hated* it. But the feeling of triumph lasted about one-and-a-half traffic lights. Then life was back to complete and utter suckage. I got stuck behind someone trying to make a left into the *Shop'n'Save* and beat on the horn. "Piece of shit motherfucker!" I screamed.

I pictured myself swinging a sledge hammer into Reinhaus's face.

It felt good.

It felt great.

Then the dumb-ass in front of me hit his brakes for no reason. I slammed on the horn again.

"Fucking loser! *God!*"

I had gone through about seventeen emotional peaks and valleys since I'd left my apartment. A crisp bourbon and ginger ale was calling my name, loudly. But I had to fight it. These were the moments when you had to fight it the most. So there I was heading into a bar. *Smart move, Jarvis Henders, smart move.*

6

BEN ORDERED A large platter of cheese sticks but I couldn't even look at them. I could barely even acknowledge they were there. They smelled like burnt socks.

"That sucks, man," he said, salting the cheese sticks.

"Yep." I took a swig of my artificial beer and wished it were real. Ben's shirt had even more Western stitching than the one he wore last time, big wide loops of white thread twirling across the plaid. Snaps instead of buttons. It was really starting to piss me off. I just thanked God he didn't have a red bandana tied around his neck. That might have been a deal breaker on the hanging out.

"Fuckin' lawyers, man," he said. "They should all be put—what's that joke about the fifty thousand lawyers at the bottom of the ocean?"

"I got that job because I want to *be* a lawyer, Tex."

Ben shook his head and took a swig of his real beer. "And what happened with Carly, now?"

"Yeah, the fight."

Talking about it made me sick. Made it real. I told him quickly about the fight, or whatever it was. How she called me a sucky weirdo and stormed out. How she slammed the door. How I've been attempting to resuscitate negotiations. Ben's eyes were darting all over the place. He was looking at the waitress's ass, at one of the TVs, at the wall. In a way, though, it didn't bother me because I didn't want to talk about any of it. So I started speculating on why Baltimore's two main pro sports teams were named after birds. The Orioles and the Ravens. No idea. One thing was sure, though—the Ravens were the only team in the NFL named for a poem.

"That we know of, anyway."

"At least it's a scary poem," Ben said.

Then I remembered again that my whole life had just bottomed out. It wasn't real. We drank our beers and sat there in silence. I pictured a gallon-sized glass of Jim Beam on the rocks. A whole row of them. I could knock them back like a production line and not have to worry about all this shit for a while.

I sat there watching Ben eat cheese sticks and I made a decision.

"You know what?"

"What?"

"From now on, man, things are going to be great and not suck."

"Um...that's cool."

"I'm making the big change from suckiness to greatness."

"Killer, dude," Ben said. "Cheers. Hey, I almost forgot. We just had to fire this guy for cussing out the customers."

"So? Is that supposed to make me feel better?"

"No, I mean I've totally got a spot open for you at the call center."

"*Call* center? I don't know, man..."

"What?"

"Don'tcha think maybe I'm a little over-qualified?"

"Nobody's over-qualified for getting a paycheck, Hoss."

"What is up with you and this cowboy thing?"

"Whadda you mean?"

"I mean calling me 'Hoss' and the outfit."

"It's not an outfit," he said, slamming his beer bottle down on the bar. The suds came oozing to the top. "At least I've got a sense of style."

"Sorry to have to break this to you, but that style went out in the—" My brain couldn't send the words to my mouth in time. Fucking zinger clog again.

Ben flipped me off. I double flipped him off. I looked down at my sea-foam green polo shirt and beige khakis I had put on in lieu of the rotten sweat pants. Okay, maybe a little preppie, but at least I wasn't pretending to be a ranch hand. I was who

I was, and maybe that person was an unemployed weirdo loser who sucked, but at least I had my own identity, whatever the fuck it was.

"Sorry, man," Ben said. "I know you're having a shitty day."

"It's cool."

After that we didn't say much, each of us staring off into our own corners of space. I didn't have the energy to be mad at Ben. I was tripping. There was no way I lost my job and my girlfriend all in the same day. No way it was real. I wanted to laugh and cry and vomit and celebrate and kill myself all at the same time. Then do it all again.

On the drive home, I was really feeling the roller coaster thing: one minute bleeding naked emotion and the next, frozen with disbelief, shaking my head. I was about to freaking implode. I got home and called Carly and got the busy signal again. I don't know how she made her cell phone do that. I threw my phone against the wall and the battery popped out. I made coffee and drank it and went to bed.

Could not sleep. All I could think about were the people who had unceremoniously ruined my life. It's just the truth: human beings are horrible people. So screw Reinhaus. Screw Carly. Screw Motorcar. Screw all of 'em. I finally fell asleep, wishing for that meteorite to show up. A big one. Texas-sized. Then the world could start over again with a fresh batch of pathetic losers.

Everything is great. Everything is extremely great. Absolutely nothing sucks whatsoever. I repeated this over and over to myself as I woke up, waiting to benefit from my optimism, which never came. My head sludged back into the pillow. Sounded like such a good philosophy, too. So easy to follow: *Everything is just fucking so great.* Embrace it. Live it. Feel it. I shook my head. My thoughts hurt. My stomach felt gross, and there weren't even any cheese sticks crammed in there. I could feel the purple-black death cloud of nuclear winter pressing on me, pushing down on my neck until every centimeter of my being was poisoned with deadness and hate. My life was a screaming invisible train wreck times a thousand. I realized that this must've been how people felt when they killed themselves. Good morning.

Everything is real, real great.

Even though I got to sleep in as late as I wanted, I was totally exhausted. I made coffee. The day turned into a day of nothing that blurred into itself—I called Carly and got a busy signal, I went and got a paper but then didn't look for a job. I swilled gallons of coffee and iced tea, took a couple long naps, didn't bother to eat much or shower. And that day blurred into another day of pretty much the same thing. And still there was zero from Carly. The busy signal was gone, but I stopped leaving messages because I didn't know what to say. I would just wait for the beep and hesitate and then hang up. I texted her: *hey. call me.* I called her at work and they said she wasn't there. On the third day of groggy nothing, I did have one accomplishment—I paid rent with a cash advance on my credit card. I had enough money in my checking account to pay it, but I wanted to play it safe.

My days were spent deep in a shell-shocked nothing zone choked with a toxic medicine fog. Everything was shutting down and the hell fumes were creeping in and enveloping my world. My head felt like a giant honey-glazed Easter ham. I didn't even care about the job thing anymore, I just wanted to know why Carly cut me off like that. But to win her back I was going to have to get another job first. A real vicious cycle. I guess I always knew deep down that she was an ice queen, but this was by far the most brutal display of her freezing royal powers yet. I wanted to melt her. I wanted a damn steak.

I drove by her apartment, but I was too chicken to stop. I'd give myself eight or ten chances, sometimes driving by fast, the next time slow, up around the corner and doing a u-turn in the Baptist church parking lot. But I never got up the courage to go to her door.

One day I woke up from one of my naps and just said fuck it and went by the realty company where she worked. It was at an office park that looked just like the one where I had my paralegal job. I never thought I'd feel emotional about an office park, but being in this place really made the getting fired thing hit home again. The imaginary letters that spelled "*LOOZER*" pulsated on my forehead. For some reason though, I wasn't as nervous as when I went by her house. I walked around in circles in the parking deck for only about twenty minutes before I went in.

The receptionist wasn't Carly. It was Fiona. I'd met her at the Christmas party. She was nice to me then. Now her eyes and lips tightened as soon as she recognized me.

"Carly...around?"

"It's her day off."

"She doesn't normally have Thursdays off."

"Well, you don't *normally* come in here, do you?"

Damn, I thought—everybody's a Zing Master but me. I wanted to say something. Something good.

"If she's back there? I'd really like to see...talk to her."

"She isn't *here*," Fiona snapped.

Somebody was coming down the hallway, not Carly, but a dude. A big, tall dude. "Fine," I said. "Whatever." I tried to slam the door on my way out, but it had one of those hydraulic things on top to slow it down and it wouldn't slam. I looked back at Fiona and she was picking up the phone. Was she calling the cops? I didn't wait around to find out.

That night, I finally got my balls together and went to Carly's apartment. I knew she was in there because her car was outside, but she wouldn't answer when I knocked. She wouldn't answer when I pounded. I knew she could hear me calling her.

"Carly, please!" *Pound, pound, pound, pound.* "Just please talk to me!" *Pound, pound, pound, pound.* "Ahhh!" Kicking the door didn't seem to have any effect either.

I walked away completely deflated, like a sack of wet fertilizer glumping in on itself. Couldn't we just go out for one last thing of meat?

Then, when she finally called, I missed it. I was out buying more coffee and I'd left my phone charging at home. It's just as well, though, because the message she left was like a knife in the face:

"Hey. Do I have to get a restraining order on you? Leave me the fuck alone." *Click.*

The floor shot up through the bottom of my stomach and it was not a good feeling. I tried to shake it off, tossing my head back and forth like a wet dog shaking off its coat.

Fuck being depressed.

Fuck this.

Fine, Carly, I will *never call you again.*

No problem.

I sat on the edge of my bed and shut my eyes. I pictured myself screaming in Carly's face. *No problem!* We're up on a high rooftop somewhere, close to the edge. I grab her by the shoulders and shake her—*Loser, huh? Weirdo, huh?*—and I throw her off. She doesn't scream, because in fantasies, things aren't always that realistic. She doesn't scream because she knows she's wrong and she deserves to be thrown off a roof. I don't go look over the edge. I turn and walk away, ready to move on with my life.

I throw her off a cliff.

I throw her off a plane.

I throw her down fifty flights of cement steps.

And every time after I throw her off of something I just turn and walk away to get a healthy fresh start. I feel alive for once.

No problem.

7

THE SHIRT COLLAR was digging into my neck like a saw. It was way too hot to be wearing a suit but Ben said I had to. He met me in the lobby. He was a little too happy to see me.

"Great to have you here, man," he said.

"Thanks."

We shook hands. It was a very professional handshake. He led me through a series of narrow hallways. The walls looked like they were made of painted cardboard. We went into a giant room with a sea of cubicles. The chatter of voices sounded fake, like a piped-in Hollywood sound effect.

"Wow," I said. "This is huge. You're in charge of all this?"

"No. Just my sector."

"How many sectors are there?"

He didn't answer. I followed him back to a little tiny glassed-in office. Glassed-in with plexi-glass. All it had was a modular desk, a chair and a guest chair. We sat down. Ben looked weird without his cowboy gear on. Wasn't used to seeing him all business casual.

"So," I said, "who all am I meeting with today?"

"Just me, myself and I, good buddy."

"Just you?"

"Well, normally you'd meet with Marguerite the HR lady, but she's still on vacation."

"You mean I got dressed up in a suit and came all the way down here just meet with *you*? We could have done this at Cogbill's."

"No, you had to come in for an interview. It's required. We don't just hire people off the street."

"But you're the only one who knows I'm here."

"Not true. They know you're here. Believe me, they know."

"Okay, fine." I loosened my tie a little. Yet another bad case of hot neck.

Ben looked at me with disapproval. "So, Jarvis," he said, "tell me: what interests you in a career in customer service?"

"Are you kidding me?"

"Come on, man."

"You already know the answer. I need a damn job!"

"Look—I have to ask you this stuff. It's just a formality."

"All right, um...yeah. Well, you know I...love people."

"Can you elaborate on that a bit?"

I shrugged. "That's pretty much it. Love people. I love the shit out of them."

"Mmm..."

"So...customer service? And me? A perfect match."

"Okay, great." He actually seemed to be taking me seriously. I looked out onto the great floor of cubicles. It was calmer, more orderly than I had imagined it. And beige. So very beige.

"I can probably get you a cubicle that's not too far from a window."

"I don't want any special treatment."

"That's the spirit."

"Was that a test?"

"I'd have to move Annie anyway, and you don't want to piss her off."

"No. I don't want to piss Annie off."

I noticed how sharp the edges were everywhere. The edge of Ben's desk, the aluminum door frame, even the edge of his computer monitor looked sharp. It was a palace of razors.

"By the way, Hoss, you look good in that suit."

"So when do I start?"

"You have to come back in and meet Marguerite first. She gets back from her cruise on the seventeenth."

"Okay. Marguerite. I'll bring my A-game to that one. You wanna grab some cheese sticks later?"

"Sure, man."

"So, let me ask you this. Is there room for advancement here? I could work circles around these punks."

"Easy, now. Let's get you hired first."

"Maybe they'll give me a sector to manage."

"The job isn't easy. You have to deal with all kinds of people and stay very...even. We've got a great staff right now. Willie, who sits on the far side by the break room? He's been here five years, going on six."

"Wow—five whole years."

"Yup."

"Sounds like a lifetime."

Ben just looked at me.

"So," I said, "how's the coffee here? Is it free?"

On the drive home I dreamed about getting into the most comfortable clothes I owned. But when I got there I felt like I didn't deserve to be comfortable, so I flopped down on the couch in the suit. I would've felt a lot better if I could've just killed everybody—thrown Carly off a cliff or skyscraper, mangled Reinhaus with a lawnmower, nuked Motorcar. At least I had the job thing squared away. Eh, whoopdee shit—a call center. And I didn't even have the job for sure. They still had to do my background check and get the "thumbs-up from HR" as Ben put it. Happy Thumbs-off Day.

Before I even knew what was happening, my face was all scrunched up. I was fucking crying. It erupted out of nowhere. I stuffed my face down into the couch cushion and scream-cried. It all came out. Cried until my face hurt. I felt like such a mega-pussy. Weirdo. *LOOZER*. I wanted to die as soon as possible. I lay there in a pile feeling sorry for myself for about an hour.

I got up off the couch and opened the blinds. The sky was overcast, and the gray light coming in actually made the room more gloomy instead of brighter. I took a deep breath and said *fuck this*: it's finally time to make things great and not suck. I heard my upstairs neighbor walking around, rushing around real fast. Then I heard a fire truck going by with its siren blaring full force. There was an oversized fly buzzing around in my kitchenette, celebrating its insect existence, looking for some bacteria to chow down on—the world was alive, godammit! It was breathing and buzzing and singing and screaming, right? Things *had* to be great. I took another deep, nourishing breath of dusty oxygen, changed into shorts and a tee-shirt, grabbed my car keys and headed to the Zoom Thru for some fucking snacks.

The thought of buying beer sparked across my mind—just a six-pack. Since it was time to celebrate the declaration of my depression being over. But I held strong. I bit my lip and just bought a bag of ice for more iced tea. I got a bag of cheese doodles and started in on them in the car on the way back. When I got home, I was exhausted. I felt like shit. I slumped on the couch and thought about how everything totally and completely super-sucked. My fingers and lips were orange with that disgusting fake cheese doodle cheese. I just wanted to curl up into a tiny ball of nothing and disappear into space. I didn't even have the energy to fantasize about killing Carly and Reinhaus and Motorcar. There was no joy in it like usual.

It was another miscellaneous afternoon. An afternoon of naps and nothingness and supreme lack of effort. A day identical to all the other days. The knock sounded like someone slamming a brick against the door about ten times. I opened it, still nap groggy. A sheriff's deputy stood there. He was wide awake.

"Mr. Henderson?"

"It's Henders."

"Sorry, Mr. Henders." He was holding a piece of paper. The first thought to shoot through my head was—he's here to arrest me. For stalking Carly. Train whistles went off in my head and a sledgehammer of panic started swinging in my chest. *Oh my god! I'm not a stalker! No! Carly! I'm sorry baby—I'm sorry!*

"So, you are Jarvis Hen—"

"I swear to God—I never, *ever* harassed her in any way. I mean, not to this level. You've got to cut me a break here."

The cop cleared his throat. Sounded like he had a steel wool pad caught in there.

"I fucking swear on the bible."

"I don't know what you're referring to, sir, but I'm here to serve you a warrant-in-debt. So you are Jarvis Henders?"

"Yeah. That's me."

He handed me the paper.

It was for the Citizen Search bill. A whopping $2,643.92. That no good bastard Reinhaus was suing me.

"Have a good day, sir," the cop said, spinning around military style for the stairs.

Have a *good day?* What the hell kind of thing was that to say! Could things get any fucking worse? I slammed door and dropped the warrant on the floor. I started pulling my hair and sucking air in through my teeth. A wave of feeling came over me, a wave of shit. I drove my fists into my temples. *Carly!* She would never call the cops on me. Would she? Not my sweet baby! And I've been fantasizing about killing her? *Oh my god!* How could I do that? I am a sick fuck! And I *was* stalking her, wasn't I? *Oh my god!* I deserved to be arrested. And shot.

I grabbed the phone and dialed her number. I had to apologize. For everything. For being a stalking weirdo loser. For dreaming about throwing her off of things. *I didn't mean it! I didn't mean it!* But her voicemail was full.

I didn't mean it!

What kind of sick freak was I? Why was I such a horrible person? My chest was seizing up with white panic. I started hyperventilating. My neck felt like it was making stratospheric re-entry. I touched it and practically burned my hand. I wanted to puke hot nails. I could feel them edging up to the top of my throat. I drove my palms into the sides of my head and clenched my face shut. This must have been the bottom. I had to have

47

hit it. There couldn't be a lower level. I was a stalker, a fantasy killer, a weirdo.

And, of course, I sucked.

It was four-thirty in the morning and I was in bed, wide awake. My stomach was churning with boiling raw sewage. For the first time, I seriously thought about what I could do to end it. Eat a bottle of pills and then lights out—Jarvis no more. The idea got my heart going. I felt alive again. Pretty fucked up when the only thing that makes you feel alive is the idea of suicide. But I didn't have the balls. And it would kill Mom. She was doing bad enough with her prescription meds and ruined mortgage.

So I just lay there, swallowing down lumps of grim depression. It tasted like ass. I thought about the warrant-in-debt again. What a kick in the groin. But at least I now had more justification for being so down. Things really *were* fucking awful. I had it on paper. Now all I needed was an injury, a broken leg or something. That's probably what would happen if I tried to kill myself—I'd jump off a building and just break my legs. And face.

4:46 am. Still wide awake. I knew I was going to spend most of the next day sleeping, but it didn't matter. I didn't have anything to do. Other than drive by Carly's to see if I could catch her coming or going. I had zero to occupy my time. Nothing to do but sleep and think. And at night, nothing to do but lie awake and think. And fantasize about mass destruction or spraying gasoline on all my enemies and lighting one gorgeous match. And think. And remember. And think some more.

8

DANIEL MOTORCAR WAS our Adventure Group Leader. He took us on canoe patrol, nature hikes and he was director of the weekly scavenger hunt. But Motorcar did things Adventure Group Leaders aren't supposed to do. We camp kids were filing into the craft shop to make papier-mâché rabbits or something. But Motorcar shuffled me off to the side for a *Super-Secret Commando Mission*, as he called it. I asked him if any other kids were going with us, but he said no, this was a two-man mission. It made me feel good when he referred to me as a man. But as we got over to an isolated spot behind the canoe shed, I found out that his only mission was to explore the contents of my underwear with his stubby little hand. He said if I told anybody about it that I'd get sent home like Jeffy. Jeffy was this messed-up kid who had spontaneous screaming tantrums and violent outbursts, such as smearing a giant handful of mac'n'cheese into this other kid's face one night at dinner. They sent him home after a few days. I thought wow, his parents are going to be furious. He's gonna be in major trouble.

I didn't want to get sent home and I didn't want to get in major trouble.

A few days later, it happened again behind the craft shop. I remember trying to get away by telling Motorcar I had to go to the bathroom. He said I could go later. I ended up not going until late the next day when my bladder was about to erupt. I was so tripped-out I couldn't pee. I was in some new zone of tripped-out. A zone of cosmic confusion. I knew what he did was wrong, but I wasn't even a hundred percent sure what the whole sex thing was about yet. He did it one more time

49

behind the canoe shed. I knew if I told on him then the police and firemen and news cameras would all come and the adults would be upset and swarming and interrogating me. There would be this giant flashing circus and all because of me. No way was I going to cause all that chaos. There were a thousand reasons not to tell anybody what Motorcar did. Anyway, even if I had wanted to, I couldn't think up the words to describe it. Eleven-year-old boys think in phrases like: "summer vacation" and "football hero." Language like "sexual molestation" and "pedophile" wasn't exactly in my word arsenal. If I couldn't put it into words in my head then how was I going to describe it to an adult? I couldn't sort any of it out. The sick lump dropped to the bottom of my stomach that first time behind the canoe shed. It sucked all the energy and joy and ability to think right out of me. A festering black death hole.

And it never left.

For the last two weeks of camp, I avoided Motorcar at all costs. Even though I knew he wasn't likely to do anything to me in the bunkhouse at night with my five bunkmates there, I slept in two pair of jeans. They were tight and I sweat all night, but I felt a lot safer in my suit of armor. The last time anything happened was the second-to-last day of camp. I was at a urinal peeing in the moldy old bathroom building and he came up behind me and started rubbing my back.

"Hello there, Jarvis," he said in this sick lady's voice. "I'll miss you." Then he left. I was so freaked out I stopped peeing and couldn't pee again until late the next day.

After I got home I knew it was less likely that I'd get into trouble, so I decided to tell Mom and Dad what happened. But every time I started to tell them, this sick freezing chill came careening up my legs and my mouth would fill up with glue. So I didn't even try. After a while the whole thing became too embarrassing to ever bring up.

I felt like such a giant failure. Before Motorcar got his hand anywhere near me I should have beaten him in the face with a canoe oar and ran screaming *Pervert! Pervert!* But I didn't.

I wimped out like a super mega-wuss. If only I had picked up that canoe paddle or a giant tree branch and knocked him out. Then I could have watched him being wheeled off to the ambulance in handcuffs, the crowd hissing him and cheering me.

If only. If the fuck only.

The next spring, my parents sat me down and asked me if I wanted to go to camp again in the coming summer. I pretended to think it over for a minute or two and then I said no, I've outgrown camp for now. They laughed. And I never went anywhere the fuck near a summer camp again.

I woke up in an ice cold death sweat. No idea what time it was. It could have been four a.m. or noon-thirty. I felt a steady blast of white hot rage screaming through my chest. My head felt like a truck accident. I wanted to kill people. I hated flimsy girlfriends, dirty cops, crooked lawyers, perverts, and fake best friends. Wanted them all dead. I rolled over and beat the pillow with my fists. Then I started crying. It was Tuesday.

Sometime later I pulled myself out of bed and made an iced tea. Clean out of coffee. I stirred the tea mixture until it was mud brown and stuck my head in the freezer. The cold air bit my ears and rushed down to the bottom of my lungs. It felt good. Real good. I was energized. It was a strange and unfamiliar feeling. I felt a tiny spark, an invisible kernel of something positive.

It turned out to be the beginnings of a little tiny idea.

For a while, it was formless. I started whistling as I poured the soap into the washing machine. Not silent whistling, but a real actual tune. I didn't know what was going on exactly, all I knew was, I was feeling a little better. For my next iced tea, I didn't measure it industrial strength like usual. Then I started up a mental to-do list for the day: finish the laundry, shower, push-ups, look for a job. But then I remembered that I didn't need to look for a job anymore, I had the gig waiting for me at the call center. That is, if I got past Marguerite. No prob—I was going to smoke her. I opened the blinds. Sunlight shot in everywhere.

But the feeling didn't last. I sat on the couch and filled up with purple-black winter. It didn't matter if things got better or if I got this new job or whatever, if I won Carly back or even got a new girlfriend—it was all going to crash to shit again no matter what I did. Just like always. It was the same thing over and over. An endless, meaningless cycle of 100% pure crap. I couldn't take it anymore. It wasn't just the highs and lows of life, either, because the highs weren't that high and the lows were unbearable pain. Something wasn't right. I just couldn't fucking go on like this anymore. This life was a colossal suck-fest. I wanted my money back from God.

I wanted justice.

I wanted *something*.

I got up and started beating my fists on the kitchen counter. All the dirty dishes were shaking and rattling like it was Armageddon. Things started falling on the floor.

"Motherfucker!"

That's when I first started picturing it:

Me, screaming in Motorcar's face. Blasting him with the harshest, most satisfying razor cold, death zinger ever spoken. Screaming in his face like a rabid drill sergeant on PCP, crystal meth and gin. Chewing him so many new assholes that he drowns in a sea of his own bullshit. Yelling into his fat wet face. *You sick motherfucker!* Getting it all out. Burning him. Frying him. Zinging him like I knew I was capable of. Really, *really* doing it. Then shooting him. Or stabbing him. Wasting him and setting his corpse on fire. Kicking it with steel-toed shoes as it burned. Then tossing his dead body out in a desert somewhere and watching the vultures swoop down for lunch. And me, laughing in a state of absolute triumphant glee.

I had the fantasies about killing Motorcar off and on for years, but this was different. This had a new air, a sense of distinct possibility. I realized for the first time that there was nothing actually stopping me from going out into the world and finding Motorcar. Giving him a faceful of boiling cold justice. When the idea fully hit me, it hit like a thousand steam whistles blowing into my neck. I imagined screaming molten zingers into his face as though it was really happening, like it was really *going* to happen. And why shouldn't it? Why couldn't I have a showdown with Motorcar? It was still a free country, last time I checked. And I had zero to lose. If I was going to kill myself anyway, why not take him down with me?

Before I knew it, I was bathing in the magical golden light of absolute decision. Everything was coming together in my head. Motorcar. That *sonofabitch!* Ruined my life! Piece of shit made me a nervous wreck alcoholic freak! I had let him off the hook for too long. Time for that filth to die!

The idea started to grow, to sink in. Exhilaration was pumping through my body like a nuclear turbine, if there was such a thing. There was now. Motorcar was going to die, for reals, and not before I totally blasted him with the world's most spectacular, most satisfying series of ice blind killer gotcha lines ever spoken by man. I was going to waste his rancid soul with super-zingers before I snuffed the life out of his pathetic body. It was going to be history's most fantastic moment of golden electric hell glory ever. And I knew that I had the power to make it real.

You stupid sack-of-shit pervert motherfucker!

Okay, but a little too common.

You disgusting, child molesting lump of human waste!

Eh. I could do better.

I asked myself why I hadn't realized this before. Why had it never occurred to me before to find Motorcar and pump him full of zingers and bullet holes? The concept was thoroughly satisfying, like a gourmet dessert. I decided to take a walk, take my new idea outside. Give it some air. Nurture it. Massage it. Any reason I couldn't do this? Anything stopping me?

Fuck no!

Taking a walk was something I never did—who the hell wants to walk through an apartment complex? But I felt good. I was onto something. Something big. Something *really* big. I didn't feel like a million bucks—I felt like a fifty billion dollar trust fund. A wheelbarrow full of stinking ten thousand dollar bills.

You worthless pedophile scum!

No, that one was terrible.

You pathetic sack of...

I hit the sidewalk and took in the oatmeal beige apartment boxes, row after duplicate row. Now they were somehow a reassuring rich light brown. At least it was *my* boring apartment complex. Things were going to change. I could feel the nuclear winter retreat an inch or two. Time for that crap to melt. I was gonna do it. I was *really* gonna do it. Motherfucker wasn't going to drag me down into his psycho loser world anymore. He wasn't gonna know what hit him. No *wonder* I became a drunk. And no wonder that my drunken stupors had been filled with evil circus clowns and flying space robots and a bunch of other stuff I couldn't remember. Like getting thrown out of places—Cogbill's, Tim Barlowe's wedding reception, college. Because Motorcar was always there. He was down at the end of a creepy hallway, laughing mad scientist laughter, always dragging me back to a life of shit behind the canoe shed. It was time to snuff him out once and for all. I was so sick of feeling tiny and vulnerable, shriveled and shaky inside, like everything was coming at me from every which way, stomping on my face. Things were going to fucking change. Things were going to change and the world was going to have to take orders from Captain Kick-Ass.

You dirty piece of...

You disgusting lump of...

You filthy worm of a sub-human...

All terrible, but I was on the right track. I had to think of something. Something good. Something *really* good.

When I got back from my walk, I went on the Internet to look for Daniel Motorcar. My heart was jack-hammering its way across the inside of my ribcage. Then, as I stared at the flashing cursor on the Internet White Pages screen, it occurred to me that I had no idea what his real name was. Sounded vaguely similar to Motorcar and that's all I knew. Was it French maybe? Or at least French-ish? Something told me it was. I started punching in all the combinations I thought it might be: *Morticar, Morticlair, Metercore.* I'd run about thirty of them before I starting getting test anxiety. My neck was raging hot. It was four o'clock, late enough to justify getting some beer to celebrate my bold new direction. I actually started to make a move for the car keys but I told myself no, I needed to stay tight to the wagon. I needed all my focus and concentration for this mission.

I punched in names for about an hour and didn't find squat. I got up and paced. I made iced tea and tried some more names. Nothing. I started getting discouraged. How was I going to find and kill the fucker if I didn't even know his name? I kept going and finally, one spelling brought up some results.

"Marticlair." There were seven of them in the United States. Two of them were in Richmond, Virginia, which was not far from the summer camp. One of them was a "D. Marticlair." That's probably him! Jackpot! But the phone number and address were unlisted. Still, the more I kept saying "Marticlair" over and over in my head, the more I was convinced that I had the name right. But the information was so freaking vague—no number, no address.

I sat there tapping my fingers. No way to find him. I started hyperventilating. I paced around the apartment some more. I ate some stale coffee cake, devouring it like I hadn't eaten in years. It tasted like moldy chalk. I turned on the TV and watched some women's tennis. Man, their legs were hot. So toned and wholesome. At least I was feeling alive again. Then I fell asleep.

I woke up and yawned and stretched. Time to resume my search. Then, while I was taking a pee I remembered something—*Citizen Search.* I could have smacked myself for not thinking of it in the first place. I raced back to the computer to have at it. Having logged on so many times at work, I easily remembered my username and password. Of course they no longer worked. I wanted to head-butt the monitor. Then I realized that I could just do it myself. So I signed up and paid for the search with my credit card. God, I love America. Within seconds a wealth of Motorcar info was laid out before me on the screen. *Citizen Search* finally did something to make up for getting me fired.

Daniel Marticlair was forty-three years old. He was the right age. He was employed as a driver for Emissary Limousine in Richmond, Virginia. And unless he was married to a seventy-two year old woman, the person listed as Margaret Marticlair was surely his mom. Living with his mom—seemed almost standard for a perv. It had to be him. I couldn't believe I'd found him. And in less than three hours. This was going to happen. I was going to be judge, jury and executioner in the royal court of Fuck You. I couldn't wait.

I got up and stretched out. Then I did fifteen push-ups. I got tired at twelve but I powered through. I was dying to tell someone about my mission, so I called Ben at work. Of course, I would have to leave out the part about killing Motorcar with my lethal fists of cosmic fury. Or shooting him. Whatever I was going to do, I knew enough about the law to know I couldn't tell anyone my ultimate intention. That could make them an accessory or something.

"This is Ben," he answered.

"Hey, Ben, it's Jarvis. Listen—I've got good news and I've got bad news."

"I've got some good news, too. Marguerite can meet you on Thursday. You might be able to start next week."

"Okay, um…that's part of the bad news."

"What do you mean?"

"I'm gonna have to delay my…when I start the job."

"What are you talking about? You don't even have the job yet. Still gotta interview with Marguerite, man. She can see you, um…hold on…"

He put me on hold. The on-hold music was a brain searing assault of synthesizers and lame jazz electric guitar. It went on forever.

"Sorry about that, Jar. Now what's the—"

"I'm taking a trip and I don't know when I'll be back. I'm going after him, Ben." Saying it out loud—I never felt so empowered.

"Going after who?"

"You know who."

He thought about it for a few seconds and then whispered: "The, um…camp counselor guy?"

"Yup."

"Oh, man—Jarvis, that is awesome! You should totally blow his brains out!"

"Ben, don't say that."

"Why not? You should. If anybody had it coming to him—"

"Is this call being recorded, like, for quality assurance purposes?"

"No, I'm not in the call center. I'm in my office."

"I thought your office was *in* a call center."

"Just—no, we're not being recorded."

"You sure?"

"Where is he? Where are you going?"

"Richmond, Virginia."

"Wow, man. That's…heavy-duty."

"It's been a long time coming."

"So what's your good news?"

"That *is* my good news."

"Shit. Mmm. Well, why don't you come in and meet Marguerite on Thursday, go down to Virginia and fuck that guy up, and then come back and start work. I mean, seriously—you're a shoo-in."

I let out a giant sigh, a huge lungful of air. It tasted like sheet metal.

"Dude," I said. "I don't know about this whole…job thing anymore."

"What!"

"I really kind of need to focus right now."

"Dude, I'll look like a maje weasel if you bail on me."

"I might be in jail."

There was a long silence.

"Yeah, that's true," he said. "Man…wow."

"If not, I mean…I feel like some changes are coming. I want to do big things, Ben. I'm not sure if telemarketing is really gonna cut it for me."

"It's not telemarketing! You don't *make* calls, you field incoming ones."

"Whatever. Look, let's just…how about I go do this thing and we'll see what's going on when I come back?"

"Okay, okay, fine, but it's not telemarketing."

"Thanks for understanding, Tex. I appreciate it."

We hung up and I went and stuck my head in the freezer. I took a couple of cold deep breaths. My neck was cooling down, but it still felt like there was a fatal car accident stuck at the bottom of my stomach. I went to the bathroom to get some Pepto, but it was fucking empty. Never worked anyway. I wondered if people at the call center knew Ben was a wannabe cowboy in his free time. Did he dress like a cowboy on casual Friday?

Oh, who gave a fuck! I was in a totally new zone. I hadn't even thought of Carly in over an hour. I was too involved with my mission. I was really going to face down Motorcar. I could feel the excitement rising off my skin like an electrified steam. The highest pinnacle of glory in my life was soon to come. It was going to be brilliant. *I* was going to be brilliant. And when I come back, if I come back, the world better look the fuck out. The world better watch its ass because Jarvis Henders was going to come back stronger, faster, bolder, better. He was going to be free. Jarvis Henders was going to come back from the sweet magnetic glory of his greatest achievement and devour the world like it was a goddam tuna salad sandwich.

9

I ACTUALLY SLEPT somewhat well that night. As I was coming to, I thought up some really good zingers to burn Motorcar with, but by the time I was fully awake I couldn't remember any of them. I tried but it was no use. Took a shower and went to the store, trying out zingers the whole time.

You disgusting, sub-mammal wad of… No.

You perverted waste of a human… Eh, no.

There's a special spot carved out for you in hell, you puke-filled sack of revolting garbage… Okay, I was improving, but I still needed work.

Whatever I ended up saying to him, the end result was this: I was going to own that piece of human waste. *Piece of human waste.* Not bad. I needed to write these down. I started making lists.

List #1: "Zingers."

List #2: "Things needed for mission."

List #3: "Affairs to be put in order."

I didn't really have any affairs. I needed to pay the cable bill. Fuck it—let the cable die. I needed a gun. I could get one at the sporting goods store. But aside from playing paintball, I had never shot a gun. Maybe that wasn't the way to go. I could strangle him but then I'd actually have to touch that disgusting piece of crap. Okay, strangling was out. Then I realized that I could wear gloves, so strangling was back in. What about poison? Too logistically difficult. Arson? He could escape before the flames got him. And I didn't really see the point in burning down his mom. She had enough problems living with her pervert loser son. When I ice him she'll be relieved of that burden, I thought. I'll be doing countless people a huge favor.

I was starting to feel overwhelmed, so I decided to focus on zingers first. I could figure out the means of death later.

I sat there with my half-baked lists, reminding myself that this was the Project of My Life. I felt like the Chosen One. Gradually, the zingers started coming.

You pathetic piece of human shit.

You worthless scumbag pervert.

Get ready to go meet Satan, ass-face!

I had three pages before I decided to take a break. I went to buy coffee and more coffee cake. I came home and drank coffee and ate coffee cake and fell asleep on the couch writing zingers. My favorite so far was *you piece of human shit,* but I had some really awful ones too, like *king of perverts.* This wasn't going to be easy.

The next day I woke up feeling amazing. I had no anger. No anger toward Carly, no anger toward Reinhaus. No fantasies of pushing Carly off the roof of a skyscraper or running over Motorcar's face with an 18-wheeler. The anger that I did have toward Motorcar was streamlined into the glorious trajectory of my mission. It had evolved from anger to purpose. I wasn't going to stay mad, I was going to get even. For once, I felt healthy. I even got started on some dishes. So this is what being healthy feels like? I thought this as I scrubbed some crust-covered plates that had been in the sink for about three months.

I picked up all the rest of the clothes off my floor and started more laundry. I washed everything. Seven full loads. The new me wasn't going to wear dirty clothes, especially in the summer. I was going to care what I smelled like. While my duds were washing, I finished the dishes. While the clothes were in the dryer, I cleaned the living room and wiped down the kitchen. I even dusted a little. I don't think I had ever dusted in my entire life. Wasn't quite sure how. I threw zingers around in my head the whole time, but nothing had stuck yet. Took a trip to the grocery store and bought a bunch of food—tuna fish, wheat bread, mayonnaise, cucumbers, orange juice, bananas and peanut butter. I wanted to be crisp and focused. I got home and made a huge tuna salad and cucumber sandwich and washed it down with ice coffee. I felt so good I wanted to hug myself, but that would've been weird.

Now I knew how all those choir boys must have felt, the ones who grew up and decided to go after their pervo priests and gun them down in the street. I could feel the sweet magic that those dudes must have felt when they made their ultimate decision. I was at peace for once. Of course, if those guys got convicted, they'd end up in a maximum security prison and God forbid they should ever "drop the soap." Seemed like that sort of defeated the purpose of the vengeance, but I didn't have time to worry about that right then. I needed to get back to work on my zinger list.

I finally came up with something that was sort of okay, I guess. *You worthless piece of human shit sperm-waste pervert motherfucking loser psycho slime ball ass-face scumbag pedophile wad of rotten feces stupid live-with-your-mother disgusting ass-neck sick-o piece of human filth!* I sat there on the couch and looked at it on the page. It was a lot to memorize. I still needed to tweak it some more. I needed the word "pathetic" in there. Did I have it? No. I needed pathetic.

I decided to go for a run, so I put on my running shoes and went outside into the blazing July heat. At least the humidity wasn't too bad. I stretched out on the grass by the sidewalk—my hamstrings, my groin, my ankles. I rolled my head around on my neck and it made a crunching sound. Then I took off. Started out at a good pace. I was running, as opposed to jogging. Jogging was for pussies. Motorcar probably jogged. Actually, I doubted that he exercised at all. He was probably a giant couch potato douche-bag. Hey—I should remember that one for my zinger list.

The run was feeling good. I took it out onto Woodfield Road and ran down the grassy shoulder, dodging dog bombs and feeling the blood pump through me. After a while I didn't even feel like I was running—I was skipping across the treetops. I owned gravity.

Then it hit me, like a surge of majestic truth—*I don't have to kill Motorcar.*

I played it over again in my mind—*I don't have to kill Motorcar.* I just needed to face him and scream at him. Get my anger out with words. That was the healthy, sensible way. Of course. I started running faster. A feeling of supreme health was rushing through me, both mentally and physically. It all made sense. I would strike him down with my killer death zingers. I would kill his soul, not his body. Then he could live with the pain of hearing my words over and over again forever in his head. This was brilliant. Now I didn't have to buy a gun or go to jail. I could do this the healthy, cathartic way. This was genius! I felt twenty pounds lighter. I felt so good I ran all the way to the Zoom Thru for a big blasting hot coffee.

My tee-shirt was gloriously soaked with sweat. The air conditioning in the Zoom Thru made me feel like I was walking into a meat freezer. I got a hot coffee and an ice cold bottle of water and stood in front of the store, alternating between the two. I looked out across the hot pavement and up at the royal blue sky and cotton-puff clouds. Everything looked so different when you weren't wallowing in sick depression like a mega-loser. Everything looked good. I never felt so fucking happy. And I had just gone from being a would-be murderer back to being a free man. But I was still going to have the full satisfaction of giving my victim the what-for. The more I thought about it, the more it made perfect sense: violence wasn't the answer, except for the brutal violence of my words. I was going to lay my burden on Motorcar and let *him* live with it. Killing him would be giving him a free pass. That bitch wasn't getting any free pass! And I was going to have a new life. Not as a murderer, not as a stalker, not as the old lame Jarvis. I was going to be the new, shiny, healthy, kick-ass Jarvis. I was going to pull the golden ring off the merry-go-round of life and make love to it. The world was going to belong to *my* ass.

Big time.

PART 2

10

MY COUSIN EVAN had lived in Richmond a long time. Maybe ten years. He'd gone to art school there but he dropped out. I didn't know what he did now—made collages out of things-found-in-the-street? The last thing I'd heard about him was he had quit his landscaping job to go on tour with a punk band. I pictured him with a torn shirt and torn jeans, lazily moving amps and drums in between smoke breaks. And by smoke breaks, I meant crack. Whenever anybody in the family talked about Evan, they always said "What a shame." I didn't know for sure about his smoking crack, but what I did know was that Evan seemed like a giant sack of wasted potential. He was always super smart and had this look of creative intelligence in his eyes, even when we were kids. But now he was just this art school drop-out freakazoid. A roadie for a punk band. "What a shame."

He and I got along great when we were kids, though. I was eight months younger but he was skinny and I punched him a lot. By the time we were teenagers he'd become a full blown death metal goth dude. When he showed up at that one Christmas with dyed long black hair and eyeliner and the piercings in his lip, we pretty much officially elected him family weirdo. It was unanimous. He looked so out of place, especially with his mom wearing her bright red Christmas sweater with the elaborate snowmen and reindeer scene on the front.

The most recent time I'd seen him was at Uncle Pie-rold's funeral three or four years back. Pie-rold's carotid arteries were so packed with butter and pie crust that he didn't make it to his fifty-third birthday. Evan showed up at the funeral looking more punk than goth, with spiky short hair and a slightly wild look in his eye. He was pretty upbeat, even smiling at times, which somehow for him didn't look out of place at a funeral. He pulled it off. Never could figure his ass out.

I only needed a crash pad for one night. I was going to be so focused on my confrontation with Motorcar that I didn't care if I had to sleep on Evan's kitchen floor amongst his sculptures of things-found-in-the-street. Being unemployed, I really didn't want to waste money on a hotel. And I didn't want to make the three-hour drive down to Richmond, do the confrontation and then drive back all in the same day either. I wanted to be relaxed and steady. I wanted plenty of extra time to case out Motorcar's house and run a final honing of my zingers.

I got Evan's number from his mom, my Aunt Pat. She wanted to know why I was calling him, but I wasn't saying squat. Just wanted to catch up with the old boy. I wasn't going to tell Evan about the real reason for my visit either. No way. No need to get into all that. So I told him I was interviewing for paralegal jobs down in Richmond as a precursor to submitting my application to several Virginia law schools.

"Nice," Evan said. "You moving here would be awesome!"

"No, well, I mean, it would just be, like, an internship. Just temporary."

"It would be great to have you down here, bro. I mean cuz."

"I really appreciate you letting me stay over."

"Don't mention it, dude. People stay here all the time. You can hang as long as you want, check out the area, whatever."

"Yeah, no. Just one night'll do."

"That's cool. Man, it'll be great to see you."

"Yeah…um, you too, Evan. For sure."

"One thing, though."

"What's that?"

"I don't go by 'Evan' anymore. I'm Shred now."

"Shred?"

"Yeah."

"Okay, Shred."

He'd sounded more congenial than I expected. Actually polite and friendly and upbeat. Bizarre. The whole "people stay here all the time thing" didn't surprise me. I pictured touring punk bands sleeping on his coffee table or transient artists living in the kitchen. For months at a time. Freaks who made obscene sculptures out of aluminum foil and snorted angel dust. I made a mental note to bring my own soap.

I had Motorcar's address memorized, a couple of Mapquest maps so I could find both his and Shred's place, a list of zingers, jar of instant iced tea and a full tank of gas. That was all I needed. And the soap. I just had to polish my paragraph of zingers to a fine sheen and I'd be good. I read it over and hated it. Too wordy. I crumpled it up and threw it in the sink. Screw it. Plenty of time to think up a new one. I started working up some new lines as soon as I got in the car.

You sleazebag mistake of a human filth...piece. Piece of...

Nuh-uh.

You disgustingly rotten slime...monster.

No—it wasn't a fucking science fiction movie. I would think of something. The day had come up quick but I still had time to construct the perfect series of zingers. I imagined them shooting out of my mouth like a magical death ray. So sweet. I just hoped that my crappy Hyundai motor wouldn't blow before I reached my state of ultimate redemption. I was going to be so healthy after this, I would have to rent a storage unit for all my extra health. Carly would be sure to notice the change, so winning her back should be easy. Potential employers were going to notice it in job interviews. The new me was going to fucking rock. I stepped on the gas pedal. The plastic had broken off leaving a metal nub but it still worked. I told her to take it easy, one mile at a time, girl. You can do it. Just get me there. As I crossed the Woodrow Wilson Bridge I looked over toward D.C., but the summer haze rising off the Potomac was so thick I could barely see the tiny Capitol and Monument. The river looked like it was about to start boiling from underneath, plotting to suck everything down with it back into the primordial slop.

I thought about the earth before the invention of time, when it was all a bunch of lava lakes and toxic ooze. They didn't have problems like perverts and stalkers back then.

I was already halfway through Fairfax County when I realized I hadn't been working on my zingers.

You gross sonofabitch.

Terrible.

You worthless piece of disgusting puke.

Worse.

I had Motorcar's street address locked down solid, but no zings. 2214 Glade Farms Way. It sounded too nice for him. Who wouldn't want the easy-going times of life on a glade farm? Why did they need a farm to grow glades anyway? Wasn't a glade just a thing of giant grass? Didn't they just grow naturally, like, in meadows and shit? The contradictions were leading me to fantasize violence, something I was really trying to get away from. What other topics could I think about? Pro football, space travel, what I would do if I won the lottery. Nothing stuck as a topic to ponder. Maybe I needed a hobby. After all this is over, I should take up a hobby. How about card tricks? No. Kung Fu? Possibility. I could always get better at paint-ball. Maybe I should try out for the local paint-ball league.

The car started making this weird zushing noise. It didn't sound bad but it didn't sound good either. Maybe there was a Canadian goose stuck under the wheel well. *Zush.* No, probably not. Wasn't sure what else it could be. *Zush...zush...zush.*

I got to the Richmond area close to sunset. I started seeing warehouses, industrial buildings, a baseball stadium, so I figured I must be getting close. I got out my directions and kept my eyes peeled for the Belvidere Street exit. It came up quick.

Richmond was a sleepy looking city. Didn't have that crisp buzz of D.C. It seemed overgrown with weeds and humidity, a city that was nestled in the depths of summer and lolled there like a lazy head in a soft pillow. There was something relaxed in the air. I liked it. The twilight made everything look yellow and red. I felt like I was driving into another time. Shred's neighborhood was supposed to be coming up on the right. I turned on Idlewood Avenue and took a left on South Laurel Street, which was his street. These were the easiest directions I'd ever followed. I took this as a good sign.

The houses were old slumping row houses, like a hundred years old. Most of them had these Wild West front porches, some with swirly ornate carvings around the tops. Most of them needed paint. Actually, all of them needed paint. And siding. Giant chunks of siding were missing in some cases, exposing the tar paper. The narrow one-way street was packed with parked cars on both sides, leaving barely enough room for my car to fit through. The porches and sidewalks were jam packed with screaming little kids, women with giant arms and angry looks on their faces and old men with sideburns and baseball caps drinking Budweiser. One of them was working on a car even though it was practically dark. This was not a neighborhood that one might describe as privileged. The strange thing was, everyone was white, from the lady in the NASCAR tee-shirt to the ten-year-old boys with no shirts who were jumping and dashing and raising general hell, to the young teenage girl I saw pushing a stroller down the street. I hoped the baby in the stroller was her little sister and not her daughter. Holy jeez.

When I saw the full spread of a Confederate flag displayed against the front of one house, anchored from the sill of a second story window for all the world to see, I knew I was in some kind of all-white, inner-city redneck ghetto. But, aside from being racists, I figured they were harmless enough. Until I got to the next intersection. There was a huge throng of late-teens and early-twenty-something bad-asses all hanging out on the sidewalk and street, their heads shaved or close cropped, mostly wearing white tee-shirts or wife-beaters and giant pants, some with their shirts off. A couple of girls were scattered in, wearing too much make-up and looking overweight and underage. Hip-hop beats blasted from a car stereo rig that probably cost more than the car it boomed from, if you subtracted the cost of the shiny, pimped-out wheels. These guys looked like they wanted nothing more than to smoke some crack and kick some ass. A few of them glared at me as I drove by. I looked straight ahead and cruised on until I found Evan's house, two long, thankful blocks from the mayhem.

I found a parking space across the street from Shred's and practically ran to the front door, even though the ruffians were long out of sight. Shred's block was a lot quieter. I saw a lady out on her front porch watering some plants. She actually looked kind of more middle class, the wooden siding on her house freshly painted light blue. What kind of fucked-up neighborhood *was* this?

The row of ancient row houses that included Shred's place sat slumping into itself, like it was in a peaceful geriatric coma. There were two front doors, so I figured it was an up-down duplex, but he hadn't told me which door was his. I took my directions out to double check. "718 S. Laurel St." There were thick blankets hanging up on the inside of the windows of the downstairs unit, so I couldn't tell if the lights were on or not. I decided to try that one first, since Shred seemed like someone who would put blankets up over the windows.

I knocked. Nothing. And again. Nothing. So I tried the other door. Nada. One of the neighborhood bad-asses sped by in their little car booming a hip-hop beat at outrageous decibels. I stepped in a little closer to the house. What was it with this redneck white boy hip-hop thing? Shouldn't they be playing Lynyrd Skynyrd? I knocked again on both doors and after a while I heard some rattling.

A guy with moppy blonde hair opened the door and stood there, hunched over on aluminum crutches. He had on the biggest broken leg cast I've ever seen in my life and a miserable smirk on his face. He was wearing a tee-shirt that said *Thirty and Dirty*. The shirt actually was dirty.

"Didn't you hear me?" he said.

"No, I didn't."

"I said 'come in' three times."

"Sorry. Um…hi. I'm Evan's cousin? I mean Shred. Shred's cousin?"

He just stared at me. It was dark, but I could see his eyes were glazed over. He smelled like wet cardboard.

"I'm Jarvis," I said, reaching out my hand.

He just looked down at his one of his crutches and then back at me. "Kenny," he said.

"So… is he around? He said I could stay here tonight?"

"Naw. He's working." Kenny let out a big sigh. It sounded painful.

"Come on in," he said, like he didn't really want me to come in. He carefully maneuvered his leg around and crutched himself down the hall.

It was a shotgun apartment, three rooms and a bathroom off a long hallway ending in a living room with the kitchen beyond that. Looked like it still had the original plaster from 1908. A smell of weird incense floated in the air, mixing with the wet cardboard. I followed crutches guy. He must have broken his leg in fifty places, the cast was so huge.

The living room was full-on zany. Walls were covered with this crazy artwork, cartoony paintings of wacky faces with their features all stretched out and crooked in strange colors. One of them looked just like our dead Uncle Pie-rold, with his eyes shut and his tongue sticking out, laying across the top of a giant toaster. There was an orange shag rug from the 70s on the floor. The coffee table, pushed up close to the couch so Kenny could reach stuff, featured the biggest mound of crap I'd ever seen. Usual items like ashtrays, car keys, beer cans, a bottle opener, CDs, bits of paper, junk mail, pens and pencils, an empty can of cashews, sunglasses, but then there was all this other stuff: a little red ceramic frog that looked really out of place, anti-itch salve, a Native American pot pipe, a small brass Buddha, an old 35mm camera, a woman's silver necklace and an open metal box that contained a variety of pill bottles and a bag of weed. When Kenny saw me looking into it he bent over and snapped the lid shut. The TV was on. Looked like something on PBS. An old air conditioner hummed and wheezed in the window, but it didn't seem to be cooling the air at all. Maybe it took some of the humidity out and that was it.

Kenny started this painful-looking process of transferring himself from crutches to couch. Now I felt bad for knocking on the door. He lifted his cast onto about seven pillows and then just stared off toward the TV with his mouth partly open. I put my backpack on the floor and sat down on the edge of an orange chair. It was a different orange than the rug. I started getting a headache.

After I couldn't take sitting there tapping my feet anymore, I said: "So…what time does Evan get home from work?"

"You mean Shred? 'Round eleven."

"How'd he get that name, anyway?"

Kenny didn't answer.

"How'd he get 'Shred' as a nickname?"

Nothing.

"'Cause he shreds it," he finally said.

"He what?"

"He rips it up."

"Oh. Okay."

I looked up at one of the paintings, a cartoony face with a purple tongue sticking out and two mismatched eyes. The background was a puke green sky with orange clouds. The frame looked like something found in a dumpster, spray painted burnt orange. Orange was big in here.

"Bong hit?" Kenny offered.

"Oh, no thanks."

"D'ya mind grabbing me the bong? It's in the corner." He pointed toward a two-foot tall, red glass bong. He wasn't that far from it, but I could see how stretching and twisting up from the couch would kill his leg.

"Sure." I went over and grabbed the ruby tower of pot-head glory.

"Careful," Kenny said. "Put it right here." I set the bong down on the floor near Kenny's head. "There's beer if you want one."

"No, thanks. I don't drink."

"I thought all lawyers drank."

"I'm not a lawyer."

"Shred said you were a lawyer."

"No, no. I am planning on going to law school, but..."

Kenny just looked at me like—*so what's the difference then?*

And yeah, with my red polo shirt and khaki shorts and flip-flops, trimmed professional law office haircut, I looked like a lawyer on my day off.

"You mind gettin' me one? They're in the fridge."

I went and got him a beer from the fridge. The kitchen looked normal. No aluminum foil sculptures featuring things-found-in-the-street, anyway. I gave Kenny his beer and sat back down. He reached into the metal box for some pharmaceuticals and washed a couple down with the beer.

After a while I asked: "So, you mind if I ask how you broke your leg?"

"Skydiving."

"Nuh-uh. Really?"

"It's more addictive than heroin and five times as expensive."

"Wow. You're like, a skydiving addict?"

"Nothing like it on earth, in hell or outer space."

"I dunno. Going to space would be pretty...cool?"

There was a heavy silence. I didn't really believe him. He probably broke it falling off a curb after a long night of drinking. I sat there and thought about how I couldn't wait to grab Motorcar by the collar and scream zingers into his face.

Kenny did his bong-hit, and I could feel myself getting high off the residuals. Or maybe I just felt strange naturally. I went to take a pee. The bathroom was actually sort of clean. When I came back, some documentary about spiders was on. Kenny readjusted his leg, sucking air in between his teeth and scrunching his face together.

Spiders. It was theorized they may have migrated from another planet, some genetic goo tucked inside the crevice of a meteor that evolved into spiders. Maybe that's where I came from. I got up to look at the bookshelf of videos and books. There were a couple of classic flicks like *Taxi Driver* and *Willy Wonka and the Chocolate Factory*, and a bunch of documentaries, like: *Sirhan & Company: Who Really Killed RFK*, *The Trilateral Commission: Fact vs. Fiction*, *The Illuminati Tapes: Secret Governments & Their Minions*. For books there was a lot of Phillip K. Dick, Robert Anton Wilson, more non-fiction stuff, *The History of Freemasonry*, *UFOs & The New World Order*, etc. Whoa. The word "kook" came to mind. No idea if the kook was Kenny or Shred though, and I didn't feel much like asking. We sat there for a while not saying anything.

Someone knocked on the front door and it scared the shit out of me. I jerked my head around.

"Don't worry," Kenny said, amused at me. "Probably just the cops."

They knocked again.

"You mind getting it?"

"Okay," and I jumped up from my seat. I headed down the hall thinking a hotel room might've been a better deal than being this guy's manservant.

I opened the door and saw two absolute freaks—a girl with tattoos all over and piercings in her nose and ears and one eyebrow, her hair molded into short spikes. She wore a black tank top, green army pants cut-offs and old ratty pair of black-and-white Chuck's. A tall, skinny guy with funeral eyes stood behind her. He was wearing a black trench coat even though it was August. The coat looked lightweight and he didn't look hot, but still.

The girl looked at me and smiled, almost a laugh. She was tiny, with a gorgeous smile of big sensuous lips and happiness creases. She had a sexy mischievous elf quality, but all the freak stuff kinda ruined it for me.

Then three dogs came charging into the house, nearly knocking me down. They hauled ass down the hallway. "Hey!"

I yelled at them, feeling like I had done something wrong by letting them in.

"Who are you?" the girl asked.

"I'm Jarvis. The Shred's cousin."

"*The* Shred?" She smiled. "I'm Summer."

The tall funeral one did not speak. We both looked at him. "This is Klavin," Summer said, hitting the guy on the sleeve of his trench coat. He nodded and we shook hands. His hand felt completely neutral, not hot, not cold. Not dry, not clammy. He seemed barely alive.

"Is Shred still at work?" Summer said.

"I...I believe so, yes."

"Is Kenny here?"

"Yes. Kenny."

"Well, um...can we come in?"

"Oh. Yeah, sure."

Summer smiled again, like I somehow amused her. I led them to the living room, where Kenny's eyes were even more glazed over than when I left him. They all said *What's up* to each other. Summer was spunky, plopping onto the couch next to Kenny with a bit too much energy.

"Ow!" Kenny screamed. "You trying to kill me?"

"Awww," she said, and started stroking his neck and saying "Poor baby." He seemed to recover pretty fast. Klavin, who was still standing, looked down at them like he might produce a .45 from under his trench coat at any minute and blow us all away. The dogs were already sitting on the floor chilling out, like they'd been there thirty-seven million times before.

What a bunch of freaks. I wondered if I was even going to recognize my own cousin when he came home. He probably had tattoos of gargoyles and griffins on his face and a beard down to his stomach, a beard inhabited with fruit flies and a family of exotic birds.

Kenny called for a round of beers, and for some reason I said I'd have one. Then I immediately wondered what the hell was I thinking.

"I thought you didn't drink," Kenny snapped.

"No, I'm…just one beer."

"He sat there ten minutes ago and said he didn't drink."

"No, I said I wasn't a lawyer."

"You're a lawyer?" Summer said.

"No! I'm not a lawyer. I'm trying to get a job in a law firm, that's all. Paralegal." It came out as testy and uptight. Followed by a painful stretch of no talking. Thank god at least the TV was on for some background noise. Now I did want to drink the beer.

Kenny offered bong-hits. Klavin handed out the cold ones, dripping cans of Pabst Blue Ribbon.

I cracked mine open and felt human again.

I looked down at the open tab on the can. The alcohol smell rose up and tweaked my nose.

No way.

I set the beer down on a rare open space on the coffee table and tried to pretend it never existed.

Summer popped up from the couch and turned off the TV. "Sorry Mister Spider," she said to the documentary. Then she sat on her knees and picked out a CD. A cloud of pot smoke wafted above, followed by Klavin's thin cough. And then the last thing I ever would have expected to emerge from the speakers came rolling out: the sound of Hank Williams. Senior. The real one. Country music from a thousand years ago. This girl Summer was obviously a punker, or some kind of goth variation on the punk theme, so I would have expected her to play some Sex Pistols or Black Flag or other hard stuff. Now I was truly in Bizarro World, where the rednecks played hip-hop and the punkers were into country. I couldn't wait until "Shred" got home so I could ask him what the fuck was going on—*hey man, why are your friends so weird?*

With all the weed smoke in there, my head started to feel like a floatation device. Kenny told a skydiving story about a guy whose chute didn't open. He lived, but broke every bone in his skeleton, had internal injuries, a concussion, months of traction. Summer talked about going to see a show at the Ditch later, which I figured was a club, though I pictured a scraggily punk band actually playing in a roadside ditch. She caught me staring at her. I had never been in such close proximity to a cute girl freak-type. She had a spider web tattoo on her shoulder, but it had a lady bug instead of a spider. On her arm was a moon with a weird cartoon face, one looked like part of a fire truck. One of them may or may not have been Satan. I couldn't tell what her other tattoos were. I thought about the kind of upscale sophistication that Carly was always trying to display. Summer didn't seem to give two craps about any of that. It struck me as kind of refreshing. Then again, maybe it was just the weed smoke thinking for me. These people didn't seem to care much about anything. Did they even work? I couldn't picture Klavin at a job. Then again, I was jobless myself, so who was I to talk?

The front door blasted open and I jumped again. Shred's grand entrance into the room was to walk in with his head down and this mischievous little smile on his face. He looked weirdly clean cut, short hair, shaven, wearing catering black and whites, except without the bow tie. He had a slightly wild bed-head hairdo, but other than that, he actually looked kind of normal.

"Jarvis!" he said. "Good to see you."

"Good to see you too." I put my hand out but he gave me a hug instead. He smelled vaguely of blue cheese and salmon.

"I guess y'all met my cousin, Jarvis, right?" he said to the room.

Only Summer said yes. Kenny and Klavin were silent.

"I need a damn beer," Shred announced. "Anybody else?"

He got his beer and came back and took a bong-hit. Summer threw on a Patsy Cline disc. Maybe she was just venturing into country oldies as an experiment. A break from the punk. Or she was being ironic. Couldn't tell for sure.

"So, Jar," Shred asked. "You wanna go to a show with us?"

"I dunno. I'm pretty tired from the drive."

"Shit—that drive's, what—it's less than three hours. Come on."

"I got up really early today."

"Bah."

Shred was no longer gloomy Evan from the Goth netherworld, now he was one of those energetic, persuading types. He had a kind of insanity in his eyes. Summer was looking at me like she was amused again.

"Yeah," I said. "Pretty beat. I'll probably just crash here on the couch, if that's cool."

"That's where Kenny sleeps. Come on, it's a great band—Burnt Thunder." He started doodling an air guitar with a manic intensity.

Kenny nodded his head to Shred's imaginary beat.

"They have a girl who plays accordion through a distortion pedal," Summer said from the floor where she was scratching one of her dogs.

"Come on," Shred pleaded.

I wasn't that tired. I just wanted to focus on my mission. I needed to practice zingers. And I actually didn't want to be seen in public with these people. I knew that was ridiculous, since no one in Richmond knew me. My stomach was swamping up, too. I just wanted to drink some coffee and go to sleep.

"If you don't go with us, you can't stay here," Shred said with a smart-ass smile.

"Are you ever gonna drink your damn beer?" Kenny said.

"You going, Kenny?" Shred asked.

Kenny answered by staring at him with his glazed-over eyes. Then he made a vague "nah" sound and looked back over toward the wall.

I realized that if I didn't go, I'd be stuck sitting here with Kenny. Plus Shred and Summer would think I was lame. Also, where the fuck was I supposed to be sleeping anyway? The sides were closing in on me.

"Okay," I said. "I'll go."

"*Yes!*" Shred said.

We piled into Summer's giant, rusted, late 70s Buick—me, Shred, Klavin, Summer, dogs and all. The chocolate lab sat on my lap and panted dog breath directly into my face. I think

I heard Summer calling him Moosie. She could barely see up over the dashboard. She needed to be sitting on some telephone books or something.

Took about four minutes to get to the Ditch, a small old brick building that stood by itself, like a box. I knew it had to be the Ditch, because the only other things around were an old warehouse-looking building across the street and a parking lot. Everything around here was so old, I half expected to see some Civil War soldiers walking up the street. The Ditch didn't even look open, until I saw tiny Christmas lights strung up across the front door. Summer parked in the parking lot and we all got out, dogs included.

"They let dogs in here?" I said.

No one answered me. Summer was smiling a little on the side of her mouth. I was so amusing.

Two dollar cover for humans. The doorman seemed to know the dogs and they got in free, disappearing into the forest of legs. The Ditch was packed with art freaks, punkers, Goths, people with blue hair, girls wearing combat boots and glitter on their cheeks and now me—a preppo in a red polo shirt. My cohorts immediately scattered into different conversations with people they knew. Shred seemed to know everybody.

I walked up to an innocuous looking spot near the end of the bar and tried to pretend I was invisible. I wanted coffee, but I didn't see any coffee pots going, only beer, liquor and a rack of soda guns. A Coke would do, but the bar was crammed with people ordering real drinks.

I started noticing some stares, not really dirty looks, but one punker dude did look at me like he wanted to kick my ass. I couldn't see Shred or his gang anywhere and it was making me nervous. Did I look like a cop? Were these people really giving me unfriendly stares or were they just weirdos and that's how they looked at people?

After fifteen minutes or so of standing there looking vaguely at the ceiling, I heard the whoops and pops and bits of feedback of the band getting ready to start burning their thunder. There was a dividing wall with two arched passageways between the bar and the stage area, so I could only see part of one band member's arm from where I stood. One of Summer's dogs squeezed by in front of me. I reached down to pet him, but he ignored me and kept going.

Starting with a crackled punch, a searing guitar sound came blasting out from the amps in a sonic death orgy of red noise and drums. It sounded like a major malfunction of equipment at a hydro-electric power plant, where all the workers were schizophrenics on meth. No way I'm gonna be able to stand here and think up zingers for Motorcar with that going on. Not that I could anyway, with all these freaks around, looking at me. What was *that*? That sound. A loud burning sound, like someone playing a lawnmower with a radioactive violin bow. I craned my head around to the see the stage through the archway, but I could only see more of the bass player's arm. Then I remembered: the girl who plays the accordion through a distortion pedal. I thought my brain was going to implode, but people seemed to like it, they were bobbing their heads. It was the strangest music I'd ever heard, a turbo-powered electric accordion throbbing against a pounding hybrid of punk and metal. Punkle? Munk? I wondered what they called it. Some pushing was going on up front near the archway, which at first I thought was a fight, but it turned out to just be a warm-up for a mosh pit.

You cock-suckin-mother-fuckin-sonofabitch.

No.

You ruined my life, you worthless piece of sub-human raw sewage.

Better, but basically terrible. Too noisy to concentrate. It was going to be less than twenty-four hours before the showdown and I couldn't think of shit. For all the zinger raw material floating around my head, the perfect combo of burning cold hit-words still eluded me.

Maybe I should just kill him instead. I chuckled to myself at the thought. Of course, I wasn't going to abandon my mature, non-violent approach—I'd come so far already. In such a short stretch of time, I'd gone from having sick execution fantasies to making this healthy verbal confrontation a *real* reality. If I could just spew out the verbal ammunition, just the right words, in just the right order—then the permanent sunbeams of righteousness would glare from my head forever, showing me the way.

I tried nodding my head to the music along with all the other rockers or punklers or whatever they were, but it didn't feel right so I stopped. I wanted coffee. I wanted iced tea. The bar was still crammed with drinkers trying to order, and now there was a biker dude with a sleeveless, spiked leather jacket taking up a bunch of the space. This was the strangest bar I'd ever been to in my life—I half expected the Village People to come popping out. I cussed myself for not having just stayed in a hotel with a pad and pen and perfected my zinger speech.

Then Summer appeared in front of me, screaming, "You like 'em?"

"Yeah," I yelled back. "*You* like em?"

"Oh yeah, they're awesome."

"I thought you were a country fan."

"What?"

"I said I thought you were a country music fan!" I screamed louder.

She looked at me like I was an idiot, then she stepped in closer to my ear: "What kind of music do you like?"

"Oh, all kinds," I said. "Billy Joel?"

Her little elf nose curled up like she smelled something bad. Then Klavin showed up and handed her a beer. She said something to him, but I couldn't tell what. Then she squeezed my elbow and leaned in again.

"We're gonna go back up front," she said.

They headed back into the wall of people. My elbow felt all warm where she touched it. What the hell was up with that? No way I could be attracted to such a freaky chick. Maybe I was just still feeling vulnerable because of the break-up thing with Carly. I started getting a little sleepy. Hard to believe someone could yawn during a heavy metal accordion solo, but I did.

81

After the show, I overheard talk of folks heading to Shred's to do bong-hits and drink more beer. These people were non-stop. Party professionals. There were two extra people for the ride back, not that Summer's giant car couldn't handle it. This time I had the golden retriever-Lassie mix half on me. Verty, I believe Summer called her. Her big eyes looked like marinated olives. Verty's other half was on Shred. Good thing this was a four-minute drive and not a road trip to Europe.

11

WE FELL UP into the house and loudly woke up Kenny, but he seemed like he was used to it. Summer immediately cranked the Burnt Thunder CD, which must have felt like a hundred jackhammers going at once in Kenny's head. That's what it sounded like in my head, anyway. The place flowed with beer and bong-hits, cigarette smoke and laughter. This was *not* the best environment to be thinking up hot zingers and honing my mission focus. Shred was acting like a nut. I couldn't understand half of what he was talking about. He kept mimicking the distorted accordion player's weird swaying arm motions. I think he had a crush on her.

"She had that, like…did you hear on 'Andalusia' that one fucked-up part where she hit the delay pedal and *Braaaang…*" He started flapping his arms like a chicken trying to fly. No one ever introduced me to the other two dudes who came. They talked to Kenny about his leg and some art festival they had all gone to. Summer played with her dogs on the floor. The little black one was trying to eat the tip of one of her Chucks.

Shred finished packing everyone their first bong-hit and came over to where I was sitting on an upside down milk crate by the orange chair.

"Come on down here, Jarvis. I wanna show you something."

We went down the hall and into one of the closed rooms. It was Shred's studio, I guess, for lack of a better word. A total mess, junk and beer cans and clothes on the floor, with half-finished paintings lying all around, his cartoony drawings taped to the wall. He led me to a crap-cluttered table and sat down to warm up his computer.

"Check this out," he said.

I thought he was going to show me his artist's website, or some astrology charts or something. For some reason, I thought he was into astrology. But what he did pull up on the screen was even weirder. It was a blown-up, slow-motion clip of the Zapruder film. Poor doomed Kennedy with his fists against his chest, and then a couple frames later, *blammo*. Gruesome, that up-close.

"Look," Shred said, running the clip back again. "They blew half his face off. See? Now check this out," he said, pulling up a string of black-and-white photographs from JFK's autopsy. "The back of his head's all blown apart, but his face is fine? Now look at the hit again."

"Think I pretty much got it."

"See? They got him in the face. The autopsy is of a wax dummy." Shred clicked back to the autopsy photo. "See how phony it looks?" He turned in his chair and looked at me, as if for approval.

"Come on, man," I laughed. "The Evan I know isn't a sucker for conspiracy theories."

"Don't ever call me that. I'm Shred now. And it's not a theory, it's a conspiracy *fact*. Patton, John Lennon, Marilyn Monroe—the government wasted all of them. The blue-blood shadow government, I mean."

"Suuuurrrre," I said. "You mind if I put on some light in here?" I hit the switch for the overhead light, which was bright as fuck. Shred was squinting like he just bit into an unripened grapefruit. "Now, why do I need to know all this? So nine guys shot Kennedy. So what?"

"Well, for one thing, being a lawyer, you should be aware of—"

"Whoa, hold on here. I'm not a lawyer."

"I thought you were down here to interview for lawyer gigs."

"No, I'm just looking for a paralegal job."

"Mom said you were in law school."

"No," I said. "I want to *go* to law school."

"Oh." Shred blinked his eyes. He looked confused.

Bursts of group laughter were coming in from the living room. "Shouldn't we get back to the party?" I asked.

We went in and I sat in the corner on the floor. There was so much pot smoke in the room now, by just sitting there for a couple of minutes and breathing, I was buck stoned. I wanted to get my instant iced tea out of my backpack and make a strong glass, but I felt like I didn't have permission to move. Summer was making herself right at home, though, playing with her dogs and laughing a lot. She had the joy of life.

I couldn't follow the conversation very well. I did catch something about a friend of theirs named Farns who drove his van up to the front of city hall to protest his high water bill with a megaphone. He spent the night in jail. Shred recounted a special on cable about Hitler's doctor injecting him with liquefied bull testicles. I didn't believe him. People were making references to things I'd never heard of, underground movies I'd never seen, music I didn't know existed. Never felt so isolated in my life. I was sure everyone could see the sterile medicine fog surrounding me. *What's that boring medical smell? Oh, look, it's that yuppie Jarvis.*

I needed to get in my own space and zing it up. I waited for Shred to go in the kitchen and followed him in.

"Thanks again for the hospitality, Ev—I mean Shred."

"You're having a good time, right?" he said, opening the fridge and looking around.

"Yeah. Tired, though, um..." I pointed vaguely toward the living room. "Place to...crash?"

"Already?"

"Well, I got that interview tomorrow."

"Oh, yeah. What time is that?" He popped open a beer and started guzzling.

"Um...four o'clock?"

"Cool, then we got time to go out for breakfast."

"So, do you have like a...sleeping bag or—"

"Kenny's room."

"Oh. So he is your roommate."

"Yeah—what do you think this is, a convalescent home for gimpos? Actually, I guess it is. Captain Gimpo sleeps on the couch. Easier on the leg."

Wow. Shred had gone from being a deadly quiet vampire to a quick-witted zing tosser in just a few years. And for a pot-smoking, hard drinking, weirdo art freak, that was pretty impressive. Damn him. I went to get the instant iced tea out of my backpack to make a glass before bed. I opened the freezer, psyched to find a bag of store ice. That was one good thing about drinkers— they usually had ice. I thought about sticking my head in, but I didn't feel the need. Plus, what if someone saw me. Back in the living room, one of the nameless dudes was on the floor playing with Summer's dogs. It also looked like he was kind of hitting on her. That bothered me for some reason.

"Watch the leg," Kenny told the guy.

Some of the party spirit seemed to have left the room. I was careful to hold my iced tea steady as I leaned over to picked up my backpack from the floor. Then I stood up straight and looked around and wondered what to say. *So pleased to have made your respective acquaintances, fine gentlefolk?* That wouldn't exactly have been audible above the music. They'd gone from Burnt Thunder to Dylan to some strange punk jazz sounding stuff to Black Sabbath, cranked.

Kenny's eyes looked like distant planets that had been tweaked off their orbits by a deranged comet. Still, he looked straight up at me and read my awkwardness.

"Didn't even touch your damn beer and now you're drinking iced tea?" he said. "That's alcohol abuse!"

"Oh…uh…sor—" I stopped myself. Apologizing sounded too weak. I put my backpack over my shoulder instead. He was right, though. My opened and full, unsipped beer sat there on the edge of the coffee table. Kenny looked down at the beer and then up at me like I'd committed high crimes against humanity. A look made all the more eerie due to his floating eyeballs.

Fortunately, Shred walked up and said: "It's down here," nodding toward the hallway.

"Are you going to sleep?" There was a sweetness in Summer's voice that seemed completely incongruous with the tattoos and piercings. I was surprised she even cared.

"Yeah, um…" I looked at Shred. "I've got an interview tomorrow, so—"

"We should go, then," she said. "Come on, Moosie."

"Oh, don't go on my account."

Everyone started to get up. Dogs too. Except Kenny, of course. I felt super lame. A party-destroying party pooper. Now I just wanted to get down to Kenny's bedroom and close the door before he made some shitty comment.

"It was very nice to meet you," Summer said. "Good luck tomorrow."

"Thanks." I couldn't stop looking at the way the edges of her smile curled up. She shook my hand. Very lady-like. "Nice to meet you, too."

"Oh, jeez," Kenny said.

Everyone said their "Laters" and their "Later ons." I followed the throng down the hallway. Shred closed the front door behind them and led me into Kenny's room. The wall was covered with skydiving posters so I guess he wasn't lying about his leg. Unless he was just extremely delusional or stoned. Aside from a pile of rotten clothes in the corner, the room was actually kind of neat. The bed was even made.

"Don't mind Kenny," Shred said. "He's going through withdrawal." He nodded toward the skydiving scenes.

"Oh, no problem. Sorry about the beer."

"Eh," he said, waving it away.

"I meant to ask you, your neighborhood here—"

"What, Oregon Hill? What about it?"

"It's a little bit…I dunno, different, huh?"

He laughed. "A little bit, yeah. What about it exactly?" He had a sort of insane wolf look in his eyes but also a tiny smile.

"Oh, nothing. Just the neighbors are kind of…not what I'm used to, I guess."

"Oh, the Hillites?"

"The who?"

"The Hillites. The natives. Aborigines."

"They're a little a bit scary. The hip-hop rednecks."

"Yeah—watch out for those fuckers. They still think it's the Wild West around here sometimes."

"But then the place across the street looks kind of…I dunno…middle class."

Shred twisted his eyes at me a bit, like he didn't quite trust me. "Well, it's mainly Hillites, then you got the yuppos who live in all the renovated places, and then the people like us."

"People like… ?" I smiled. For some reason I wanted him to admit he was the filthy outcast art freak that I was so infinitely superior to.

He bugged his eyes out and said, in this kind of Satanic dungeon voice: "We are the ones from the backwards electric netherworld called Yes-no. We walk the night and eat the brains of small children and live in your pants. We harken—"

"Okay, okay," I said. "I need to hit the sack."

Shred pointed at me with two index fingers. "Breakfast tomorrow."

"We'll see." I kicked off my flip-flops.

"We'll *see*? I thought your interview wasn't until four?"

"I have to—I have some preparation I have to go through first, might take a while. Law firm stuff."

He looked at me like I was ridiculous. "Yeah," he said. "Well, if you can fit it in, we'll hit the diner. My treat."

"Oh, no. You don't have to treat."

Now he looked pissed. Why did I say that?

"I mean, no, yeah," I said. "That'd be cool. The diner."

"All right, Jarvis. Sleep tight."

"Goodnight."

I saw a smirk on his lips as he shut the door. I guess I annoyed him. But I didn't have time to worry about "Shred."

I sat on the edge of the bed and shut my eyes.

You insufferable worthless piece of scumbag.

No.

You tractor trailer full of disgusting scum.

God awful.

You crappy excuse for a human worm.

Oh, no. Hell no.

A pile of rotten dogshit is a better person than you'll ever be, you disgusting degenerate pedophile ass face. Hey—that one was a great one. Hell yeah. Almost perfect. Write it down *now*, I told myself. But it was short so I knew I could memorize it.

A piece of dog shit is a better person than you'll ever be, you disgusting pedophile ass face.

I said it again.

And again.

Got it. I turned the overhead light off and chugged the rest of my iced tea, then threw the comforter off to the side and got under the sheet.

Piece of dog shit is a glorious king compared to you.

Piece of dog—face.

You rotten piece of degenerate…

…and I was out

12

THE SMELL OF coffee woke me up. It was the Big Day. Biggest day of my life. And I was armed with an awesome zinger. Or so I thought. All I could remember was something about comparing him to dogshit. I pounded the mattress with my fists. Was the word "degenerate" in there? I couldn't remember. Fuck!

"Fuck!" I yelled. *Degenerate dogshit*—what kind of zinger is *that?* Why didn't I write it down! It was the absolute perfect zinger. "Shit!"

Someone tapped on the door. "You okay in there, Jarvis?" It was Shred.

"Yeah. Fine."

"Um…there's coffee out here if you want. Cock-a-doodle-don't."

"Cool. Yeah, I'll be up in a minute."

I reached into my backpack and got out my cell phone. It was 11:37. I wondered how the hell I could have slept so late. There wasn't much time.

It was hot as shit. Any air that began to move was immediately stopped dead by the walls of humidity. Searing sunlight hit the parachute posters and the glare was painful. I pulled a clean shirt out of my backpack and slid it on over the film of sweat on my skin. At least my beige cookie-cutter apartment had good a/c, not like this place.

Out in the living room, Shred was wearing this huge, blood-red terry cloth bathrobe with giant lapels. It was monogrammed "CM" in swirly white letters. Way regal. Kenny was sitting on the couch, smirking at the TV. He already looked high.

The air smelled like burning plastic. The apartment looked much crappier in the daylight—plaster hanging off the ceiling, crooked window frames, old rough wooden floors with ship-sized splinters rising from them. But it had a kind of run-down charm I guess. Rustic maybe. In the bathrobe, Shred looked like a wealthy eccentric, the original bohemian.

I followed him into the kitchen and asked him what the "CM" on his robe stood for.

"Cantaloupe Master," he said, very matter-of-factly.

"Where are the cantaloupes?" I started to look around his kitchen.

Shred pinched the lapel of the robe. "Thrift store find."

"Oh."

The coffee was stronger than is allowed by law. Nearly motor oil. Perfect. They didn't have any half'n'half, but I didn't care. Coffee at all seemed like a luxurious amenity in this bohemian death trap. For me, of course, I had to have it or my brain would fall out, so I wasn't complaining. We sat down at his kitchen table.

"So what's been new, there, Cousin Jarvis?"

"Oh," I said. "Not a whole lot."

"Gotta girlfriend?"

"We just broke up."

"Yeah. Me too." He started shaking his head. "Womens..."

"Yeah. You can't live with 'em and you can't, what is it... shoot 'em?"

"Oh, but you can," he said. "I strangled her, though. Body's still in the trunk."

"Sure it is."

We sat there sipping our coffees. The kitchen was somewhat normal looking. There was even a hanging basket of onions.

"So which law firm is your interview with?" Shred asked.

"Oh, you wouldn't know. One of these Richmond firms."

"Yeah, I know all of them from catering. Is it Barton Weil?"

"Um...I can't remember right now. It's written down in the car?" I felt my neck getting hot, test anxiety hot. My stomach was swishing. I threw back the rest of my coffee and burped. It hurt my throat.

"You have an interview at a law firm and you don't even know the name?"

"I'm applying at a bunch of other ones, and I guess I'm getting the names all mixed up together." I felt like the 800-pound idiot in the room.

Shred smiled. He could tell I was somehow full of shit, but he seemed more amused than offended. I thought maybe I should just tell him the truth, but I didn't want the distraction. Plus I'd have to go into the whole story of the abuse and my quest for catharsis and everything. And I was pretty sure that Shred wouldn't be able to relate. He didn't seem like the type of guy who would be doing any of this. He seemed like he really knew how to let stuff go. Nothing bothered him. Shred and his crew were cutting edge mad artists, they knew how to roll freestyle and all that crap.

"Earth to Jarvis," he said.

"Huh? Sorry."

"You hungry?"

"Yeah. I'm starving, actually."

"Gotcha covered, daddy-o." He stood up and chugged the rest of his coffee. Then he smacked his lips and said: "Let's go to Second Street."

"Sounds good, Cantaloupe Master."

I helped lift Kenny into the back of Shred's rusting Dodge van. Thing was ancient. You could have fit a basketball through the rust holes. Kenny settled into a bean bag chair that seemed to have been set up for him, pillows and all. We cruised slowly. Shred seemed very conscious of bumps and potholes. Still, his van needed shocks.

"Fuck!" Kenny screamed. "Godammit—take it easy!"

I looked back at him and he sneered at me. What a jerk. After I helped lift him into the van he has to sneer at me.

I secretly wished that Shred would drive through a series of cavernous potholes. I took a deep breath. Something smelled like rotten socks. Maybe it was rotten socks.

Richmond was gorgeous in the daytime, big exploding trees and high cottony clouds. Aside from a couple of modern buildings and the cars and asphalt, everything looked way old. That red brick and the ornate iron work—it coulda been 1890. We pulled up to Second Street Diner, another old-ass place in between Shred's hood and the downtown of tiny skyscrapers. Took us about an hour to get Kenny out of the van and into the place.

The diner was packed, a bustling summit of rednecks, yuppies, a couple of church ladies, a few black people and some art freaks. The pale hospital green paint job in there somehow worked. Maybe it was balanced out by the chrome-lined walls and quirky faux antique signs that were up everywhere. Signs like: *Coca-Cola Beverage Department*, *Mom's Home Baked Pie's* and a big one that said: *Biscuits: 15 Cents*. Its perfectly square pat of butter was just about to slide off the side of the biscuit. I was starving. All the smells in there, particularly the bacon, were killing me. Kenny took another three hours to get his leg situated in the booth. I hated him and his stupid leg in that moment. I had to admit, though, he was pretty freaking brave for jumping out of airplanes multiple times. Willingly. That's mega-balls, no denying it. Then again, what I was going to do later was pretty damn brave. That's right. I was no pussy. The reality that I was really going through with it was starting to solidify. It was making me nervous. My hunger was starting to give way to that old familiar feeling of rotten lagoon stomach.

Shred and I sat down across the table from Kenny. His cast was touching my leg. I wanted to die. We ordered coffee and all-American breakfasts from an artsy waitress with an array of pencils sticking out of her hair bun. She reminded me of a punker Audrey Hepburn. Shred called her "Alison." This dude knew everybody. We sat there for a while not saying anything. The silence was making me uncomfortable.

"So, uh..." I looked at Shred. "Ever sold any of those paintings of yours?"

"Yeah, actually. I've done a couple of local shows, sold a few."

"Really? How much did you make?"

He gave me an extended blank look. Kenny rolled his eyes. I guess it was kind of a superficial question. Not that I could ever see Shred turning down ten grand for one of his sideways cartoon canvases, though.

"I walked away with three million in cashier's checks that night," Shred dead-panned.

I almost said: *Really?*

"Yeah," Kenny said. "Three million cents. Negative cents." They both laughed.

"Three million cents would still be...let's see...ten thousand dollars," I said. "That's not oh-so bad." My comment was met with an Arctic silence. Kenny and Shred looked at each other. Then at me. I felt like the biggest mega-dork ever sprouted. A couple of people came over to the table to say whutsup. Some guy named Hatchet and another dude whose name I didn't get. They asked Kenny how his leg was doing.

"It's doing," he smirked. "Still attached." The one called Hatchet asked when someone named "Farns" was coming back to town, which I guessed was short for Farnsworth, but maybe it was a nickname. Seemed like half the people in this town had some nickname.

"This is my cousin, Jarvis," Shred told the dudes. "Hey, Cousin Jarvis." Maybe that was going to be my nickname. I could be *Zing Master Cuz J* for short.

The meat and eggs came. Slathering globs of butter on my goldish pancakes. Three huge eggs over-easy. Shiny bacon. Real Southern grease. I was stoked. We chowed. We chowed like men. I ordered and drank three coffees and downed them in rapid succession. Our waitress seemed both annoyed and impressed.

After a while, I said: "That girl Summer—I almost expect to see her around. This seems like her kind of place." I said.

"They won't let her in with her dogs anymore," Shred said.

"She's vegan anyway," Kenny said. "Not much on the menu for her."

"She eats their salad."

"I like her," I said. "She's a righteous babe."

Kenny's eyes tightened at me. He looked like he was trying to bite his own teeth. His leg must have really hurt.

Shred chewed his bacon thoughtfully. "You know, JFK wasn't the only president since World War II to be brought down by the Illuminati. They all were."

"Uh-oh," Kenny said. "Here we go again."

"How so?" I said.

"Don't encourage him," Kenny said.

"It's all a system. They prop them up as needed and then knock them down like ducks in a shooting gallery." He paused dramatically, and added: "As needed."

"Oh jeez," Kenny said, smearing his face with a napkin.

"What about Reagan?" I said.

"They shot him in '81. He was a stoned CIA zombie puppet after that."

"Jimmy Carter? He wasn't taken down."

"Iranian hostage crisis. They used it to paralyze him."

"So, who is 'they' exactly?"

Shred smiled at me like I was a fool not to know. "The evil secret government of the military-industrial corporate death masters. The Illuminati. The blue-bloods who really run everything."

"What did I tell you about staying off the Internet," Kenny said in a mock scolding tone.

"Don't worry about it."

"Maybe it's time to face the fact that you're retarded with a capital D."

"So," I said, "how about Monica Lewinsky? She was like what, some type of FBI-planted robot?"

"An FBI blow-up doll," Kenny said.

Shred looked pissed. "Come on, dude. Be real."

"No, you're right," Kenny reasoned. "I agree. The Illuminati sucks butt."

"Fine—you don't want to know how the world *really* runs. That's cool."

"The world runs and I sit." Kenny shrugged.

"Wouldn't kill you to have at least a little concern for the hypocrisy that plays itself out every day, right in front of your face."

"Perhaps you've mistaken me for someone else," Kenny deadpanned, "but I can't imagine them giving a shit either."

I was trying not to laugh. Shred seemed to take this kook-job stuff pretty seriously and I didn't want to be rude. So I looked around the place. Some rednecks at a table across the way looked like they were laughing at us, probably at Shred's bed-head. Kenny was staring vaguely at the ceiling, like he was thinking about being somewhere else, maybe free-falling through the clouds with two mighty femurs under him, pulling his chute at the last possible minute for that extra blind rush.

We continued chewing in silence for a while.

"So Farns is coming back today?" Kenny asked.

"Today or tomorrow."

"He's the guy who drove his truck onto the sidewalk in front of Richmond City Hall to protest his gas bill, right?" I asked.

"Van."

"And it was his water bill, not gas."

"We had a hard freeze and his pipe burst," Kenny said.

"That's what she said."

"Ha fucking ha."

"Actually," Shred explained, "the city did some work by his house and broke the line and didn't realize it. Then they charged him for all the water on his water bill."

"Something like that," Kenny said.

"Farns isn't one to take injustice lightly," Shred said.

"No, he is not."

They started discussing something I couldn't follow at all. Then Shred made a random comment about a boat ride with

Farns and they both laughed. So I asked what was up with the boat ride. He said that a couple of years back, Farns had just finished fixing up this boat of his.

"Nice one, too, " Shred said. "A thirty-one foot Wellcraft Steplift with a blasting T-225 Evinrude. He named her Lava Neck, and Farns had her all ready to go. But there was a bad drought that year. All summer it had only rained like twice, so the water level was too low to take her out on the river. Farns had been promising everyone boat rides for months. He couldn't fucking stand it, so he gathered up a bunch of us, like nine people, and we partied in the boat while Farns pulled it around the roads of Richmond behind his van. There we were at three in the morning drinking beer and smoking weed in the back of a land boat, laughing and screaming. Still can't believe we didn't get caught."

"Let alone killed," Kenny said.

"Oh, check out Captain Safety here," Shred laughed.

"Skydiving is way safer than getting thrown around in a boat being driven down the street by a drunken lunatic," Kenny said.

"Ten-four. I admit the boat ride on the street was a mad hazard. Peg leg."

I laughed, but I cut it short because Kenny looked at me like I wasn't qualified to laugh at this.

"Farns lived to regret it, too," Shred said.

"Yeah?" I said. "How so?"

"Trailer got fucked up somehow. Boy was he pissed. You don't want to be around him when he's pissed off."

"He sounds like a real character," I said. "A real hero type, huh?"

"Well," Shred said, "he may not be a hero, but he's, um…I'll tell you one thing—sonofabitch is honest. Doesn't candy coat anything."

"Not a candy coater," Kenny added, shaking his head.

"He'll speak the truth, no matter how much it offends anyone."

"He actually enjoys offending people."

"Yeah, he does."

They talked about him like he was some kind of rebel guru, their anti-establishment punk rock superman. Whatever.

"Speaking of skydiving," Kenny said, "one time this guy crapped his jumpsuit." He said it so deadpan that Shred and I both laughed for about twenty minutes. I almost choked on a length of bacon.

Seemed like we were at the diner forever. I may have killed twelve cups of coffee, which was a lot even for me in one sitting. I went to pee and when I came out, they were finally getting up to go. I walked over to the cake and pie case that ran along the counter and I stared into a decadent, lopsided German chocolate cake. Almost down to the wire and I still had no knock-out zinger. I was getting really nervous. My stomach felt like it was filled with drowning fish, flip-flopping around, gasping for water. What the hell was I going to say to him? I dropped my forehead against the glass case and it made a loud *bonk* sound. People were looking at me. I closed my eyes and tried to pretend I didn't exist.

"You okay, man?" Shred asked.

"Oh, yeah. Fine." I got out my wallet.

"Put that away. My treat."

"Sure?"

He just smiled and paid a cashier with a bouffant hairdo. Shred seemed like a sophisticated gentleman in that moment, not an artsy whacko at all. It was strange. Everything was strange. The world was strange. And in spite of being surrounded by the biggest collection of oddballs I had ever met in my life, I felt like the oddest oddball to ever set foot on the face of the globe.

13

ON THE WAY back from the diner, Shred talked about his latest painting, a giant head being pulled by balloons across a landscape of rabid orange and green bobcats. He was psyched about finishing it today. I was glad he'd be occupied. All I wanted to do was get into the zone, think up a zinger and focus.

Kenny worked his way down onto the couch and cracked a beer and started organizing his pharmaceuticals. Shred went into his studio to paint. I sat on the lounge chair and got out my Mapquest map. I took a deep breath. The room smelled like dust and mildew. Then Shred stormed back out, all hyper.

"Paint's set up," he said, clapping his hands together once for effect. "Time for a bong-hit." He shook his head like a dog with a wet coat. Very wound-up all of a sudden, as though a few too many volts were plugged into his breaker box. He took his bong-hit and disappeared. The room smelled better, but I didn't want to get a residual high so I took my maps and my backpack and went down to Kenny's room and shut the door.

I sat on the edge of the bed and looked over the map and directions and it was all pretty straightforward. Finding Motorcar's house was going to be the easy part, but what the fuck was I gonna say when I got there? *Stupid pervert loser ass-neck!* Oh lord—I was regressing!

Shred called me from the hallway: "Hey Jarvis, you want a Bloody Mary?"

I pictured him in his Cantaloupe Master robe, holding up his glass and swirling the ice cubes, lecturing on the many conspiratorial events surrounding the reign of Mary Queen of Scots. I wanted one. Bad. I knew it would help. A good strong drink would loosen me up and help my balls grow. The zingers would probably start flowing. I felt a lump crawling up my throat. But no, I couldn't.

"No, thanks. I don't drink, remember?"

"Oh, yeah. Sorry, man. I just didn't want to be rude."

"No problem."

"Shit—what am I thinking? You can't drink before your interview, anyway." He opened the door and popped his head in. He had a goofy smile on his face. Like one of his cartoon paintings. "Don't you have to take a shower and put on a suit and stuff? You kinda need a shave."

"That stuff's out in the car. I was just getting ready to go out there and get it."

His smile dropped. He looked like he didn't believe me.

"Damn—I hope you brought your own towel. Let me know if you need anything. I mean, other than a clean towel. Sorry, I should've done laundry." And he unpopped his head back out though the door and shut it.

Yeesh, I thought. I considered just telling Shred about the whole deal and buying myself a few hours of peace before dark. Then I wouldn't have to go through with this whole charade. But I didn't want to tell anyone. At least not until afterwards when all was resolved and I got my self-esteem and mojo back in working order.

I decided the best thing to do would be to just leave. I could go somewhere, find a diner or a café, load up on some coffee, devise a few perfect zingers and calm down these butterflies, swamp fish and sinking cinderblocks. I could always call Shred later and tell him the whole deal and apologize for not saying goodbye. He would understand such a spontaneous and rude action.

My moves were quick and decisive: I went to the kitchen and got my jar of instant iced tea, stuffed that and my maps into my backpack, zipped up the pocket and headed out the front door.

I was feeling good. I headed down the brick sidewalk thinking today was the day. Today was *my* day. The world better look the fuck out.

That's when I saw them.

They were half a block down Shred's street, a bunch of the hip-hop redneck Oregon Hill punks. Ten or twelve of them. They looked like a younger group than the ones I saw the day before hanging out around their cars a couple of blocks down. These dudes were on foot, wearing their white tee-shirts or wife-beaters or no shirt at all, their pants baggy and drooping. One of them yelled: "Look at the college pussy!" I heard shards of menacing laughter. A lump of clay formed in my throat. To walk to my car I had to walk *toward* them. So like an idiot I just stood there. Like a mark. Bad call. They started running toward me, yelling: "Woo-hoo!" and "Faggot-ass!" I turned to run for Shred's when something hit me in the shoulder. I looked down and saw it was a half-piece of brick.

"Got him! Fuckin pussy!" They cheered and laughed.

It didn't really hurt, but like an even bigger idiot I turned to look back at them to see how close they were. That's when it hit me in the face. A rock or piece of brick. Right in the eye. I almost fell over, but I kept running for Shred's. I couldn't believe it.

"Nice one!"

"Sweet!"

"Yo college bitch!"

"Ha ha!"

I kept my hand up on my eye and blasted through Shred's front door. Slammed it and turned the dead bolt and dropped my backpack on the hallway floor. "Shit!" I was breathing so hard I thought my lungs were going to pop. My eye felt numb and wet. And then—BAM! A rock hit the house.

"What the fuck is that!" Kenny yelled from down the long hallway. Then another rock hit the house, this time on the door.

Shred came charging out into the hallway. "What is that? Holy shit, Jarvis—what happened?"

Another rock hit. "They're going to kill us all!" I yelled. I started heading down the hall toward the safe interior of the house. Shred got in my face and pulled my hand away from my eye.

"Holy fuck," he said. "This is bad."

"It feels bad."

"What happened?"

"Your neighbors attacked me with rocks!"

"No shit! I told you to watch out for them."

"You did?"

"You're gonna need stitches. Wow."

"Fuck!"

"Don't squint your eye shut so hard—you're making it bleed more. Come on." And he led me down the hall and into the living room. "I'll be right back."

I tried not squinting, but my eye started to sting and then twitch. My brain was probably filling up with blood. I was going to catch a fatal brain infection and die right there in Shred's crappy duplex. I heard him running some water in the kitchen.

"What ever so happened to your face?" Kenny said sarcastically.

I didn't say anything. I should have said: "I dunno—what happened to your leg, Colonel Limpy?" But I was in the zinger desert as usual.

Shred came out and led me into the kitchen. He put a wad of damp paper towel to my eye and applied pressure. I felt a dull ache but that was about it.

"You've got a nasty cut," he said. "I'm gonna run you down to MCV to get it sewn up."

"MC what?"

"Emergency room."

"God this *sucks!*"

I heard Kenny in the other room, laughing.

Shred took the paper towel off to look. "They really hit the bull's-eye here. Gory."

"Thanks," I said. My whole face was starting to hurt.

"What the fuck happened?" Kenny yelled from the couch.

"The Hillites got Jarvis. With a rock."

"Oh," he said, like it happened every day. "That's what I thought."

"I'm gonna call the cops," I said.

"Don't bother. They won't do anything." He went to the sink and started washing his hands.

"Great."

I couldn't fucking believe it. Instead of going to Motorcar's to slam him with zingers, I was going to the hospital. But it was just a delay. I would resume the mission as soon as they sewed up my face. Shred gave me a fresh wad of paper towel for my eye. I took off the old wad and blinked. I could kind of see through the blood, so I figured I wouldn't be blind at least. We went down the hall and out onto the front porch. No sign of the rock throwers. Shred picked up one of the brick pieces that had been thrown at the house and he studied it, as though it might yield some vital information. I wasn't too psyched about going out there, but I guess I needed stitches. He led me across the street to his van. My head was on a swivel, looking all over, but I didn't see any of them.

Shred started the van up and hit the gas pedal hard. "Sorry about the asshole neighbor kids. Those dicks."

"Sorry you have to live in such a bad neighborhood."

He looked pissed. "It's really not that bad. You just have to know how to handle those punks. The rent around here is super cheap."

"I can see why."

"I'm sorry, Jar. And you're like the first family member to ever come visit me here and look what happens. This really fucking disrupts my personal electricity."

"Your what?"

"My personal electricity. Y'know, my vibe. My flow."

"Cosmic," I said. "Is that what you shred?"

"Huh?"

"Personal electricity? Is that what you shred up?"

"Farns gave me that nickname. First it was 'The Shredder' and now it's just 'Shred' for short."

"Killer, dude."

"How's your eye?"

"It's been better."

"Oh, man—your job interview!"

"Yeah. So much for that."

"That sucks."

Maybe it was the adrenalin rushing through my body, working like some kind of truth serum in me. Or the sheer animal experience of getting pelted by rocks and bricks. Whatever it was, something compelled me to clear away the bullshit and administer a cold splash of truth.

Shred stopped at a stoplight.

"There is no job interview, actually. I made that up."

"I knew it!" His eyes were bugging out. "So why are you here? I know it ain't just to visit *my* ass. Is it a girl?"

"Well...I'm on a mission. Kind of."

"What mission?"

"I came here to...basically to have a confrontation with someone. From the past."

"Ex-girlfriend?"

"I'll tell you about it later."

"Come on. Just gimme the basics. Real quick."

"My brains are leaking out over here. Can it wait a while?"

"No, they're not. You have a cut above your eye. A bad cut, but you're gonna be fine."

"We'll see."

"So tell me—why are you here, Jarvis?"

"I'm here to see someone." I looked out the window with my one eye.

"All right, Lieutenant Mystery."

"Are we gonna be to the emergency room soon?"

"We're not going til you tell me. Just kidding!"

"I'm going to have a confrontation with someone who did something fucked up to me when I was little, okay?"

"Okay."

We didn't speak for a couple of minutes and I thought I was off the hook. I hoped there wouldn't be a long wait at the emergency room. Shred wasn't done yet, though.

"A child molester?" he said.

"Yes, actually. How did you know?"

"Man, I am hitting 'em out of the park! And you came here to fuck him up? That is *awesome*."

"Not to fuck him up. I plan on having a healthy, verbal confro—"

"What did he do exactly?"

We stopped at a red light and The Shredder looked at me with the whacko eyes of a psycho murderer. He was way more worked up than I was, and I just had a rock thrown into my face.

"I really don't like talking about it," I said. "He fondled my package, okay? A camp counselor. You happy now?"

"That twisted fucking pervert bitch! He is *not* getting away with this!"

I did not want to accept the fact that Shred had just spontaneously produced a world class zinger. I had been trying to think of one for weeks and I had nothing.

"You gonna kill him?" he said. "Gonna fuck him up good, right?" He looked like an animal who could smell meat.

"No, of course not. I'm just going to express my, verbally express my anger and…it's going to be, like, really healthy." I pushed the bloody wad of paper towel tighter to my eye.

"Jesus—he deserves to have his fucking face blown off! Did you bring a piece?"

"A *piece*? Are you kidding?"

"How're you gonna do it?"

"I'm not gonna *do* anything. I just want to talk to him."

"Talk to him? If I were you I'd blow his ass into about a gazillion pieces, y'know? That low-life shit-neck."

My head was starting to feel like a watermelon that had been dropped down a flight of concrete steps. The pain was dull and sharp at the same time.

"As shitty as this world is, it's way too good of a place for that motherfucker. You should shank him. In the face. Hell, I'll help you. I'll pitchfork his ass about a thousand times."

"Okay, okay. I'll nuke him for you."

"Now you're talking."

We turned into the hospital complex. I never thought I'd be so glad to go to a hospital. Getting my eyebrow sewn back together was gonna be way more comfortable than this conversation.

"They should take people like that and cut off their hands and shove them down their throat," he said, pulling up to the ER entrance. He was more pissed off about it than I ever was. It did feel kind of good to hear someone taking my side. He let me out and said he'd be right in after he parked the van. Right before I shut the van door, he leaned over and said: "I'll totally help you kill him."

"Thanks," I said. "I'll take care of it."

"I'm there for you, man. I gotchyer back."

I shut the door and he and zoomed off.

14

THE PAPER TOWEL wasn't paper towel anymore, it was more like a mass of bloody pulp. The bleeding seemed to have slowed down, but I kept it up there. My eye was stinging like a mofo. A sign above the sliding glass doors to the emergency room said: *Medical College of Virginia.* I pictured teams of wacky, incompetent young medical students running around and botching everything they touched. Why couldn't Shred have taken me to a *real* hospital? Was this place even accredited?

The giant waiting room was slam full of people, none of whom appeared to be bleeding from the head, so I hoped I would get fast service. I registered with a lady at a little open cubicle. She took my name and asked if it was my eye.

"It's like, right above my eye."

She smirked and wrote something down.

I realized I should have said it was my eye to speed up the process. She wasn't in any hurry at all. Then she told me to go wait in the waiting area and they would call my name. Before I got a chance to ask her how long the wait would be, she took her clipboard and left.

There weren't any seats available, so I stood against the wall. My brain was swirling. After a while, Shred showed up. He was all sweaty and jittery, like he was allergic to hospitals or something.

"Man, parking was a bitch," he said. "How is it? Has it stopped bleeding yet?"

"Pretty much, I guess."

"I just can't believe this shit. I mean, I do believe it, but it's still so fucked up."

"I think your neighbors need a rec center or something."

"No, man, I mean the sicko guy. Your pervert."

"Let's not talk about that in here, okay?"

"Why? You know any of these people?"

"I'd appreciate it if you'd just stop talking about the whole thing. It's kinda, you know…personal?"

"Don't worry, chief," Shred said, wiping the sweat off his forehead with his tee-shirt. "I'm in this with you a thousand percent."

"But there's nothing to be 'in' with me with! Just drop it, okay? Please? It's my…"

"Your what?"

"Never mind."

"I gotta hit the john."

Shred disappeared through some swinging doors. I sat there for about twenty minutes. Not only was my name not called, but *nobody's* name was being called. Shred reappeared looking like he'd been trapped in some wild animal's cave.

"Did you find the can?"

"Yeah, but I got lost. Place is a maze."

We stood there for another ten minutes, not talking. I was grateful. Shred looked deep in thought, which had me worried. Finally, the check-in lady with the clipboard was back.

"Mister Henderson? They're ready to see you."

"It's *Henders*," Shred corrected her, annoyed. "There's no 'son' at the end."

"Oh, I am so sorry, *sir*," the lady snipped. "You want to come with me Mr. Hender?" I think she left the "s" off on purpose.

"I'll be right here, cuz."

The doctor was about my age. His youth reminded me that I should have been a lawyer by now. Nine stitches. Doc Junior had to shave off half my eyebrow. The bandage was big and it pushed down on my eyelid, so my eye was half shut. How was I gonna see Motorcar now? Find his house? Stare him down with my death glare when I had only one eye available? I felt raw panic pulling the sides of my chest open like meat hooks. Something was punching me in the stomach, but from the inside.

I had developed a screaming headache and my whole face hurt, but Doogie Howser refused to prescribe me anything.

"Just get some Extra Strength Tylenol."

"I'm not sure that'll do it."

"That ought to do it."

I should have said: *You ever get hit in the face with a rock, pal?* But I didn't think of it in time. At least they gave me some free bandages and anti-biotic ointment. Then the lady at the pay window took my insurance card from the law firm. Old Reinhaus-and-crew must have forgotten to cancel it. That gave me a warm feeling inside.

Shred drove back just as fast as he had driven us there. "Don't worry about your face-ache, man. Kenny has a whole box full of pain meds."

"I noticed."

"I've still got a ton of vodka left, too."

"Look—you should probably stop offering me drinks. I'm an alcoholic."

"A *recovering* alcoholic."

"That, too."

Shred's lips tightened and his knuckles started going white on the steering wheel. "The only reason you're an alcoholic is because of that pervert. That sonofabitch!"

"There's more to it than that."

"We could go get a shot right now if it wasn't for that motherfucker."

"Heaven knows I could use one."

"It's not your fault you're all fucked up."

I didn't say anything.

"And I'm gonna help you, too, man."

"I don't need help."

"*God*, I hate pervert child molesters!" He hit the steering wheel as he screamed.

"Yeah. Don't we all."

We turned back into Oregon Hill and headed down the dilapidated NASCAR block. I saw the rock throwing gang, or at least some dudes who looked like them. I slumped down in the seat below dashboard level.

"Hey, don't do that. They can smell fear. Like dogs."

I sat back up a little. They were all out of sight by the time we parked, but I felt pretty paranoid getting out of the van. I could just hear them in my head—*let's get the college pussy again!*

Inside, Kenny was watching the news, plumes of fresh weed smoke hanging under the ceiling.

"They fucked up your face, huh?" Kenny said with obvious glee.

"Apparently," I said.

"Try having your leg broken in six places."

"I didn't voluntarily jump out of an airplane."

I sat down and let the pain take over my head and face. Even my shoulders hurt. I was going to have to feel better soon if I was going to go find Motorcar. Damn those punks—I'd have been crushing Motorcar with a series of perfect steel cold zingers by now if they hadn't attacked me.

"Hey, Kenny," I said. "Shred mentioned that you might, um…loan me one of those pain pills you got."

"*Loan* you one?"

"Well, I mean let me have one, I guess."

He reached over and pulled a big blue pill out of his drug box. "Here."

"Thanks."

I stood up and put the pill in my pocket and went to take a pee. I was expecting Kenny to make a shitty comment about putting the pill in my pocket but he didn't say anything. When I came out of the bathroom, I got my iced tea jar out of my back pack and went into the kitchen to stir some up. The pill went down like an aircraft carrier that refused to be sunk. After three straight glasses of chugged iced tea, it was still lodged in the center of my neck. I went back to the living room and sat down. I swallowed a couple of times and felt the pill begin to make its way down.

Shred came down the hall and darted into the kitchen and started banging things around. Then he bolted back through the living room and halfway down the hall but then stopped and came back.

"So, you gonna go see your friend tonight?" he said. "I'll drive."

"I don't know. I'm gonna see how I feel after this pain pill kicks in."

"You sure as hell ain't goin' anywhere *tonight*," Kenny said.

"What do you mean?" I said.

Kenny looked at Shred and nodded. "Landmine."

"You gave him a blue landmine? Oh, jeez."

Shred put his hand on my shoulder. "So the perv gets to live another day. You can stay here as long as you need to get the job done."

"Thanks, but I'd appreciate it if you wouldn't talk about it here."

"Talk about what?" Kenny said.

"Nothing," I said.

"What perv?"

Shred looked at Kenny like he was about to tell him. But I shook my head and thankfully he didn't.

"What?" Kenny said again.

Shred looked at my bandage. "Looks like it's holding up. I'll be right back." And he left the house. I sat there and tried to pretend I was interested in what was on TV. Looked like a commercial for car insurance.

"You're not here for a job interview, are you?" Kenny said.

"Yes, I am."

"You can tell me after that blue elephant kicks in."

"I thought it was a landmine."

"It's a truth serum. You'll tell me later."

We sat there. I kept expecting a throng of party people to come rushing in, but no one did. A show about inmates in the Missouri state prison system was coming on. Cheerful. Kenny shifted his leg on the pillow. "There you go, boy," he told it.

Inmates who are psychologically unfit to co-exist with the others in the general population are sent to live in the notorious Section E... That's where I was. Section E. I should have known this whole Motorcar thing wasn't going to be easy. I tried to think up a zinger. Nothing.

Inmates who previously suffered from psychological instability are likely to have those tendencies exacerbated during incarceration.

"No shit, Captain Genius-neck," Kenny said to the TV.

A psyche ward was bad enough, but a psyche ward inside a maximum security prison? Yikes. They were interviewing one guy who'd stabbed his own mother thirty-six times with a steak knife because her soul was apparently infested by hell demons. Imagine being cell-mates with *that* freak. I'd rather be attacked by an evil swirl of flying space robots, crushing my skull with their electronic death grip and swirling my carcass off to some distant...planet...somewhere. The pill was beginning to kick in. My face and head didn't hurt anymore and the prison nut ward suddenly didn't look so bad. It actually started to look like a kind of paradise. So clean and organized. The orange jumpsuits, so comfortable. At some point, I managed to stand up and make my way down the blurry hallway. I think I heard Kenny laughing at me but it could have just been the sound of my own insanity. Whatever it was, when I got to his room I collapsed on the bed and proceeded to dissolve into thirty-seven gazillion tiny invisible particles. For once I felt at peace, but I was only awake another fourteen seconds to enjoy it.

15

I WOKE UP thinking about Carly. I thought I was over her, but it hit me like the proverbial ton'o'bricks. Maybe if I took care of this Motorcar thing, and it restored my sense of self-worth and self-esteem and all that, maybe that would really work like a glowing power force around me and I really could win her back. Then again, she was kind of an ice cold beeyotch. Her neck was so sexy, though. I wanted to eat it. I wanted to have enthusiastic make-up sex with her in the stairwell of her apartment. She could be dressed like Snow White and I would wear an orange prison jumpsuit. I started to beat off but it made my face hurt. I needed coffee. My head was bloated with fog. No more painkillers, that was for damn sure. No more blue aircraft carriers or whatever the hell that thing was. What I really needed was a shower. The odor rising off me was probably visible.

Kenny was on the couch with his eyes half shut. Major surprise. The TV was on but muted. No sign of Shred. His studio door was open, but he wasn't in there. I looked into his bedroom. Also Shredless. I started poking around in the kitchen, looking for the make-coffee-stuff. Why not make myself at home? It was my cousin's place after all. My fucked-up eye was sort of my license to be there. I earned it. I found a bag of coffee grounds in the back of the fridge. It looked old but I didn't care.

Getting Shred's old coffee maker bubbling and brewing felt like a major accomplishment. I took in the aroma. My injury felt weird, and it hurt, but the fog in my head started lifting and overall I felt pretty good. This was the perfect time to work on my Motorcar speech. I started thinking that maybe the rock throwing attack was a blessing in that I had more time to come up with a prime zinger. I stirred the sugar into my coffee. Today was my day.

You dirty sack of...

You perv mother...

Son of a...

Then the TV sound came on. Threw me off completely. Not that I was getting anywhere. I touched my eye bandage. It felt pretty solid. The cut hurt but it could have been worse. I downed my coffee and poured another.

You disgusting pervert bitch-ass...

I heard a commotion down the hall. I stepped out into the living room to see what was up. Summer's dogs, all three of them, were charging. She'd apparently let herself in. One of them jumped up on the couch to say hello to Kenny. He screamed, though I don't see how he could feel pain. His blood had more painkillers running through it than most pharmacies had on their shelves.

Summer looked very smiley and lively. She came right up to me and put her little hand on the side of my head in a very gentle, Nurse Nightingale sort of way.

"You poor thing!"

"So, you know about me getting hit with the rock?"

"Hey," Kenny said. "Where's *my* sympathy?"

"I'm sympathied-out on you. Besides, you did that to yourself. Jarvis got attacked."

"I was attacked. By the earth."

"You want a cup of coffee?" I asked her.

"Sure."

"You never offered me any," Kenny said. "And it's *my* coffee. Cyclops."

Summer gave Kenny a dirty look. I liked that. I went back into the kitchen and started washing out some cups. Summer followed me.

"I'm on my way to go thrift store shopping if you want to go."

"Um...sure, okay. I have to take a shower first, though."

She put her hand on my arm and smiled at me. I felt the double whammy of hand and smile. I wasn't sure how a wild tattooed punker chick could be so nice. Summer was blowing my mind.

"I don't care about that," she said. "It's like ninety-something outside anyway."

Her hand was still on my arm. My stomach started gurgling. I tried to picture her as a normal person, with no tattoos or piercings, no Goth *grrrl* make-up, maybe wearing a smart gray business suit and some normal colored lipstick. A tingle shot down my legs.

"Hey, Kenny," I called. "What do you take in your coffee?"

He didn't answer, so I went out in the living room and asked him again.

"Don't want any."

"But I thought you said—"

"Don't need your room service, thanks."

Summer and I sat in the living room and drank our coffees pretty fast. The dogs were spread out on the floor, panting from the heat. Kenny was watching some show about extreme motor biking at a very high volume. It was all *vrooom, vrooom* and no one said much.

Out front, I half-expected flying projectiles to be criss-crossing through the air. But it was quiet. No white tee-shirts or wife-beaters anywhere nearby. We got into Summer's giant car and one of her pooches immediately jumped into the front seat and started wagging its tail against my bandage. We started rolling along. I was still on the look-out for the Oregon Hillites. But it was only noon-ish. Maybe they weren't awake yet, still groggy, nursing their meth hangovers.

"Those little bitches," Summer said. I guessed she sensed me looking around for them. "Sorry they did that to you. Not the best introduction to Richmond."

"They don't bother you?"

"They know better."

"And you've got the dogs for protection."

"I carry a corkscrew. It's legal and it tears up your victim's internal organs when you pull it out."

"Wow."

"Yeah." She smiled.

"Ever use it on anybody?"

"Maybe."

I made a mental note to never piss her off. One visit to the hospital on this trip was enough. We pulled into the parking lot of the Vietnam Veterans Family Discount Outlet, and she asked me to help her roll up her windows just enough so the dogs couldn't get out. It was hot but there was a good breeze and we parked near the building in some shade.

I was never a big thrift store aficionado. Always bought new. There was a big Goodwill not too far from my apartment, but I'd never been. I just didn't see the point of buying someone else's skanked-out throwaways when you could drop a few extra bucks and buy something crisp and fresh. Something that hadn't been sweat in already. But if Summer had wanted to go to a slaughterhouse, I probably would have been an enthusiastic tag-along. I was pretty psyched to have a cute girl paying attention to me, especially after having woken up thinking about Carly.

The store was huge but the air inside was dense and humid, like the a/c system was ailing, if not totally broken. It smelled like an old grandmother's musty basement, which made sense. That was where most of the crap probably came from. Summer led me straight back to the junky stuff, bypassing all the clothes, which I had thought was going to be her destination. It was a world unto itself back there: ancient alarm clocks, an Elvis mirror, candy dishes, ashtrays, candlesticks, a little ceramic Jesus, a small plate celebrating the existence of Butte, Montana. I was surrounded by an alternately sparkling and not-so-sparkling world of wonder. Summer started going through a bin of artwork, mostly bad prints of 19th Century masters in gaudy frames.

"They look like they came out of a dead podiatrist's office," I said.

Summer laughed. Making her laugh felt like some huge accomplishment. Her full smile was fully gorgeous. My stomach started flip-flopping around once again. I liked her, I really liked her, and I didn't give a shit if she was a tattooed punker. I suddenly felt liberated in a way I'd never felt before. Alive, for the first time in forever. I decided to play it cool and walk over to another aisle. I watched her with my one available eye. I could see she was fascinated by a paint-by-numbers clown portrait from probably the 70s. I started looking around. I was checking out an ancient tin snack tray with a picture of pink roses on it when she called me over. The snack tray seemed appropriately tacky, so I brought it with me.

"Tell me this isn't to kill for," she said, holding the clown painting in my face. It actually scared me a little bit, making me realize I may have had a long-repressed pathological fear of clowns to add to all my other stupid-ass problems.

"Interesting," I said.

"What's that?"

I showed her the tray.

She made a hesitant face, as in: *wrong*.

"No?"

"It's close. If they were yellow roses I'd get it. Not much of a pink fan."

I should have figured. Hates pink. Her enthusiasm for the whole *junque aesthetic* was starting to rub off. I'd just never taken the time before to appreciate all this cool, quirky stuff. It made me realize that I had absolutely nothing interesting in my apartment. Or in my life, for that matter. I had that Times Square ashtray, but it wasn't an antique or anything, just touristy.

"I'm going over to the shoes," she said.

"Okay. I'll be over here in the…stuff."

She held her smile on me again for an extra bit and then took off with the clown portrait. I was in a daze, hungry, wanting more coffee, watching my new girlfriend walk to the shoe section. This is how it always happened for me—fast. I met someone and then after a couple of well-timed smiles thrown in my direction, I was a goner. I was in love, hopeless, a walking train wreck.

Summer bought the clown painting and a pair of men's brown wingtips. I asked her if she was going to wear them but she didn't answer. They looked small enough to fit her.

"Those don't look giant enough to be clown shoes, but I believe you can make it work."

She smiled. I felt like I was on a roll. We got back to the car and she let the dogs out to run around the parking lot for a minute.

"I'd say let's go to another one, but it's too hot for the dogs. I'm a bad dog mother."

"You're a champion dog mother."

"Can I quote you on that?"

"Only on opposite Tuesdays."

"How's your boo-boo?"

"It hurts. The bandage is annoying."

"Aw, that sucks."

"Thanks for asking."

We got in the car and she fired up the mighty engine.

"Are you hungry?" she asked.

"Starving."

"I've got some lentil salad at my house. It's really good."

Lentils were those nasty little hippie beans. I liked that she was inviting me over, but the idea of lentil salad wasn't doing it for me.

"How would it be if...do you want to eat out instead? My treat."

"All right. Second Street okay? It's a diner over by—"

"Yeah. We ate there yesterday."

"I just have to drop off the dogs."

Summer explained that the dogs weren't allowed in the diner anymore after one of them ate a customer's open-faced roast beef sandwich right off their plate. I couldn't believe they were ever allowed in there in the first place. She probably never asked permission. We headed back to Oregon Hill and I made a conscious decision not to look for the Hillites, but there they were, hanging out on the corner near Summer's house, being unemployed and not in school. I was unemployed and not in school too, but at least I didn't attack people with rocks. We pulled up in front of her house, which wasn't that far from the gang. Great.

"I'll be right back," she said.

"Need any help?"

"No, I'm good, thanks."

"Okay."

She smiled again. Sure did smile a lot for someone who looked like the picture of an angst-ridden punker artiste. Her morose lipstick made her teeth really white. She got the dogs and clown painting and shoes into the house and was back in the car pretty fast. Then she drove right by the white gangsters and came to a complete stop at the stop sign. She stared them down. There was nowhere for me to hide. It was a calm moment. I think they were afraid of her. As we pulled off, the whoops and hollers started. I didn't hear them yell "college pussy" or anything, but I was pretty sure they knew it was me.

"Boy...uh...that was a crowd I didn't need to see," I said in a voice that came out high-pitched.

Summer seemed a little too amused by all this. "You can't show your fear to these jerks. They can smell it out like dogs."

"That's exactly what Shred told me."

We pulled out of the neighborhood and onto Route One. The wind came rushing through the car windows and I could feel it drying my sweat.

"So, what was Shred like when he was little?"

I felt a little twinge of jealousy like a pair of needle-nosed pliers nipping at my lower intestines. "You mean when he was just 'Evan?' Well, he was actually really quiet. Kinda dark. Not like now. Hyper-ass."

"Mmm," she said.

"He was always kinda weird, though."

"So, nothing much has changed." We both laughed.

We didn't talk the rest of the way. By the time we got there, I was jonesing for coffee so bad my hair hurt. Summer knew everybody at the diner, of course. It was nice that she was introducing me as "Jarvis" instead of "Shred's cousin Jarvis." I was developing my own identity. It was also nice when the social wave blew over and we sat down and she started asking me questions about me—where I was from, what I was into. My answers seemed so boring before they came out, I felt like I had to spice them up: I liked sports, but extreme sports. Music? I liked all different kinds. Did I have a girlfriend? No, we just broke up.

"I'm sorry to hear that."

"She left me for a hang-gliding Zulu bond trader from Portugal." I didn't know where this quick-wittiness was coming from, but I was in the zone. The waitress arrived and I ordered coffee and iced tea. I was getting ready to ask Summer where she was from and what she was into, but before the words came out, a looming figure stood over the table.

"Farns!" Summer shouted, jumping up out of the booth. She hugged him, looking like a toy baby doll in the arms of a grizzly bear man-child.

"I missed you, you big piece of shit!" Summer said. Farns seemed to have no intention of freeing her from the hug. He wore a flannel shirt with the sleeves cut off, jeans and construction boots. Looked more like a typical redneck than the mythical cool guy everyone had made him out to be. He had a beer gut and thinning hair, but big, powerful forearms and a thick, tough-guy neck. He had to be at least thirty-five. I was unimpressed. And I didn't like the way he was hugging the new love of my life.

When he finally let her go, she sat down and patted the bench seat next to her. Shit, I thought, this guy is joining us. It was like someone had parked a tractor-trailer on my picnic blanket.

"Who are you?" he asked me, and not in a friendly way.

"Farns!" Summer scolded. "You be nice. This is Shreddie's cousin from Maryland. Jarvis, this is Farns."

I held my hand out and he squeezed until it hurt. He didn't make much effort to hide the fact that he was sizing me up. And by the dismissive look on his face, it appeared that he had come to the conclusion that I was a major douche-bag. He turned to Summer, who asked him how New Orleans was. It was too hot, he said, and he drank too much and had too much fun. The guy was a real extremist.

People started coming up to the table to pay their respects, treating him like he was back from a heroic expedition to save mankind from itself. They were all ignoring me. I could see our waitress trying to get through to take our order, and then giving up. The irritation was teeming through my veins. My guts were curdling like an environmental disaster. I was so hungry my head felt like it was about to break away and float off.

When the welcoming committee finally settled down, Farns was beaming. He obviously loved the attention. I finally got to order my French toast. Summer ordered a Caesar salad. Farns went with a double bacon cheeseburger with extra Swiss and extra fried onions and a side of onion rings.

"So, Farns," I said. "Is that short for Farnsworth?"

"No," he snipped. Then there was this pregnant silence, pregnant with Siamese twins conjoined at the head, with red eyes and horns.

"I gotta piss," he said, and got up. He smelled like burned motor oil.

"What's wrong?" Summer asked.

"Oh, nothing. I just…I don't like aggressive people that much."

"Who, Farnsy? He's a big teddy bear underneath all that macho bullshit."

"Oh, I'm sure. He's great."

I couldn't swallow down the lump of goo that had congealed in my throat. The waitress never brought us waters. Farns came back and they started talking about people I didn't know. I sort of zoned out. Felt like everybody in the diner was looking at me, the goofball one-eyed yuppie. Then the food and coffee and water all came. I was psyched until I realized that my French toast was gray. It looked like planks of flattened vomit. I wanted to disappear. Farns dove into his burger like he was having grudge sex with it. Summer ate very delicately. I covered up the grayness of my French toast with a lot of fake maple syrup and took a bite. It tasted like floor.

"Happened to your eye?" Farns said, chewing with his mouth open.

"Oh, um, the kids in Shred's neighborhood threw rocks and bricks at me yesterday."

Farns laughed. A laugh of joyous hilarity. What an asshole. A little piece of pink burger fell out of his mouth landed on his plate. Disgusting.

"Farns, you play nice," Summer said.

He finished laughing and wiped his mouth. He actually used a napkin. "They gotcha pretty good there, huh?"

"They got me all right."

Farns chuckled at me. "What'd you throw back at 'em?"

"Oh, nothing," I said. Immediately I realized I should have said something witty, like *a car* or *Shred's house. I threw a house at them.*

Now Farns had this little smile on, like he was amused with me. He had these little tiny horizontal scars on the upper part of his cheeks. They were barely noticeable, but they looked like they might have been old scars from fighting. He probably liked to beat people up so he could laugh at them while they squirmed on the ground in mortal pain.

Summer started telling Farns about the *Burnt Thunder* show. How killer it was. The band had sounded to me like a series of fatal accidents at a chain saw factory, but they were both enthusiasts for the *Thunder*. Farns said he was bummed he missed it, but he had caught them in Philly back in April. A real globetrotter, this guy.

Klavin came up to the table, the corpse guy. He wasn't wearing his black trench coat, only a tee-shirt that said *OSTRICH*. He didn't even say hi or anything, he just stood there.

"Hey, honey bunches," Summer said. It made me jealous. Were they going out? Was he even capable of the sex act? Was

Summer some kind of necrophiliac? Farns looked at Klavin with a face of searing contempt, then went back to making out with his burger. That made me feel good—I wasn't the only one despised by Farns.

"What are you doing today?" Summer said.

"Nothing." Klavin could just as easily have said: *Oh, going back to my coffin.*

Summer smiled at him. Her lips were so delicious. Klavin took off and she looked at me. She had big brown eyes like a deer. I wished that all of these other people would vaporize and we could be alone together.

"So where you from again, Jerry?" Farns said

"Jarvis. Towson, Maryland."

He chuckled at me again. He was a chuckler. "I'll be right back." And he took off.

"So, come here often?" I asked Summer.

She laughed. It made me feel better. She'd only eaten about half her salad. My French toast was down to a couple of French rinds.

"Hey," I said, "not to be a spoil-sport, but my eye is feeling pretty crusty. I think I need to change the bandage."

"Okay, we can go soon."

The waitress had put the check on the table when she brought the food. I grabbed it. It was covered with grease spots. The Farns showed back up and plopped his big ass back down next to Summer. "You guys aren't leaving, are you?"

"Yeah," Summer said. "He's gotta—"

"C'mon, stay a while. I was thinking about getting a little afternoon drinky-drink."

I started to say that I needed to go change my bandage, but then Farns would have pegged me as a pussy for sure. I just wanted to stab him in the face with that corkscrew of Summer's and get out of there. I had shit to do. Bandages to change. Zingers to invent. Uncomfortable situations to escape from.

"Stay a little bit longer?" Summer said to me.

I shrugged. "Sure. Why not?"

"Your eye will be okay, right?"

"What, your eye hurts?" Farns asked.

"No, it's cool. I mean, yeah, it hurts a little but I really just need to change the bandage."

Farns rolled his eyes and almost started to laugh. "Rip that bandage off, you'll probably feel a lot better."

The waitress came over and Farns ordered a PBR. Summer's choice was a vodka and cranberry. I asked if they had any non-alcoholic beer and she said yes.

"You actually *drink* that crap?" Farns sneered.

"I'm an alcoholic," I said, thinking I would somehow seem cool or mature, but instead sounding uptight.

"Sheeeeeit..." Farns said. "All the alcoholics I know drink bourbon and gin."

I had no comeback for this and Summer didn't scold him this time. There was another unbearably pregnant silence. Sextuplet alien devil babies from space hell this time. The kind the doctors are morally obligated by God to euthanize as soon as they emerge from the demon birth mother. The waitress brought drinks. Farns smirked at my near-beer, as if he was offended to share the booth with it.

Thankfully, a red-headed dude came up to the table and wanted Farns to come see his new car, a freshly painted '68 Chevy Impala, he said. Farns chugged his beer and zipped off.

"You're drinking that awfully fast," Summer said.

"That's the beauty of it—you don't have to worry about getting zonked."

"How's it taste?"

"Like a finely carbonated toilet water." Then I drained it. "Mmm..."

She laughed. "Want to leave?"

I nodded, which made my head hurt.

The waitress looked busy, carrying about five plates of food to a group of construction workers, guys who looked like they would order chili on top of everything. So we went up to pay the cashier directly. She was this thirty-something lady with a flower print blouse and cat-eye glasses.

"Farns said not to let you guys pay," she said. "He's getting it."

"Aww," Summer said. "That was sweet of him."

"Yeah," I said, seething inside. "Sweet." I was supposed to be the one buying her lunch. That S.O.B. bested me. I hated Richmond and all of its inhabitants at that moment. "I'll leave the tip." I went over and put a fiver on the table. Then I thought about it and I put down three more singles.

Summer had to say goodbyes to a couple different groups of people. Took forever. We finally went outside and the gods must have been smiling on me because Farns was nowhere to be seen. He must have been around the corner looking at the Chevy, dispensing his expert opinion on what was cool and what wasn't. We got into Summer's car and I had to slump down. Not to hide from anyone, but because the vinyl seat was scorching and I didn't want the backs of my legs to fry.

"My friend Nelly is coming over in a bit, so I need to get home. She's bringing me a mannequin."

"A who?"

"A mannequin. I collect them."

"Weird," I said. "I mean—yeah, cool. What, um...why do you collect mannequins?"

"I just like them. Paint 'em and dress 'em up. Glue stuff on them."

"That's really bizarre. But, yeah, like...awesome?"

"It's okay if you think it's weird. I know it is. That's why I like it. You wanna come over and see?"

"Yeah, definitely. I just have to change my eye thing first."

"Oh, yeah. Sorry, I keep forgetting."

Then I remembered that scene in *Chinatown* where Faye Dunaway helps Nicholson with his nose wound, and what happens after.

"You know, it's not so bad," I said. "It can wait."

"You sure?"

"Yeah."

We stopped at a red light, and for some reason the lack of talking was making me uncomfortable.

"So, uh...what do you do for a living?" It came out way too adult.

"Bartender at the Ditch."

"Oh, okay. The Ditch. So the other night at *Burnt Thunder*, that was your night off?"

"One of them. I work three nights a week."

I thought *wow*, the bohemian lifestyle down here was something to behold. Three nights a week. Shred didn't seem to work much either. This place was Slackylvania for sure. I heard a warning bell go off in my head, an alert to the pitfalls of wayward lives devoid of accomplishment. But then I thought of, say, Steve Reinhaus the lawyer, a major world class jerkface. What were his accomplishments? Screwing people over? Living the American dream of being a rich asshole with a big front lawn, snot-ass kids in private school and a trophy wife who banged the young Ecuadorian gardener every afternoon in the greenhouse behind the orchids? At least Summer and Shred were making art. That seemed like a much more tangible accomplishment than anything Reinhaus ever did.

16

BACK IN THE hood, there was no sign of the Hillites, which was good since I was trying not to think about them. Summer parked in front of her duplex, and the dogs must have known the sound because I could hear them barking from inside. Poor dudes were having separation anxiety.

"Do you take the dogs with you to work?" I asked as we got out of the car.

"No, silly." But I didn't think it was a silly question.

We went right into her apartment. She hadn't even locked the door. The dogs went nuts, jumping, barking, licking, banging into each other, sprinting up and down the hall. We went down to her living room. The place was like a thrift store boutique. The first thing I noticed was a mannequin in the corner, naked, painted purple and green, serving as a coat rack. The coats and a jacket were hanging from her hands. "She" wore a blond curly wig and really set the tone for the whole room. There was a leopard skin covered sofa, black candles across the mantle of a defunct fireplace, posters of bands I'd never heard of on the walls. There was also a completely bizarro thrift store art collection: an African batik of native peoples playing primitive instruments, an amateur oil painting of ancient Egyptian temples, a big greenish Picasso print of one of his French carnival models wearing a funny pointed hat. Its frame was hand-painted red, probably Summer's handiwork. I wondered where she was going to put the new clown painting. It didn't look like there was room for it anywhere. In the corner sat a hamster cage on top of some milk crates. Above it was taped a hand-painted sign that said: *Hamsterdammit*. There were also strange things hanging from the ceiling: a monkey doll on one side of the room and a scary red and black piñata that looked like a devil dog on the other. A thick smell of opium flavored incense saturated the room. I felt like I was in another country. On another planet. Shit, galaxy.

"You want something to drink?"

"No thanks," I said, thinking I wasn't in the mood for any raw asparagus juice at the moment. I went over to *Hamsterdammit*, but I didn't see any hamsters.

"Jerome died a couple months ago," Summer said.

"I'm sorry."

"That's okay. He had a long, rich hamster life."

"What are the dogs' names?"

"Moosie, Vertigo and Soup." She pointed at each one as she said their name but I knew I wouldn't remember.

"Nice."

Summer went into her kitchen. I looked at a framed picture on top of her TV, an old faded photo of two hippie parents holding up a baby with garland on its head. The dad wore a tye-dyed tee-shirt and had long hair. The mom had flowers in hers.

"Are these your parents? Here on the TV?"

"Yep. That's Henry and Lisa."

What a rebel. She was so cute I wanted to die. I started thinking about getting the bandages and ointment I had at Shred's and getting her to help me change it. He only lived two blocks away, but I might run into the Hillites again. I should've brought the stuff with me when we left for the thrift store. I went into her bathroom to take a pee. The walls were painted pink, which was strange since she claimed to hate pink. This was a woman of complex contradictions. Made me hot. I made sure to put the toilet seat down when I was done. I started washing my hands and I realized my armpits smelled worse than a fast food dumpster at three p.m. in August. If the Hillites can smell fear, my armpit reek would surely mask any fear odors. Otherwise, I felt like a prisoner. Then I said to myself: *fuck* this. I'm not going to let a bunch of inner-city redneck drop-outs dictate my moves. Any more than they already had, anyway.

When I came out, Summer was in the living room drinking something that looked like cranberry juice. She was petting one of her dogs and asking it, in baby-talk: "Whatchoo doin? Whatchoo doin?"

"Summer," I said, "my bandage is feeling kind of fucked-up. I think I'm gonna run back to Shred's and change it. Maybe jump in the shower real quick."

"Cool. You gonna come back?"

"Definitely." Then I just stood there. I should have turned and just strutted out cool-like, but I stood there like I was waiting for her to say something else. It was an extra ten seconds of awkwardness added to my life that I had no use for.

"Okay, um…see you?" I said, and made a little half-ass wave and left.

I stepped out onto her front porch and looked around. All clear. I felt pretty sure Summer liked me, but why would she? I wasn't a hipster or artsy in the slightest. I took a deep breath of hot, humid air and reminded myself of my mission. No rock in the face was going to keep me from confronting Motorcar and giving him a faceful of ice hot zingers. I could think of an ice hot zinger on the drive over to his house. I had time. My confidence was growing and with it, the belief that I would come up with something before the deadline. As soon as it got dark, I'd be on my way. I felt good. In control. In the mean time, this Summer thing was making me feel pretty damn all right and I was going to enjoy it.

From the sidewalk a few members of the White Tee-shirt Brigade were visible from around the corner. Loitering, hanging out, probably waiting for their next victim. I tried to tell myself, well, what's the worst they can do, blind me in the other eye? All I had to do was cross the street, go down the alley and take the back way to Shred's. They would still see me, but if they gave chase at least I'd have a decent lead on them. I took another deep inhale of humid air, told myself not to exude the aroma of fear, and ventured forth.

I made it across the street and headed down the sidewalk. Until I cut into the alley, I was actually walking almost toward them for a minute. They were about a stone's throw away, which was what worried me. I tried not to look but I couldn't help it. I tried to radiate total confidence, sticking my chest out, holding up my head with a slight tilt that showed I didn't care about anything in the world outside of my own awesomeness. My heart was pounding like a Keith Moon drum fill, my neck and ears burning with test anxiety. I could tell they saw me. Just before I ducked into the alley, I saw in my peripheral vision the unmistakable sight of heads turned in my direction. I expected to hear the Rebel Yell shouted out, the sound of feet pounding, clouds of gravel dust swirling up from the alley floor as they swooped down on me for the kill. But, nothing. When I got halfway down the alleyway I looked back. Nothing. They didn't even care. At first I felt relieved, but then I realized it kind of hurt my feelings. They ignored me. Not that I wanted to get my ass kicked, but I was expecting a little more life out of them. No shouts, no name-calling, nothing. They must have been coming down off of their afternoon crack highs.

When I got down to Shred's his van was gone, but I figured Kenny would be inside. I hated to knock on the door and make him get up out of his coma, so I just turned the knob and let myself in.

"Hello?" I called. I walked down the hall and Kenny was asleep on the couch. His face was twisted into a cartoon grimace. Maybe he was dreaming about pain. I got my backpack and went into the bathroom and took off my clothes. They were so dirty, they were almost crunchy. I turned on the tub faucets and hit the shower knob. The hot water came right away and the water pressure was excellent. Way better than at my apartment. I stepped into my shower thinking how much I hated my place. It had no style or flair or water pressure. And I probably paid twice as much for it as Shred paid for his. Aside from having to avoid getting water near my cut, the shower was the best I'd ever had. It was almost sex. And there was even soap, so I didn't need to break out the bar I brought. After I lathered and rinsed, I stood there in the hot water and just let it massage me. I tried to picture all my troubles going down the drain along with the sudsy gray water. I washed my armpits like three times. I tried to focus on a zing for Motorcar. *Bastard sonofa*...but the water just felt too good to think up zingers. I had plenty of time. Then a vision shot up through me, up through the night crawlers in my stomach and straight up to my brain: Motorcar stretched out on a huge Medieval torture rack, chains binding his wrists and ankles, little altar boys in black robes stabbing him with corkscrews. It was lovely. Motorcar's girlish screams were vibrating the iron bars in the dark windows of the torture chamber. So sweet. The idea of lowering him into a vat of boiling Clorox, or watching as his entire body is eaten live by West African fire ants while he's handcuffed to a sticker bush was so satisfying. So much easier than composing a zinger speech. But, whatever—I didn't have any fire ants to throw on him or a vat to boil Clorox in. I had my words, whatever they were going to be. I was on the right track, the healthy track. I had to make my words into boiling Clorox.

The showdown was coming. I was alive, godammit!

I stepped out of the tub and grabbed the rolled up towel from my backpack. I started drying off when I realized my bandage felt funny. The steam and hot water had gotten under the tape and it was coming off. I wiped the steam off the bathroom mirror and started pulling gently on the bandage. It came right off, no pain at all. My cut was sick looking—a purple and pink crusty line of gore overtop a dark bruise. Swollen. The stitches were the clear kind, like fishing line. Maybe it *was* fishing line. State hospital cutbacks. I'd have to change the bandage there and figure out some other way to get Summer to make out with me. I dabbed some ointment on the gore and taped on the new bandage. Then I wrapped the towel around my waist and headed for Kenny's room.

For clothes, all I brought was another pair of navy blue khaki shorts and another polo shirt, this one tan. I held it up tan one. What was my problem? Tan was just a slightly darker version of beige. I had been a willing participant in the beige lifestyle. I just couldn't wear this damn shirt. So I put on a pair of briefs and the shorts, stepped into my flip-flops, and went out into the hall shirtless.

I stepped slowly into Shred's bedroom. I wondered why Shred got the art studio room and a bedroom, but Kenny only got a bedroom. Maybe Shred paid more rent. Maybe they flipped for it. Shred's clothes were piled up on several mountains across the floor. His mattress had no sheets. There was a giant fake plastic terra cotta pot with a dead ficus tree in it, dead brown little ficus leaves on the floor all around it. I made my way over to an old dresser covered with magazines and old clothes. In the third drawer I opened there were three tee-shirts, miraculously clean and folded. The first one was dark blue with a Confederate flag iron-on done with African colors: red, yellow and green. Was this supposed to be some kind of joke? Probably, I thought, but I still wasn't brave enough to wear it. I wasn't going to provoke the rednecks if I didn't have to. Maybe that's why it was still in the drawer. The next one I looked at was light blue and said: NEWTON CHEESE FARMS. Suitable in a quirky way, but I didn't feel I was quite up to that level of backwards cool yet. Plus it had an ink stain on the sleeve, and I wanted to look my best. The last one was a band tee, some group I had never heard of called *Spentilator*. It was way huge, like X-Large. I decided to make it work, so I put it on and tucked it into my shorts. It was kind of like wearing a tent, but it beat the hell out of my polo shirt, so I went with it.

Out in the living room, Kenny's eyes were shut, but he still said: "What's up, Jarvis?" I was surprised by his congeniality.

"Not too much," I said. "You?"

"You mind grabbing me a beer?"

"Sure." I went into the kitchen and got him a PBR out of the fridge and myself a glass of water, which I chugged at the sink. When I handed Kenny the beer, his eyes were still shut. There was only one eye operating between the two of us.

"So how's that old leg doin' there?"

"It's fuckin' great. Wanna saw it off for me?"

"Okay." There was an awkward pause, but somehow it was made better by Kenny's eyes being shut. "So, where's the Shredster today?"

"Band practice."

"Really? He's in a band?"

Kenny didn't answer.

"I didn't know that. What's he play?"

"Bass."

"What's his band called?"

"*Killabeaties.*"

"What does that mean? Like, killer beats?"

"Yeah, and diabetes."

"That's so cool!"

Kenny just smirked, as in, *big deal, I've seen it all.*

"Is that what he shreds?"

"What?"

"Is that how he got the nickname? By shredding it on the bass?"

"Shreds everything. Boy is outta control."

"Okay, um…I'm going back over to Summer's. She invited me over."

"Congratulations."

"You need anything else, chief?"

"*Chief?*" he snickered. "Yeah, *chief,* you could get me another beer for when this one runs out."

"Won't it get warm, though?"

He didn't answer. So I got him another beer. I set it on the table and left. He didn't even say thanks.

So Shred was a musician, too. Dude was blowing my mind. As soon as I got halfway down the block, I was in a full-on sweat. The late afternoon high was brutal. I took my same route back, down the alley, and when I emerged onto the sidewalk,

I saw that most of the rock throwers were gone from their hang-out corner. I felt a sort of serene triumph. I knocked on Summer's front door, setting off the rumbling stampede of barkers. A girl opened the door. She was tiny like Summer, but she had a big hive of hair up in a crazy bun, filled with the biggest collection of hair things I'd ever seen: different colored clips, barrettes, those girlie rubber bands, and a couple of black plastic chopsticks lodged in the back, impaling the bun. She had more going on in her hair than most people had going on in their lives.

"Hi," she said. "I'm Nellie." She was cute, too, but she rocked a more elegant kind of cute than Summer, who was more button cute or elf cute. Nellie's face was sculpted, high cheek bones, a delicate line of chin. Classy.

"I'm Jarvis," I said. "Nice to meet you." I stepped inside as the dogs lined up to alternately say hello and smell my crotch. Summer was in her mannequin studio. It was the creepiest place I'd ever seen in my life. There were a dozen or so mannequins standing around, painted in different crazy colors, dressed in various punk and other weird fashions, some with random objects glued to them. One appeared to be completely covered with things found in the street! Stove knobs, pieces of metal tubing, twisted bits of wire, crumpled aluminum foil, a chunk of asphalt. So it wasn't just things found in the street, it *was* the street. There were also random arms, legs and heads everywhere. Some of the appendages were hanging from hooks on the ceiling, mostly legs. It was like a scene from hell. In addition to the mannequin bodies and body parts, there was all kinds of cloth piled around—gingham, lace, checkers, retro prints. Summer was messing around with a loose arm on a naked, flesh-colored mannequin, and I figured that was the one Nellie brought over.

"She's in her element," Nellie said.

"I see."

They were both painfully attractive, these girls. That Shred had it made, hanging out with these wild cute babes all the time.

I wondered if he'd ever managed a threesome with them. Hot. Then I thought—why not me? Maybe I would be the lucky third. I felt the tingling early stages of a boner just thinking about it.

Summer proclaimed that the new mannequin's name would be "Francine." I asked if the others had names but I didn't get an answer.

We went into the living room and sat down on the sofa. The dogs were by far the centers of attention. I thought about how awesome life would be if I was a dog. Then Summer and Nellie started talking about things I didn't know about, people, music, events. I guess I was starting to get used to it, like being in a strange country and you just have to put up with people speaking in a foreign language all the time. You want to shake them and go: "What are you saying! Speak English!" But you know if you do then you'll get thrown into some dingy foreign jail with rats crawling over you and sewer water to drink.

After a while, Summer suggested we all go to Avalon for happy hour. I guess she didn't realize it wasn't exactly super cool to invite an alcoholic to happy hour but maybe she wasn't used to being around one. A recovering one, that is. Most of the people in their scene looked to me like they were already drowning in the lake. It reminded me of a tee-shirt I saw once: *I'm not an alcoholic. I'm a drunk. Alcoholics go to meetings.* I hadn't been to a meeting since my AA sponsor tried to hang himself in his grandparent's basement. Poor Jeff, he fell off the wagon and couldn't deal with the guilt. Couldn't deal with killing himself either. He ended up only bruising his neck and then he moved to Albuquerque.

"Sure," I said. "Happy hour sounds good."

Avalon was a dark and classy place with candles on the tables. The walls featured framed photographs from the 30s, 40s and 50s, Humphrey Bogart, Marilyn Monroe, Will Rogers, who reminded me of Ben. The air conditioning was excellent, maybe even too cold. Summer didn't bring the dogs. We sat at a table near the bar. The girls knew the waitress. I wondered how anyone got away with anything in this town. Summer ordered a Long Island iced tea and Nellie, an apple-tini. I got a Sprite with a lemon wedge so I could feel like part of the group.

"So what brings you to Richmond?" Nellie asked. I was immediately psyched that she asked me something, rather than letting me sit there squirming while they discussed incomprehensible topics.

"I was looking for a job down here, but that's a bust for the moment." I pointed at my eye.

"Yeah, what happened? If you don't mind me asking."

"Hill kids threw rocks at him," Summer answered for me.

"Oh…" Nellie said, with instant understanding. "Those dirtbags should all get jobs."

"They have jobs," Summer said. "Smoking meth and stealing car stereos."

"They should be Major League pitchers," I said. "Really good at throwing things." They laughed, and I was glad to be navigating the conversation so well. But then it turned to other topics: the inherent spirituality of polar bears, how Republicans suck, and Democrats too for that matter, *Burnt Thunder* again, some guy they knew named Freebone got a DUI, how Farns is back from his trip, how dogs and mannequins are better than people. That I agreed with.

They ordered a second round of drinks and I guess I was feeling all right. But I could really smell the alcohol in Summer's Long Island. It partly repulsed me and partly called out to me: *Drink, drink, my young apprentice, drink me.* I really wanted one, but I held tight. Being on this trip and around these people was no place to fall off the wagon. I could go completely crazy, drink fifty drinks and end up in a straight jacket. Stuck in that medical college place with med students poking me with metal probes while I wrestled with the helicopter spins and space robots and giant imaginary Satans. The very thought of it made me want to do a shot of Jägermeister. What an evil circle.

After a couple more rounds, they had a pain-free buzz going and I had a sugar rush. They talked about a couple of weird indie films I'd never heard of, but other than that, I kept up pretty well. We cruised back to Summer's and Nellie took off. Technically, Summer was drunk driving, but I didn't say anything. Who was I, Billy Graham here? She playfully bumped into me a couple times on the way into her house, causing bottle rockets of possibility to shoot all through me in all crazy directions. Something was happening. Her little soft neck with the wisps of hair floating around the back of it—I was a complete and utter goner.

"Wanna watch a movie?" she said.

"Sure."

This was good. A movie. Sitting on the couch together. There were opportunities for snuggling. This was very good. Summer listened to her messages and sent a couple of texts. Then someone knocked on the door, dammit. I went to answer it but the door opened before I even got there. It was Klavin, looking like he overslept in his grave. He just came right on in like he lived there. Major cock block. I hated him in that moment.

"Hey, Klavy-Klav!" Summer was so glad to see him, it made me physically sick.

"Hey," he said like a beached fish.

I couldn't see how or why this cool interesting girl could possibly be friends with someone whose personality level was absolute zero. Or maybe they were more than just friends. That fucker, moving in on my game.

"We're gonna watch *Stranger Than Paradise*," Summer said. "Is that okay?"

Klavin didn't answer. She popped in the DVD and sat on the couch between me and Klavin. So at least I didn't have to sit next to the guy. The movie was in black'n'white.

"Old movie, huh? Cool."

"Not really."

I guess it was an art film. Of *course* it was an art film. What else? As the movie got going, I realized it was the oddest, driest and most nonsensical thing I'd ever seen. But it was funny. Not belly laugh funny but subtle funny. I think I was getting it, but I had no way to be sure. When it ended I felt like I'd just woken up from a strange dream, suddenly transported somewhere else. Cleveland maybe?

"How'd you like it?" Summer asked.

"It was good. Funny."

"Yeah. It's my all-time favorite movie."

Klavin got up and just stood there. I guess it was his way of saying: *Had a great time guys. Take it easy.*

"You going?" Summer said.

He nodded. Before he cruised, she gave him a big hug and kiss on the cheek. I hated to see that but at least he was leaving.

She put on some music. Something mellow and atmospheric. Then she sat on the couch next to me, close. Dangerously close.

"Who's this?"

"*Stereolab.*"

"Cool." I liked it. I put my arm over the back of the couch behind her and fished for something to say. "Thanks for showing me the movie." I couldn't come up with anything better.

"You're welcome." She smiled.

I was done. That was it.

Without even thinking about it, I leaned in to kiss her.

And she kissed back.

Her mouth and lips and tongue were so soft and generous, I was immediately swimming on ribbons of warm liquid velvet. I barely even noticed that her tongue was pierced. That was a first for me. I kissed her neck and I kissed her face. I tried not to let my bandage interfere, but that was impossible. She didn't seem to care though. Carly would have cared. Carly would have said: *No way I'm kissing you with that bandage on.* But why the fuck was I thinking about her? Summer's neck was so soft and luscious, I was in golden electric heaven. She was breathing fast. Something quite serious was going on in my shorts. I started running my hand up her thigh, heading for the promised land but she steered it away. I tried again and she pushed it away again. Now we were kissing very deeply, and I was really checking out the hunk of metal lodged in her tongue. So crazy. I felt like I was being transported to another place again, only this time it wasn't Cleveland at all.

Then, like a robot arm over which I had no control, like it was on automatic, I reached up even further, with even more determination. But she pushed my hand away even harder.

Then she stopped kissing me altogether.

"This is going a little fast for me," she said.

"Oh, I'm sorry. I just thought…you were…um…you know."

"You just thought I was what?"

"Nothing."

"That didn't sound like nothing."

"I just, I dunno, your piercings and tattoos and all that…"

I felt her stiffen up. She pulled away from me.

"What, that makes me a slut or something?"

"No. No. I didn't mean that at all." Wow, I thought—I am really fucking up here.

"Then what *did* you mean?"

"I didn't mean anything. I'm sorry." I leaned in to try to kiss her again, but she pushed my shoulder back.

"I've got an idea," she said. "Why don't you just get the fuck out?" She had a meanness in her voice that I hadn't heard before.

She was mega-pissed.

"But I didn't mean anything—"

"Get the fuck out!" she yelled, and then she kicked me in the knee with her construction boot heel.

"Ouch!" I stood up and rubbed my knee. She got it good.

One of the dogs got up from its spot on the floor. Another one growled a little.

"I'm sorry," I repeated.

"Don't worry about it—just go."

"Okay," I said as timidly as possible. I stood up. I still had a boner, but it was fading at record speed. I walked down her hallway with my head down. How could I be such a stupid idiot moron? Everything was going so great. It was all my hand's fault. Stupid fucking hand. And my stupid mouth.

I stepped out front and shut the door behind me. It was twilight. An ominous purple and pink twilight. A white hot panic started shooting through me in every direction. How could I *do* that! How could I *say* that! I really liked her and now she hated my guts. I wanted to die right there. I headed down the sidewalk to Shred's, hoping a neighborhood posse would pop out and beat me until my head was a bloody wad of pulp.

I deserved it.

What the hell was I *doing?* I should have spent all this time and energy preparing for Motorcar, planning my verbal assault, logistics, psyching myself up. My knee really hurt. I stopped and rubbed it. Bending over there on the sidewalk, I was hit with the feeling that I had no right to confront Motorcar. Who did I think I was? I deserved to be molested and abused. I was such a piece of human shit. *You piece of human shit!* That was actually a pretty decent zinger. Great—I finally decide on a good zinger and it was directed at myself. *Piece of human shit!*

I came up to Shred's house and noticed a funny odor, a burning mechanical smell. Like someone had been driving around with their parking brake on. Couldn't tell where it was coming from. I got on the porch and tried to pull it together. I felt horrible about Summer but I couldn't let it ruin my mission. I just couldn't. I felt like I was being tested. I had to do this. I had to overcome these obstacles and face my demon. Motorcar was the piece of shit, not me. Okay, maybe we both were, but he was worse. I took in a deep breath and refocused: I was going to go into Shred's, grab my back-pack, go have my showdown and start living my damn life.

17

I WENT IN. Seemed darker than usual. I heard talking. I went down to the living room where Shred and Kenny and Farns were seated in a sort of triangle around the coffee table, Kenny on the couch in his usual spot, Shred and Farns in chairs. There was no music playing, which seemed odd. A bottle of Jim Beam sat on the table. They were drinking it on-the-rocks. They all looked really somber and heavy, like they were having a séance, waiting for some dead friend's soul to come back and give them final instructions.

"There he is," Shred said like a good-ol' boy.

"There's the man of the hour," Farns said. "How y'doin?" He nodded. Farns was being way friendly. Strange. What, were they sitting there snorting horse tranquilizer or something? Probably.

"You guys having a funeral?"

Shred looked at Farns and then up at me. They were all looking at me. What the fuck?

"Have a seat, Jar," Shred said.

Now I felt like I was at a business meeting, the agenda for which included me getting fired. I almost expected to see Reinhaus pop out of the kitchen and fire me again. *Piece of human shit!*

No one was saying anything.

"What's going on?"

Nothing.

"Did I do something wrong?"

"Jarvis," Shred said very seriously, "we've been talking about how to help you, y'know, with…your thing."

"What thing?"

"You can't just go about something like this on your own," he went on. "It's too dangerous."

"What are you talking about?" I said.

"You know what we're talking about," Farns said like a kindly father.

"I do?"

"The guy," Shred said. "The guy you came here to see."

"Dude!" I yelled at Shred. "I told you not to tell anybody!" My heart was in my neck, like a dry ball of bread dough pressing on my chin.

"You gotta be careful with this kind of thing," Farns said. "I've heard of priests packing guns these days, ready to shoot if some kid they were a pervert to comes back for revenge."

I just looked at him like, *do I know you?* "Who else did you tell, Shred?"

"If it wasn't for my leg," Kenny said, "I'd totally help you kick the guy's ass."

"Who else did you tell?"

"All fucking perverts should be lined up and shot," Farns said. "Damn right."

"But like, tortured first."

"Evan!" I yelled. "Who else?"

"Hey—don't ever call me that. I hate that name."

"Death by blow torch," Farns continued.

"Oh my God," I said.

"Jarvis, you're my cousin. We're family. You can't just go and do this on your own. You need a posse at your back. And we are that posse."

Farns nodded. "That's right."

"If you don't tell me who else you told, I swear I'm gonna pop you one."

"Hey," Farns said, puffing up in his seat like he was ready to fight me.

Shred raised his hands in a *calm-down* gesture. "Everybody just chill. I only told people who were cool, Jar. I didn't go blabbing it all over town or anything."

I wanted to kill him.

"We were just talking about some of the options we do have here," Farns said. "We can duct tape him up, throw him in my van and move him to my shop. Ice him there. Or we could… have you cased out his crib yet?"

"Hold on just a minute here," I said. "I never said anything about kidnapping the guy. Let alone killing him. Are you fucking kidding me? I just wanted to have a healthy verbal confrontation."

Farns laughed. "A *what*?"

Shred threw his hands out to the sides. "Oh, come on, man!"

"Shred told us you wanted to take the guy's head off," Farns said.

I looked at Shred. He just had this look on his face that said: Well, you *should* want to take his head off, so you might as well have said it.

"I'm getting the fuck out of here. You people are crazy."

"No—man—no—you can't go—can't leave now," Shred and Farns both said, their words all mixed up and overlapping.

Kenny was just sitting there, observing. He probably didn't care one way or the other about me or Motorcar or any of it, but he seemed to be enjoying this spectacle, watching with his far away, painkiller eyes.

"Tell me who else you told."

"You can't just leave," Shred pleaded. "You gotta at least face the guy and speak your peace thing. Punch him maybe. With a shovel. In the fucking face. I sure wouldn't mind getting a piece of him myself."

"Can't let this stand," Farns said. "Sonofabitch raped you and you're just gonna let him walk the streets?"

"*Raped* me?" I said. "Where the hell did you get that?" I looked at Shred. He just shrugged. "Look—I never got raped and I don't want to kill anybody. I don't even really want to hurt him. That's not the point."

"There's nothing wrong with admitting you got raped, man. It's not your fault."

"But I didn't get—"

"Let's rethink this a little bit here," Farns said. "You don't want to kill him. Fine." He appeared to be thinking things over, rubbing his chin. "There's more than one way to lay down a cold plate special on someone's ass."

"A what?"

"A cold plate special, brother."

"What do you mean? Like, cheese and grapes?"

"Means revenge," Shred explained. "From that old saying: 'Revenge is a dish best served cold.' I'm pretty sure that's it."

"Khan says it in *Star Trek II: The Wrath of Khan*," Farns added.

"I heard it on *The Simpsons*," Kenny chimed in. "Mister Burns says it."

"I think it's in some book from the seventeen-hundreds."

I just sat there, a sore red nub, my innermost places probed and poked at by these dudes I barely knew. My eye hurt. My knee hurt. My life hurt. I just wanted to vaporize myself into an invisible space gas and float away.

"Well," Farns said, "if you don't want to kill him or kick his ass, we can always do a *Wash the Car* on him."

"What's that?"

"You crack a dozen eggs and mix them up real good with a bottle of bleach. It creates this sticky evil shit that has the worst death smell ever invented, once it all starts to rot together. You pour it into the grill of their car and that's it. Car's toast. It reeks so bad, they can't even sell it. They have to throw the car away."

"That's so awesome," Shred laughed.

"Probably one of the worst fucking smells on the earth," Farns said.

"I know someone else I might do that to," Kenny said. "Soon as my leg's better."

"Definitely a good one," Shred said. "But this situation really calls for something harsher. I say we kill him."

"Would you please stop with this? It's not a situation."

"We can *Flare Gun* him," Farns said, "where you scare them with a flare gun and then shoot it off right by their head. Scary as shit and it's legal."

"That is *not* legal," I said.

"How about if you take the flare gun and shoot him in the face?" Shred asked. "How's that for legal?"

"That might kill him."

"Or burn his face off," Kenny said.

"Stop it!" I yelled. "You people are insane! I never should have told you about this. Don't you realize this is a personal thing? A very private thing?"

"You don't have to suffer in silence about this, Jar. Me and Farns and Kenny are all here for you, man."

"But I don't want you to be here for me—you're missing the whole point. This is something I have to do on my own."

"What if the perv has a gun, though?" Farns said. "What're you gonna do then?"

"You could always just take a lead pipe to his head," Shred said. "That'll get your frustration out. There are some random lengths of pipe out in the back yard you can use."

"Look," I said, "believe me—I have thought many times about killing him, a thousand different ways. But it's just not—"

"Good," Farns said. "That's good."

"Yeah," Shred agreed. "See? You *do* want to kill him."

"No, I *don't*."

"Kill!" Kenny said. "Kill them all! *Muuuur-der...*"

"Shut the fuck up, Kenny," Shred told him.

"Look," I said, "are you gonna tell me who else you told about this? My private business?"

"No one. I mean, just these guys. And a couple of other...people."

"Who!" I yelled. "Tell me!"

"Only cool people, Jarvis. You'll never meet a better man than Farns here, and Kenny—what did you want me to do? Make him take a walk around the block on his broken leg while we talk? He won't tell anybody."

"I won't tell anybody," Kenny said, smiling.

"Okay," I said, "but aside from these guys, who else did you talk to about this?"

"No one, except—"

"Who did you tell!"

"Okay, okay—but I only told Rojo Peterson and Summer and this really cool lady from work, Eileen. She's like a mom type. I didn't say anything to her about killing him, though."

"You told *Summer?*" I said.

Shred nodded. It felt like a rain of cinder blocks dropping to the bottom of my stomach swamp.

"She's solid peeps, dude," he said. "No worries."

Now I didn't want to disappear, I just wanted to go ahead straight to dying. No wonder Summer was being so nice to me. I started going back over our whole day together, re-thinking events through the filter of her knowing about Motorcar. She didn't really like me for me, she just felt sorry for me. She only acted like she liked me because I'm damaged fucking goods. I was a project. And then I even screwed that up! Death please come *now!*

"I still like the idea of torturing him with some of my welding equipment," Farns said.

I couldn't believe Shred told Summer. I never felt so exposed, so violated. Naked. I couldn't fucking handle it. I put my head down in my hands. The sick frozen nuclear winter was blowing its ice wind, the purple-black death cloud breathing through me. The flying space robots were swarming, whole divisions of them. Whole armies. It was too much. Way too much. I reached for the bottle of Jim Beam and threw back a giant shot.

"There y'go," Farns said.

"Man needs a *drink*, that's all," Kenny said.

Shred just sat there, nodding his head.

I coughed a little and wiped my mouth on my shirt sleeve. Then I took another. No one said anything. No one tried to stop me. I took a third shot, a big one, and then I felt something I hadn't felt in a long, long time.

I felt human again.

Chapter (*b*)x-1#13.7

SWIRLISHY BLUE-GREEN MEDICINE fog spank-out, floating in on the heels of a backwards electric space drizzle, drizzling sidewards, and people are really just puppets, and the Puppet Master is union. Can't be fired. If he is fired, there will be an arbitration, overlorded by a federal mediator who has a thirteen-hundred million thousand dollar per diem fee, and the Puppet Master will be reinstated. Though perhaps he will lose his back pay for the time he was suspended to make it all fair. So you can't fire the electric Puppet Master or make people into not puppets. But you can bang the puppets' heads together and it won't hurt. You can tell them secrets and they'll never tell because their mouths are made out of wood. But then there are the goddam helicopters, and the puppet strings get caught in the helicopter blades, and all hell breaks. Steel death birds popping up over the horizon with no warning. And then the Puppet Master is screwed, the strings all twisted around all going all crazy, and the little puppet is in a convulsive death dance, spinning, punching itself. *If you confront the perpetrator and speak your vengeance, he might instantly dissolve into a toxic green space gas, and then there'll be trouble, buster. Sorry, but our time is up. Sorry, but our time is up. Sorry. Time's up. Mister Henders? Mr. Henderson? Are you there? Are you there at all?*

Space Captain Jarvis the Lucifer sits belted into his captain's turbo-chair, his proton death ship topping out at double light speed times nine. He is on his way to battle the army of flying electric space robots who've attacked the peaceful spice mining colony on Vorlox 13 with toxic z-rays. The robots only have three metal fingers on each hand, but they're still cold when they touch you on the no-no place. But Space Captain Jarvis is free, free like the broken glass spraying out in slow motion from a shattered window. He's cut his puppet strings with a pair of steel kitchen shears, the kind you use to cut the strings on a tied-up turkey or trim the fat off a New York strip steak. Potatoes and onions. Chocolate crunchies and candied apples. Cooling off in the cinder block rain. *Do you like the special pot holder I made for you while I was away at camp, Mommy? Do you like it? Do you? I made it special. Please don't kill me tonight for what I did.*

Space Captain Jarvis: holy son of the frozen proton clouds. Soon to be elected High Lord of the Galactic Mind Realm, Ruler of all Vagrant Space Robots, Master of the Puppet Master, Mediator of the Gosh Danged. He flies with the fishes and swims with the birds. He drinks his milk directly from cow. He doesn't walk on the sidewalk, he skips across the magnetic treetops, doing a hundred miles every fifteen parsecs, never falling through somehow. Too fast. Too fleet-footed. And then in flight, all the blue-green medicine fog is washed away, blown to oblivion by the icy space winds, the cleansing whip of cold metallic breezes swirling around in a trillion mile-wide cone of dead, empty zero-ness. The absolute freedom of absolute zilch—the sweet endless backwards atomic French kiss of nothing.

Otherwise known as *Space Love…*

17.2

THESE GUYS WERE so fucking cool. They were my new dad, these guys. Even Kenny, old gimpy boy. These guys were cool. I'm cool. Why was I being such a tight ass?

"Can we play some music?" I said. "Got anything normal? Like Billy Joel?"

They laughed. I loved to make people laugh. Shred put on a CD of something. Never heard it before. Weird guitars getting blurred and stretched all over the place. Muffled drums that sounded like they were in another room away from the rest of the instruments.

"So what's it like jumping off planes?" I asked Kenny.

"Like nothing else. Like flying."

"Better than sex?"

"Mmm...a very close second."

"I haven't had sex in weeks," I said.

"Congratulations."

"My girlfriend sucks. She dumped me."

Shred brought me a small glass with ice and poured me a bourbon, the mellow, charred-barrel life juice of corrupt French kings and courtiers and what, or dudes from Kentucky anyway. Colonel Beam. What a lovely, whiskered old man, sitting on his Southern porch, launching bon mots of timeless Kentucky wisdom at the gathering of raggedy field hands, hungry for any spark of divine knowledge he might spew. King of his plantation, and he freed all his slaves on a whim of mercy and followed the call of his calling—to make the best liquor known to God.

"Crank it up!" I said. It was music. I think I liked it. I wanted to like it.

Shred put his hand on my shoulder. I squirmed away. "Me and Farns want to go with you to case out the perv's house tomorrow."

"Ah, fuck that!" I yelled. "Wanna help me? Wanna help me out? Then let's party. That's what I wanna do. Let's go out and cele-fucking-brate."

"There's an early show down at the Ditch," Farns said.

"Let's do it!" I screamed. "Woo-hoo!" I drained my glass of Beam and poured another. Some of it went all over the table.

"Easy there," Kenny said.

"*Easy there!*" I mocked him. "Listen to you—Colonel Careful!" Then I got up from my chair and plopped clumsily down on the couch right next to him.

"Ahhhhh!" Kenny screamed. "My leg!"

"You know what you are, Mister Kenny-Ken? You're good people. A person people."

"You fucking bastard!" Kenny said in agony. "Ooooo…"

I felt something under my armpits. It was hands. Farns's hands pulling me up from the couch.

"Doesn't take much to get you wasted, does it?"

"Wasted? Pasted maybe. Tasted. Let's go out." I laughed. I started to fall backward, but Shred caught me.

"You're already too fucked up to go out, dude. Damn."

"No, I'm not. No, I'm not." I stood as still and as quiet as I could so they'd let me go out. I love these guys, I said to myself. And they love me. They are beautiful people. And so is Summer. *Summer!* Where did we go wrong? Oh, I hope she doesn't hate me. I love her special muches. Maybe she'll be at the Ditch thing place. I want to make out with her some more. I should've kissed her neck more. Did I really kiss her neck? I need more. I love neck.

I picked up my glass for some more liquid soul power, but Shred tried to block me.

"Whoa, whoa now. I think you're quite done."

"Nuh-uh," I said. "Don't treat me like a red-headed step-child. I don't have strep throat."

"What the hell're you talking about?"

"Are we going out or what? Y'all are a bunch of lame-o's. Lame, lame, lame. I thought y'all were party professionals, like full-time. You're lettin' me down."

"Get him out of here!" Kenny yelled. "Fucking prick."

"Okay. Let's boogie."

Farns had a beat-to-hell old Chevy van. They made me get in the back. It was full of crap, equipment, junk, but I didn't care. Farns immediately started hauling ass, and I felt like floating delicious nothing. Nothing could touch me. Farns would slam on the brakes at stop signs or a traffic light, throwing me into some piece of steel equipment or his big metal toolbox, but it didn't hurt. I couldn't feel a goddam thing. I think I was singing.

We got to the Ditch and I climbed out through the back doors and it didn't go so well. All of a sudden I was kind of down there on the pavement. But they picked me up.

"Thanks, Farnsworth."

"Don't call me that, dickface."

"How'd you get that name 'Farns,' anyway? Huh, Farnsworthy?"

"It's my last name, you jerk."

"Your Farnsworthiness. No nickname for you? You need nicknames. Here's one. Wait, I got one. How about Ringling Brothers and Farnsworth and Bailey?" I laughed.

"Shut your fucking neck hole, Jarvis," Shred yelled.

We got up near the Ditch, and I had to kind of negotiate a curb and try not to lay myself out again. And while knowing that rising and swimming through the air in slow motion is impossible, I felt it was possible. To air-swim. To swim the impossible swim. The door guy said three dollar cover. I got out my wallet.

"It's on me, bros."

I couldn't get my bills together, they were all crumpled and sideways and all folded all wrong and wouldn't count up right. So Shred and Farns just paid their own way and went in, disappearing into the throng.

I finally got some money to the guy, and then there I was, all up in it. The band was screaming. Literally. Guitarist and bass player were both screaming outrageous harmonies, whacky backwards guitar sounds coming out of the amps, blaring distortion, nuclear holocaust. I loved the organized chaos of it. The place was crowded, too, so you could stumble if you needed to, y'know—the whole losing-your-balance thing—it was okay because you could just fall into people if you needed to, as you make your way to the bar.

Bourbon.

Paid.

Drained it.

Bourbon.

Paid.

Drained she.

I thought I saw one of Shred's friends walk by, maybe someone I met at the diner, so I raised my glass and nodded to him in the party spirit of a good ol' raise-em-high toast, but he just looked at me like I was a moron and walked off. Hey, fuck him if he can't take a joke—I was only trying to be friendly. "Fuck you!"

The Space Master must at all times be knowledgeable of the ways of the bad flying space robots, so that he can know how to successfully battle them real good. In space. A mosh pit was going. I smiled at the insane power-buzz mania going on in there, the wild smashing of bodies together, like an unsupervised high school football practice for punkers. And they didn't care: it didn't hurt, so they were free. I'd never fallen up into a mosh pit before, that is, not that I ever remember. I watched them mosh-pitting it up on TV once or twice on VH1, but nobody here in the Ditch place was doing the famous stage dives…

I busted full force all up through some humanoids and climbed onto a little table. I was the tallest one in the room, über-manning the secret all-original fulcrum of Einstein's triple magnetic space-time grid thing, diamond high above the rolling fields of electric hell screams. I stretched out with swimming arms, screamed a holy death yell of absolute balls-out Legageddon forever (way worse than Armageddon) and let my personal electricity fly: and I flew, flew like a blue goddam ribbon Olympic paratrooper champion with a giant magic silver parachute at my back, arching into the crazy sea of crashing bobble-head doll heads, all while wearing no death helmet whatsoever, launching myself away from the shit mess of the world and all common sense, which I left far, far behind, somewhere deep in the Vorzidian dust caves of Planet Yes-No.

18

CRUNCHY.
The wafer on my head.
Feels crunchy.
Wafer.
But wait...it's a wafer, but—no: *paper?*
I woke up gradually. On Kenny's bed. I heard feet shuffling in the hallway. I guess that's what woke me up. There were some stiff pieces of paper towel attached to my forehead for some reason. My head felt like a watermelon. Swollen. Everywhere in and on my body hurt like holy hell. Sunlight was blaring in through the window in a strange way. It was yelling at me. I touched my face and it made my fingers hurt. My face felt crusty. Something was quite wrong but I didn't quite know what.

The door to Kenny's room opened. There was Farns. He opened the door and *then* knocked, in backwards order. I was just lying there, touching the wafery paper towel on my face.

"Can I come in?" he said, already in. "Dude, how you feeling?"

"It's crunchy." Speaking made my jaw hurt. My lips hurt. Then the pain spread from my jaw like a box of marbles getting poured out on a hardwood floor. I couldn't move. Oh my god. I was dead. Did I have all my teeth?

"Boy, you are looking *rough.*" Farns was smiling. He was big and looming, seeming to block all the light out of the room. "You must have a helluva hangover, too."

I somehow sat up on the edge of the bed. "Actually, no. That's part of my problem. Don't get hangovers."

"Must be nice."

"Yeah. Real nice."

I brushed at a flap of paper towel that was hanging in front of my eye and then touched the edge of my jaw. It was swollen. So was my chin. My whole face was scabby and swollen and sore.

"What is up," I mumbled, "with this paper towel?"

"Shred put it on there to dress your wounds."

"Why do I have wounds?"

"You don't remember?"

"I don't remember anything."

"Getting thrown out of the Ditch?"

"Oh, shit."

"Yeah," he chuckled. "It was *not* pretty."

"It doesn't sound very pretty. Jesus."

"You really don't remember the fight or anything?"

The *Spentilator* tee-shirt was ripped. Covered with dried blood. My brain started throbbing. My whole body felt like one large bruise.

"Man, you *must* be an alcoholic. You were wasted!"

I couldn't tell if he was scolding me or giving congratulations.

"So…Jeez. Who was I fighting?"

"Oh, like three or four people. One of them was a girl." He chuckled.

"No fucking way. I didn't hurt her, did I?"

"Not at all."

"That's good."

"She kicked you in the face."

"Was it Summer?"

Farns laughed. "No."

I didn't remember any of this. Everything went black after the stage dive. Zilcho. All memory, fried. Data tapes, fully erased. I did it. I fucked up. I drank. Failed to execute my mission. *Failed.* I ran a corner of the crunchy paper towel between my fingers. I tried to pull on it but it was stuck to my forehead with blood.

"Your head got cut when they threw you into the iron fence next to the Ditch. We decided it wasn't bad enough for stitches."

"Iron fence? What'd they do that for?"

"Well, you throw someone out of a bar three times and they keep trying to get back in, over and over, after a while you throw them into an iron fence."

"Oh. I see."

"You're lucky no one decked you in your fucked-up eyebrow."

"Yeah. Super-duper lucky. I gotta go to the bathroom." I stood up. My legs felt like two telephone poles soaked in glue. I wobbled. Someone must have punched me in the stomach. And in my ribs. And my neck.

"Reason I came by was to take you to case out the pervert's house."

"Oh, Jesus," I said, stepping by him. "I gotta go to the can."

I grabbed my backpack and headed down the hall, thinking: *Mayday...mayday—must escape...must go home. Mission: disaster. Abort immediately. Must tell Farns: Sorry, but I've got some getting the fuck out of here to do.*

When I looked in the bathroom mirror, I almost laughed. The way insane people laugh maniacally before their laughter morphs into crying, and then full-on bawling hysterics. I had really gotten an ass-kicking. My face was half-covered with dried blood. My jaw was swollen and light gray down the right side and most of the left. My gums hurt. I had several crusted-over cuts on my cheeks and forehead and dried blood on my neck mixed with smears of dirt. Scrapes everywhere. Patches of scrapes. I pulled the stuck paper towel back and looked at my eyebrow. The rock throwing wound had obviously bled again but the stitches were still holding it together. Loosely. My knee still hurt from when Summer kicked it. My other knee hurt from I wasn't sure what. My whole body was throbbing. Wanting to die was easy because I was already nine-tenths of the way there. I was the bruised, cut and swollen physical embodiment of the humiliation and regret that lived inside of me like black mold on a basement ceiling. This was torture. The worst kind. The kind that you do to yourself.

So much for my goal of two full years sober. And blacking out—not so grand either. The last time I blacked out I lost my wallet, and so I reached around to check for it and sure enough—thing was *gone*! Keys too. Cell phone. Everything. Maybe they were somewhere in the house, but I knew they were more likely underneath a bench seat in the Ditch, or in the trash, or part of some art student's collage of things found in the street. Maybe Summer had glued them to a mannequin's face. Oh well, I figured, at least going the next two years sober should be no problem. All I'd ever have to do is think back to last night as a deterrent.

What a total pathetic failure this whole stupid trip was, and now here was Farns intruding in my private business again. That was the last thing I needed right now. So damned embarrassing. Now everyone in Richmond knew I was a child molester victim. And that it bothered me. I felt naked and stepped-on. Literally stepped-on. Kicked in the face. What I needed was to be out of this living day-mare. If I was going to do anything at all before I left, it would be apologize to Summer. If my face doesn't scare her off. Maybe she won't recognize me and she'll corkscrew me. Maybe she *will* recognize me and corkscrew me.

With a little warm water, the paper towel came right off. There was a line of cuts coming down across the center of my forehead. They were wide and not deep, more like large scrapes, but they ran across this sick purple-black death bruise. My eyes looked like dried peach pits. Basically, my face looked like a pan of burnt lasagna.

This is why I don't drink. See?

I knew there had to be a reason.

I got my antibiotic ointment and started slathering it on. Then I taped the rest of my bandages onto my face. In a haphazard fashion. I looked ridiculous so I tore them all off and threw them on the floor. I stepped over to take a pee and I thought: boy, *this* day sure did start out in the toilet. I came down here to fix my life and fucked it up even more than it already was. And to top it all off, my pee was pink, which probably meant it had some blood in it. I cried for a second while I was peeing but then pulled myself together.

Good thing I was in so much physical pain, because at least it distracted me from the searing pain of my stupidity. I pulled the *Spentilator* tee-shirt off and threw it into the bathtub. I had bruises all over my chest and ribcage. The death cloud of my personal nuclear winter was now visible—I was wearing it on the outside. I put on my beige polo shirt and went down to the living room, where Farns was sitting with Kenny.

"How y'doin, wildman?" Farns said.

I shook my head. I wanted no praise whatsoever for being a "wildman."

"You look like Frankenstein, bro," Kenny said. He actually looked awake and alert for once.

"Yeah?" I said. "Well, I wouldn't mind crawling back into the grave, actually."

"No, man," Farns said. "No grave for you. We're gonna go find your pervert. You got his address and shit, right?"

"Bong hit?" Kenny asked Farns.

"Sure."

"I don't suppose you guys have seen my wallet and keys or cell phone, huh?"

"Nope."

"Nada."

I went down to Kenny's room and looked in the bed, under the bed, everywhere. It was very painful. Nothing. Now I was trapped. No way to get home. I did find my flip-flops. They were both blown out and had dried blood and beer and some kind of goo on them. I went back out to the living room where Farns was blowing out a giant lungful of pot smoke.

"Where's Shred?" I asked. "He around?"

Nobody answered.

"So," Kenny said, "looks like you had yourself an interesting night out. Sorry I missed it."

"I wish I'd missed it."

"Wanna get some breakfast, dude?" Farns said. "I'll buy."

"No. No thanks. I'm just…I'm not hungry." I was actually starving. I just wanted coffee. And death.

"C'mon, man," Farns said, sounding pissed.

"You know, this trip hasn't exactly gone as planned. I mean, look at my face. I'm hurting all over. I should just go back home and regroup. I'll come back in a few weeks when I'm feeling better."

Farns stood up. It was a threatening gesture somehow, even though it was just a guy standing up.

"You shouldn't put this off, Jerry. It's not healthy."

"Jarvis."

Kenny chuckled.

I hated these guys.

"If you go back now, then you'll have gotten your face smashed in for nothing."

Deep down in my guts, underneath the worm swamp of nerves where the truth lived, I knew Farns was right. Didn't want to admit it.

"I'm just gonna go home."

"Well, at least go out for goddam breakfast with me, then. I'm fucking inviting you. Kenny, you coming?"

"No, man. I had some toast earlier."

"You're turning into a real fucking degenerate junkie, Ken. You know that?"

"Thanks, Mom."

"All right," Farns said to me. "Let's go." He said it like I had already agreed to go. This Farns would have made a good lawyer. In a zoo. Down at Zoo Court. I figured, well, it was either go with Farns and get some food or sit there with Kenny and starve. So I picked the lesser of two assholes and went to fix my flip-flops.

"You got the guy's address and shit, right?" Farns yelled down the hall.

"Yeah, yeah. Memorized. But I don't want to go there today." I came back into the living room. "Kenny," I said.

"Yes, ma'am?"

"Can I have a purple Titanic?"

"A what?"

"One of those super-pills? I'm dying."

"What's in it for me?"

"Give him a damn pill," Farns said. "Can't ya see he needs it?"

"I only got four blue landmines left."

Farns looked pissed. It felt good that he was helping me out. Even though I basically hated him.

"Give him the fucking pill or I'm gonna sit on your leg."

He gave it to me.

"You owe me."

"Thanks, Kenny."

I went into the kitchen and downed it with three glasses of water. In that moment I swore to myself, on my grandmother's holy grave, that I would never, ever, ever again drink or do any kind of drug or narcotic. I felt good about this. I felt the glowing kernel of a fresh start. Now it was time for some coffee.

Farns' old van had all kinds of punk rock stickers on the back: Black Flag, D.O.A., Dead Kennedys. Was this guy a redneck or a punker? I gave up on trying to figure out what kind of alternate universe I'd fallen into here. As I crawled up into the seat, the smell of ball bearing grease and peat moss hit me like a heavy death fog. My eyes stung. The hot air was brutal. No breeze. I couldn't get comfortable in the seat. Even my ass hurt.

Farns cranked some psycho punk metal on the stereo and hit the gas. The reckless way he drove and the grinding noise of his van made me feel like I was on a beat-up carnival ride that had broken loose from its moorings. We finally stopped, sitting there rumbling at a stop light. It seemed out of character for him to stop. Anything less than screeching tires and his van up on two wheels seemed too normal. We pulled up to another intersection and he pointed at an old hardware store on the opposite corner. It sat in a row of stores that had to date back to 1903.

"That's one of my signs there," he yelled over the music, pointing to the sign above the big plate glass window. *Roys' Boys Hardware.* The retro-looking black letters were set in bold contrast against a white background with shock-red trim. It really screamed at you.

"*Roys' Boys,* huh? That's, like, a mom'n'pop place?"

"No. It's a billion-dollar conglomerate chain. Duh."

I couldn't believe he was able to string together such a clever set of words. I was starting to get this sick feeling that Farns was a lot smarter than I had been giving him credit for. I don't know why it bothered me, but it did.

"The apostrophe isn't in the right spot, though," I said.

"What?"

"It should go after the 'y,' unless there's more than one *Roy.*"

"Fuck you."

"I'm just saying. I did a lot of proofreading at my last job."

"Proofread *this*, motherfucker." He flipped me off.

"Sorry, I didn't mean anything by—"

"That's how the old sign was."

"No, it's a great sign. Really."

"Glad I have your approval."

He hit the gas hard. It hurt. I couldn't wait for the red brontosaurus pill to kick in.

"Hell, if you want I'll show you the best sign I've ever done. Or what's left of it."

"Can we get coffee first? I'm dying."

"Won't take long."

I didn't want to see his sign. I didn't want anything. I didn't feel anything but pain. We drove for a while and the houses started to get nicer. Actually gorgeous. Beautiful turn-of-the-century brick homes with white columns and giant porches. It seemed like a part of town that Farns wouldn't be allowed in. We kept going and not talking and it was starting to bother me.

"So, I heard about your boat, driving the boat around with the people in the back? That is one cool story."

His lips tightened. His eyes zeroed straight ahead. He looked pissed.

"Well, what the fuck is so funny about that?"

"I dunno—it just—I didn't say it was funny, really."

"*I dunno*," he mocked me.

I must have really sandpapered a sore spot. He looked like he was getting ready to spit. Then he threw his head back and laughed. He was just fucking with me. I felt like a moron.

"You sonofabitch," I said. I meant to sound playful, but it came out too hard. He gave me a shit look. I guess I didn't know him well enough to call him a sonofabitch yet. But then I thought: and he knows me well enough to stick his nose up the ass of my personal business? Farns *is* a sonofabitch.

We came to a traffic circle at the center of which sat a huge statue of a Civil War dude on his horse. It said *Stonewall Jackson* on the white granite base. Wow, I thought, I really am in the South. If only Ben the Cowboy could see me now, riding around in an old van with a redneck punker, cruising by giant Confederate monuments. He wouldn't last five minutes down here with that goofy-ass cowboy deal of his. Either that or he'd be a big hit. We pulled out onto a main drag, Broad Street, and cruised through a few intersections. Then he pulled into the parking lot of a big Lowe's hardware store and stopped.

"See the *L* on that Lowe's sign?" he said.

"You made the sign for Lowe's? Yeah, *right*."

"No. I made it better. Look at the *L*. See those two little marks on the side?"

"Yeah."

"I made a big fake *B* and painted it blue and hauled it up there one night. Welded it next to the *L*."

"Um…okay. I don't get it."

"So it said: *BLOWE'S*."

"No you did not."

"I swear on my mama's bible. I got a picture of it somewhere. It made the paper."

"Nuh-uh. Why would you do something like that anyway?"

"Wouldn't let me return these shit two-by-fours."

I didn't believe him. Those big stores always take stuff back.

"So why'd you buy them in the first place if they were so shitty?"

"I'll give you some advice."

"What's that?"

"Don't ever send Wallace to Lowe's to buy two-by-fours."

"I'll make a mental note."

"So where's this pervert guy live? Let's go check him out."

"I thought we were getting breakfast. Coffee."

"All in good time. Let's take care of business first."

"There's no business."

"We gotta case his place out, dude. You can't just fall up into this thing blind."

"Farns, with all due respect, this is my own personal thing. I'll handle it my own way."

"I'm just trying to help you out, man."

"Can we just get some coffee? I am dying for a cup of fucking coffee."

"What's the guy's address? What street?"

Farns wasn't budging. I wanted nothing to do with any of this but my tank was empty. I just wanted to get one last cup of java and die.

"2214 Glade Farms Way."

"Glade Farms. That's on Southside."

I shrugged, which hurt.

We got to Motorcar's neighborhood in about twenty minutes. Richmond isn't that big. As we turned into the subdivision, I was starting to get really nervous. My stomach was a squirming pile of swamp knots. I felt totally exposed. I wasn't hyperventilating, but I was close. Thankfully the blue landmine had started to kick in. My seventeen headaches had gone down to about five, and three of those were from caffeine withdrawal.

We took a left then a right then another left. I left my map in my backpack back at Shred's. Farns just drove around Glade

Farms until he found the right street. I saw the limousine from about ten houses away.

"This is it coming up," I said. "The one with the limousine. Up here."

We stopped about three houses away, across the street.

"You sure?"

"Yeah. He drives for a limo company."

"How you know all this?" he said with one eye cocked.

"I used to work at a law firm. You can find out anything about anybody."

"Huh," Farns said. He smiled. "Maybe you're not such a dumb-ass."

Then it occurred to me that if the limo was out front, that meant Motorcar was probably home.

He was in there.

It started freaking me out.

"That's it," I said through my swollen face. "That's all I need to see. Let's get out of here."

"You sure? You don't wanna stake him out first? Make a positive ID?"

"I'm positive. That's gotta be his house. I'll come back later and do what I need to do."

"You want to be sure, though. You don't want to end up killing the wrong guy."

"I'm not going to kill anybody."

"Positive 'bout that?"

I was starting to feel panic. My neck was hot. Now I *was* hyperventilating.

"Please. Can we just go? Thank you for your help."

"Look, man. I'll tell you something that nobody knows. If you promise not to tell anybody?"

"Okay."

"Seriously—promise?"

"Fine! I promise."

"I've got a gun under the seat here, Jerry. You want to go in there and do this now, you can use it."

"No! And my name's not Jerry, it's Jarvis."

"You sure?"

"Yes, I know my name. And I'm sure I don't want to kill anybody. Jesus—you have a *gun* in here?"

"Well, it's just a flare gun, but it could really fuck him up."

"Jeez."

"What?"

"Nothing."

"Why do you think the limo's here at his house. He work nights?"

"I don't know. Maybe he's on lunch or 'on call' or something."

"Or he's taking the day off to hide in the bushes and molest cub scouts."

"Come on, man—that's sick."

"Damn right it is. The truth is a sick fuck."

I didn't say anything. He started to pull off. We drove slowly by the front of Motorcar's house.

"Fucking pervert filth," Farns said under his breath.

We headed out of the subdivision. Farns said breakfast. I said yes. We turned onto a main drag, a road with all the same identical plastic signs and logos as every other cross-town main drag in the nation—fast food chains, retail chains, restaurant chains. It was comforting somehow. Farns whipped onto a side road and started hauling ass. Before long we were in an industrial area. Everything was so old, we could easily have been spit out of the other end of a time machine. Looked like an area where people were brought to be killed. I saw big white rusted oil tanks and fuel truck fueling stations, concrete supply houses, warehouses with slumping loading docks running along their backs. He finally pulled into the gravel parking lot of this dive country restaurant. It didn't look like a restaurant—just a box. Farns was already out of the van before the dust cloud he'd made even settled down. It took me a while just to make a move for the door handle.

The place was a total shack. Looked like it was built out of leftover wood and metal scraps. On the side of the building there was sloppily painted sign that said: *Sallys*. Again with the apostrophe mistakes.

We went in. Could have been 1968 in there. The scuffed and chipped tile floors, the ancient chairs and tables, the old Coca-Cola clock stuck at 9:37. The weirdest thing though was the mismatching patches of fake wood paneling on the ceiling. An older black man sat at the end of the counter. He was wearing a plaid flannel shirt—in this hot weather! There was an old air conditioner up in a tiny window, but it was exhaling like it had asthma and barely getting the humidity out of the room. There were a few other people in the booths, then I realized—everyone in here was black but me and Farns. They all seemed friendly but they were still looking at us funny. I thought Farns was this blue collar Southern redneck, and here we are in this place? Nothing made sense anymore.

The sizzling sounds coming off the grill and the smells of bacon and butter and coffee gave the place a real grandma feeling. Part of me was starting to feel alive.

"Hey, Pearline," Farns said to the lady at the grill. She turned her head to see us.

"Hey, sweetie," the lady said. "How you doin'?" Her voice poured out of her mouth with the most syrupy Southern accent I'd ever heard in my life.

"Oh, not too bad," Farns said. "'Bout yourself?"

"Pretty good, pretty good." Pearline looked at me and smiled, then went back to her cooking. Didn't seem to phase her one iota that my face was smashed all to hell.

I couldn't believe this Farns. He could hang with the punkers, the rednecks and the sweet black lady at *Sallys*. Like he had a secret passport to everywhere. I never knew such a person even existed. We ordered bacon, egg and cheese sandwiches with coffees to go. She wrapped up our sandwiches in wax paper, put them in bags and gave us our coffees in big white styrofoam cups.

"Thank you," I said to Pearline.

"You're welcome, sweetie."

I got called "sweetie!" This day was actually starting to get better.

When Farns and I got back into his van, the waves of deliciousness were rising off my sandwich and calling me. I tore in. About a third of the way into the first bite, I knew that this was easily *the* absolute best bacon, egg and cheese mother mcfucking breakfast sandwich I had ever tasted in my life. The hot golden cheese mixing with the farm fresh egg and crisp bacon flavors, the giant fresh-baked biscuit—oh my *lord!*—I thought such experiences only existed in dreams. Yes, it hurt my jaw to chew and hurt my neck to swallow, but I'm talking hands down, *the best* in the history of the solar system.

"Man," I said, chewing. "Pearline's a goddess."

"You got *that* right."

"A bacon goddess."

"She's the breakfast sandwich queen of Central Virginia, no doubt."

We rode on as I devoured my sandwich and coffee. I had no idea where we were. Farns turned down some alley. He pulled in behind this building, a big, ugly cinder block thing with a rusted steel bay door. Weeds were coming up in between the cracks of the asphalt, exploding into weed bushes.

"I need to go into my shop real quick."

"Sure. I'll just wait here."

"No. Come in."

"That's okay."

"Seriously, you can't sit out here."

I didn't have the energy to argue. We went in through a regular door next to the bay door. Inside it was dark. He flicked on the overhead fluorescents. The smell of paint and paint thinner, grease and fresh lumber floated in the air. Farns threw his sandwich on a big steel work table and stretched out his back before he started eating. My sandwich was long gone, so I just looked around. It was a big place, cluttered with all kinds of junk, stacks of two-by-fours and plywood, paint cans and painting equipment, wall racks holding long steel rods and channel iron, all kinds of power tools, a giant jigsaw, welding stuff. Along the back wall sat five or six refrigerators.

"What's with the fridges?"

"Huh?" he said, chewing.

"The refrigerators?"

"I like my beer and I like it cold."

Wow, I thought, this dude is a real professional alcoholic, but nobody has five refrigerators full of beer. Body parts, maybe. Bodies of people he'd killed. Dead perverts, dead yuppies, dead store owners who didn't pay for their *Joes Coffee Shop* sign. Dead proofreaders. He finished his sandwich and chugged his coffee and let fly a throaty wet burp. Disgusting. He seemed proud of it too. He turned on a dilapidated boom box and some old jazz from the 50s came bopping out. I guess it was from the 50s—what did I know? Then he got out some weed and starting rolling a joint.

"So, what are you gonna do to the pervo when you confront him tonight?"

"I don't know if that's gonna go down tonight. I feel like complete crap. Might just come back in a few weeks and do it then."

Farns chuckled and lit his joint. He took a long, slow drag. Guy had mega-lungs. He held it in for a while and then blew a mushroom cloud of smoke into my face.

"What would you do, though, if you *were* going tonight?"

"I dunno, man. Yell some brutal insults at him. A couple of freezing hot zingers."

He smiled. "Freezing hot zingers. I like that."

"Thanks."

"Tell you what. Nothing insults a man's pride like an aluminum baseball bat…"

"Violence isn't the answer."

"…to the neck."

He offered me a hit off the joint, but I shook my head no.

"You sure?" he said. "It'll make you forget about your face."

"I don't want to forget. Remembering will keep me from drinking again."

He chuckled again. "So, you go back to little Maryland and get your beauty rest. Or in your case, your ugly rest."

"Thanks."

"Me and Shred'll make sure this motherfucker pays."

"What? Are you kidding me?"

"Know where he lives now."

"But this is my…operation."

"You think we're just gonna stand by and let a pervert walk the streets of Richmond?" Farns squinted his eyes. He showed his teeth. "I have friends who have kids."

I wondered how I could have let this happen. I felt so naked. Naked and beaten and splayed out for all to see. And trapped—I couldn't even walk out of that place, I had no idea where I was or how to get back to Shred's.

"Farns—this is something I have to do. Myself. In my own time."

"Let's do it tonight, then. Pretty sure Shred's off work."

"I don't need help!"

"Okay, okay. Don't get your panties in a bunch."

"Look—this is something I have to do as a man. Face this sick perv ass-wipe as a man and do it on my own. Know what I mean?"

Farns seemed to respect that. He nodded. I was flooded with relief. But now I felt locked in to doing it that night, no matter how beat up I was.

"Pretty cool gig you got here," I said. "You get a lot of business?"

"I'm the best."

"I'm sure."

"I turn business away."

"That's great."

"You're goddam right it's great." He exhaled with pride and held his head up like an alpha lion. He rode the moment for as long as it lasted.

"Hey, can you do me a favor?"

I said sure, and the next thing I knew I was holding these big sheets of plywood steady at the end of his work table while he drilled a hole in each corner. The plywood was real heavy and

I kept losing my footing. He kept yelling: "Hold tighter! Hold tighter!" He had eight pieces of plywood to drill. When that was done, he had me help him move these heavy-ass steel rods from a pile on the floor up onto the wall racks. It was a complete bitch. My hands were filthy and totally sore. He made me work for like an hour.

As we drove back to Shred's and my neck started to cool down, it was starting to hit me—I had seen Motorcar's house. I had been probably less than thirty yards from Motorcar himself, where he was inside, probably whacking off to kiddie porn or something. The whole thing had shifted from concept to reality. And now I *had* to go face him—*tonight!*— or Farns and Shred might kill him before I got a chance to get it off my chest and rip him with zingers. Then I'd never be able to get my shit together. So it was settled. I was inspired anew. Inspired or provoked. Either way, this was it.

As we turned onto Shred's street, Farns had half a smile on his face. Then he slammed on the brakes, jerking me around just enough to make every part of my body hurt like a motherfucker in spite of the blue landmine.

"All right, man," he said. "Thanks for helping me out in the shop."

"No problem."

"Good luck tonight."

"Um…thanks."

"How you getting over there without your keys?"

"Yeah, I don't know. I can always hot-wire my Hyundai."

"You know how to hot-wire a car?"

"Not really."

"Well, either you know how or you don't."

"Maybe Shred will let me borrow his van."

He looked like he was thinking something over. "Actually…" Then he reached over and opened his glove compartment. "These might help." And he pulled out my keys.

I looked at them. They weren't covered with dried blood or beer but they were mine.

"Dude! Why didn't you tell me you had these?"

"They yours?"

"Yes. Thank you!"

He shrugged.

"No sign of my wallet or cell phone, huh?"

"You lost those, too?" He laughed.

"Yeah, remember?"

"So when are you going over there? To kill the guy."

"If I was going to kill him, you'd be the first to know."

"Just call me or Shred if you change your mind and want any back-up. Okay, man?"

"Will do. But I think I got this."

"You think or you're sure?"

"I'm sure. A million percent."

I opened the van door and climbed out.

I made a peace sign at him.

"Peace," I said.

"Peace off," he snapped. His van motor was coughing and spewing before he kicked it up to a hell roar and blasted down Laurel Street, the punk rock stickers fading into the hazy summer distance.

19

THE DOOR WAS unlocked, as usual. No one was home. It was weird to see Kenny not there. The couch had a big blank space on it. Maybe he was at the doctor. Where the hell else would he go? Oh yeah—the pharmacy.

I took a shower. I decided to just let the hot water hit all my cuts and scrapes. The beige polo shirt was covered with sweat, sawdust and grease. No way I was putting that back on. I held it up and looked at it. God, I hated beige. I stuffed it into Shred's kitchen trash can. The trash was kind of full, so I tied up the bag and took out back to the super-can. I felt like I lived there. And had for years. I couldn't find a new trash bag to put in the can. Figures. I got the NEWTON CHEESE FARMS shirt from Shred's room and put it on. Then I went back into Kenny's bedroom and stretched out, touched my toes. It didn't feel that great. The pain pill was working but I was actually hoping it would wear off soon. I wanted my head to be clear. I had to focus, *focus*.

I sat on the edge of Kenny's bed. Sweat started running down my forehead. I felt horrible about Summer. Why did I insinuate that she was some kind of slut? She was a nice girl, godammit. So she had tattoos and piercings and wore weird make-up—that makes a girl promiscuous? I was such a fucking idiot.

It was something I had to do—I had to apologize to her and make things right. If she was going to corkscrew me then I had to take it. I made four glasses of black iced tea and chugged them. Took a pee and headed out the front door and down the street with my puffy lasagna face and broken body. Didn't give a singular damn about the Hillites. Her car was out front. I didn't want to go up there, but if I didn't, I knew I was going to call myself a piece of human shit the whole way home. I stood on her porch and shuffled from foot to foot. Then I bumped into a milk crate that had a potted plant on it, and her dogs went wild barking. I knocked.

Summer opened the door. Her mouth fell open about an inch. Her forehead scrunched up. She was feeling my pain, absorbing my face.

"Oh no!" she said. They were the sweetest sounding words I'd ever heard in my entire crappy life. "Come in."

She grabbed my hand and led me down the hallway. I guess she wasn't mad at me anymore. Thank God. She sat me down on the couch.

"I heard about what happened to you. Those assholes."

"Eh, I probably deserved it."

"No, you didn't."

She put her hand on my thigh. I flinched a little. I guess I was traumatized or something. She patted me on my leg and then sprang up from the couch.

"Summer, I am *really sorry* about what I said yesterday. I didn't mean it."

"I'm sorry, too. Hold on, we're gonna fix you up." She headed to the bathroom.

She was sorry, too? Then I remembered—she probably just felt sorry for me about the whole Motorcar thing. Oh well, I thought, sympathy was a lot better than getting booted in the knee.

She came back with a washcloth.

"I'm really sorry," I said.

"It's okay. Here." She took the cool, wet washcloth to my face, just to dab some of the sweat and crust off. There was real concern in her eyes. I hadn't felt so pampered since the diaper years. A guy should get his ass kicked more often. Now she was smearing anti-biotic cream on me, touching my face. Pure heaven.

"That feels good."

A dog growled.

"I'm really sorry about what I said. You're a nice girl."

"Blah. Sometimes I am."

"All the time."

"You don't know me that well yet."

"I feel like I do."

"I shouldn't have been so rough on you. I know you've had some...hard things to go through."

"I can't believe that douche-bag," I said, thinking of how Shred spread my personal business all over town like a crop duster.

"Yeah, that pervert motherfucker!"

"No, I mean Shred. I told him not to tell anybody about that."

"Oh."

"And then he immediately went and told everyone he knew. Kind of embarrassing."

Summer dabbed some more Neosporin on the cut above my eye, the old one with the stitches. The rock throwing incident already seemed like a hundred years ago.

"It's nothing to be ashamed of," she said.

"Oh, I'm not ashamed. I just—"

"It's not your fault. It's something that happened to you. You didn't cause it."

"I know. It's cool, it's cool." But it wasn't cool. I was cringing.

She looked at me dead on and put her hands on my shoulders. "You know it's not your fault, right? That it's not your fault?"

"It's actually not that big of a deal."

"If it's not that big of a deal, then why are you here? Why did you come to Richmond?"

Damn, I thought, any one of these crazy Richmond artist musician punk-necks would have been better at cross-examination than me.

"I don't know," I said. "Just to yell at him and get it all off my chest."

"Well, that sounds like a pretty big deal to me. What are you gonna say?"

"I'm not sure yet. Something good. I haven't had time to think it up yet."

"Mmm?"

"How about…" I cleared my throat and in my best Brando said: *"I'm an errand boy sent by grocery clerks to collect an overdue laundry bill."*

"What?" she said, looking perplexed. "Isn't that from *Apocalypse Now?*"

"Yes, ma'am. Kinda sorta." We laughed a little bit, then we just sat there for a minute. She put her arm around me. I was beat to shit, but her arm over my shoulder in that moment very well could have been the best feeling I'd ever had.

Not far from the end of Shred's block, Oregon Hill became an open air park of grass fields and a couple of giant old trees. One was an ancient magnolia. Across a street the woodsy land dropped in a steep slope to the river. You could see bits of the river water, a sparkle here and there through the trees and brush. This was real Mark Twain looking crap. To the right was an old cemetery rising up on a hill, old stone monuments and headstones poking up between its trees. Summer said it was called *Hollywood Cemetery.* I thought that was hilarious for some reason.

"J.E.B. Stuart is buried up in there."

"Wow."

"And Jefferson Davis."

"No shit, huh?"

"Sometimes the rednecks put little Confederate flags on their graves."

We sat down on a park bench by the magnolia.

"Perfect time of day to come down here," she said. "Not too hot."

"Yeah, not so hot."

Her dogs were running around, pooping, peeing, barking, playing tag with each other. There were no other people anywhere in sight. It all felt so free. And Summer—so spunky and sweet and hot and bad-ass and smart—I felt like we already had this huge history. In reality, I barely knew her, but I felt something. Some kind of substance that I never had with Carly. And the feeling must have been real, because three days ago I would never, I mean *never* have seen myself with a punker art chick. Now it easily felt like the most natural thing in the world.

The sun was getting ready to drop, the sky beginning to turn purple-orange. Summer pressed her shoulder into me. A feeling ran through me, like warm embers from a sleepy campfire. Something must have been wrong because for once I didn't feel nervous. Maybe it was the blue landmine, but that thing had pretty much worn off. She grabbed my wrist and squeezed, actually kind of hard said: "You don't really seem like a lawyer type. What made you decide on that?"

I thought about it for a minute, but my answer sucked. *To get rich. To screw people over. To be a professional asshole.* I looked out into the trees and the shiny bits of river. I really didn't have an answer.

"What do you mean exactly by not the lawyer type?"

She started running her finger along the edge of my ear. "You just seem...I dunno...the way you say things, the way you think. You have more of a creative sort of mind."

"Seriously? Like how?"

"You just have a unique sort of take on things. It's different."

"You think *I'm* different? Ha! I thought I was Mr. Super Beige."

She laughed.

"A real beige-hole."

"All the guys I know try to be so cool and indie and hip. You don't seem to care about any of that." She smiled again. The skin crinkled on the sides of her eyes. She really was gorgeous.

"Actually, I do care," I said. "I'm just a failure at *hip.*"

"Nuh-uh."

I started to tell her I liked her, but the words piled up in my mouth like falling cinderblocks. All I was able to get out was: "I—"

Next thing I knew, our mouths were swimming in that warm blue aquarium of deep-sea lusciousness, that endless place where nothing matters, nothing matters except you and the other person kissing. But I wasn't thinking any of this. I was there in the moment, living through lips and tongue and campfire embers. And it was good. It was very, very good.

We kissed for a while, until a couple of rap-pounding redneck Hillite kids cruised by in their boom-boom cars, staring at us. I tried not to give off the smell of fear, but rather the alpha smells of danger and lust and reckless abandon. I also didn't stare back exactly. I stared off into the sky like I didn't notice them. It seemed to work okay. After they moved on, we started kissing again. When we got to a mutual stopping place, I realized I was breathing very heavily. But this time I was a gentleman with my hands.

We sat there as the horizon turned purple. After a while, Summer whistled for her dogs. She was a good whistler, she did it the two-fingers-in-the-mouth method. The doggies scrambled up and we headed back toward her house.

"Will you teach me how to whistle like that sometime? I never learned how."

"Sure."

One thing's for sure, I thought—she sure does laugh more than Carly. Then I told myself to stop comparing them.

We got to her porch.

"Well," I said. "I guess I should go get psyched up."

"Come by the Ditch later and tell me how it went. I'm going in for a few hours to help Freebone."

"Okay."

She reached for something in her pocket. "Here," she said. "Take this." And she handed me her corkscrew.

"Oh, no. No, thanks. I don't need it. I'm gonna stick it to him with my words."

She pressed it into my palm. "No, take it. Just in case."

"Thanks."

"Jarvis?"

"What?"

She narrowed her eyes. "You should rip his pervert head off and ram it up his fucking corn chute."

She said it serious as a corpse.

Harsh. I swallowed. It was so…un-ladylike? I guess it was the tattoo punk rock kick-him-with-your-combat-boots in her coming out. I liked it, though. Summer had major balls.

"Yeah," I said. "He's a piece of…fucking loser neck."

"Good luck." She kissed me on a carefully chosen spot near my chin, then she just went inside without saying anything. She shut the door and I was still standing there like we were going to keep saying goodbye some more. Summer was at least 10,000 times cooler than I was. As I limped out onto the sidewalk, I felt like everybody in the free world was watching me and knew exactly how cool I wasn't.

I carried my ass down the street, looking out for rock throwers, space robots, child molesters, crazy punk-neck ass-kickers, shady lawyers, screaming parents, deranged ex-girlfriends. Luckily, I didn't see any of them. This time. I reached down in my pocket and felt Summer's corkscrew. I ran my finger up and down the curls of steel screw. Try me, motherfuckers. Just try me.

20

I KNOCKED AND went into Shred's. "Hello?" I called. Nothing. Music was playing and the TV was on with no sound. Shred stood in the kitchen doorway.

"Wassup?" he yelled. His eyes were bugged out and his hair was super short, very patchy and spiky. He'd definitely cut it himself. Or gotten a one-eyed drunk man to do it.

"What did you do to your head?"

Kenny was sitting on the couch like a robot with its power shut off, staring blankly at the wall next to the TV.

Shred ran up to me. "Man, look at you!" he panted. "I tried to stop 'em, but you kept coming back for more."

"I really don't remember much. None of it, actually."

"Maybe that's for the best."

"I'm really sorry about the whole thing."

Kenny laughed.

"How's that cut?" He inspected my rock injury. "Mmm... holding together. You need to get some bandages on this other stuff. Damn."

Shred looked very wound up. He kept nodding his head and biting his lip. Looked like his personal electricity was about to blow. "So, you going to go fuck him up tonight? I mean... speak, speak to him?"

"Yes," I tried to say calmly.

"So what's going on with you and Summer, huh?"

It seemed to come out of nowhere. Kenny looked up at me—dead blank cold. News gets around fast in this town. My confrontation with Motorcar was probably going to be on the local news.

"What? Nothing?" I smiled.

He turned and bounced into the kitchen. "Better tell me!"

"So why you doin' this, anyway?" Kenny snapped.

"Doing what?" I said.

"What's the fucking point? Yelling at him? *Scolding* him? Isn't gonna change anything. A pervert's always gonna be a pervert."

At this point, I'd had it with Kenny's negative crap. He hated me, fine, but he was hating me *and* sticking his head all up in my business. I felt a hot wire shooting up the back of my neck, lighting my head up.

"What the fuck do *you* care? Why don't you just climb back up on your space cloud and space off."

I couldn't believe it. This was the absolute best, most well-timed, perfectly slung zinger I had ever laid on anyone in my entire life. My words and delivery had completely frozen Kenny. He couldn't say jack. I was in shock myself. And then I waited the perfect amount of time and said: "I'm out," and I took off down the hall and grabbed my backpack from Kenny's room and went out the front door. I didn't say goodbye to Shred, but he never seemed to say hello or goodbye.

I went out into the street thinking *bring the rocks and bricks, motherfuckers*, but nobody was out there. I got into the Hyundai and started her up. What a smoking cold zinger I just laid on Kenny though. I was feeling zinger joy and loving it. I *do* have it in me. Now I had the confidence that a brutal purple-black death zinger would rise up when I needed it to. Something spot-on that I could scream into Motorcar's face. A professional-grade toxic hazard mongo-gotcha. Maybe thinking one up ahead of time and memorizing it wasn't the way to go after all. I had to trust my capacity for spontaneous brilliance. Yeah. I felt great. I was beat to hell and still standing. I had an awesome girl in my corner. I was ready. I was adrenaline ready. All I needed was to be able to find Motorcar's house and get the balls together to knock on his front door.

And then the shit will fly.

Motorcar's house wasn't so easy to find at night. I couldn't find the map I'd printed out. I thought I'd remember the way, but it was dark and the swelling over my eye made it hard to see. And I may have been suffering from post-traumatic brain stress. First I couldn't find the grocery store I had picked out earlier as a landmark. Then when I finally found Motorcar's subdivision, I immediately got lost. I saw Glade Farms Lane, Glade Farms Circle, Glade Farms Road, turned up and back around saw them all again. But I wasn't freaking out, I was thinking—I can't believe it, I can't believe I'm doing this. I'm going to have the face-down, the righteous, cleansing face-down with sicko boy.

It was real.

It was crap-your-pants real.

I was finally doing something with my life.

And I wasn't scared, either. Nervous as hell, yes, but not scared. I was running on straight adrenaline. I felt like someone else. And even though I didn't have a pre-set series of insults and gotchas to launch, I felt like I wielded the power of the zinger. I knew somehow that at the crucial moment, the words would arise like a spontaneous silver fountain of electrified space dust. Screw a bunch of rehearsed speeches anyway. I was a creative sonofabitch now. These thoughts were pretty clear as I drove around Glade Farms lost, but when I finally found Motorcar's street and actually pictured myself knocking on his door, my mind went purple. There were no more barriers. There was his house. There was the limo he drove. My stomach waters started bubbling. D-Day had arrived. D-Hour and D-Minute. I parked a couple houses away and sat there in the dark.

Motorcar's place had a decayed look. It was the national headquarters of creepiness. Some lights were on inside. Creepy lights. Pervert neck was probably in there, standing at the stove in his socks and underwear, fixing his mother some warm milk. Suddenly I wanted to bash his face in with the old baseball bat. Then I pictured my words, coming out of my mouth in slow motion and physically bludgeoning his face.

Piece of human…sonofabitch.

No! Stop thinking.

I squeezed the steering wheel and took a long, deep breath. The death army of flying space robots was mine. I was their space general. My personal electricity rocking full blast.

It was time.

It was time to chew aluminum foil and spit glass.

It was electric adrenaline space time.

Time to swim the impossible.

If I don't go now I'll never go, I said to myself, sitting there.

I could still cruise. Leave and get out of there. I opened the car door instead. Just a crack. I looked down at the pavement. Then I shut the door. I had completely psyched myself down somehow. I don't know how long I sat there. Probably a year. Then I thought: what if I had the wrong Motorcar? What if it's not him? Then I guess I'll apologize and start all over again. Right after I kill myself.

Finally, when all thought and feeling had drained out of me and onto Glade Farms Way, and all that was left was the feeling of wanting to smash my head against a cinder block a thousand times, I opened the door and got out.

The dried summer grass of Motorcar's yard was crunchy. Loud and crunchy. The knobs on all my senses were turned to *eleven*. Then the aluminum and plexi-glass screen door was there in front of me.

This was it.

Moment X.

Shit.

My lips were tight. Every muscle in my body was clenched. Neck, hot. Stomach, a bottomless nerve hole. I tried to take a deep breath, but my lungs were locked up and it didn't go all the way down.

"…three…two…one…"

And I rang the door bell.

After about a hundred-thousand years, I heard a couple of creaking sounds. Someone was coming.

The front door made a strange vacuum sucking sound when it opened. Like the place was a hermetically sealed perv chamber. The door opened about two inches.

There was a hand and a creepy eye.

"Who is it?"

It was him. I could tell from his high-pitched, wet voice. I remembered it to a tee.

"Daniel Marticlair?"

"Who is it?"

"Are you Daniel Marticlair?"

"No," he said in a snippy weasel tone. "Who are you?"

"It's Jarvis Henders."

"I don't know you."

"Yes, you do, Daniel."

"No, I don't. Never seen you before in my life."

"Maybe you'd recognize me if my face wasn't bashed in."

"I doubt it."

"Can you please open the door and come outside? I want to speak to you about something."

"No. I'm not coming out there."

"I just want to talk to you for one minute."

"What about?"

"Just come out here and I'll tell you. I know you're Daniel Motorcar."

"Don't call me that."

"So, you are him."

"No, I am not. He's deceased. You should leave right now."

"Yeah? Well, how do you know he's deceased if you're not him?" That was almost a zinger. I was gearing up.

He didn't say anything.

"If you don't come out here and talk to me, I'm going to wake up your mother. Do you want me to tell her what you did?" I said the last part kind of loud.

"I didn't do anything."

"Just come outside. I'm not gonna hurt you. I swear on the Bible."

"I'm not coming out there. You should go away."

"Mrs. Motorcar!"

"Shhhh!"

"Daniel?" I heard an older woman's voice calling from inside the house. "Who's there?"

"Nobody, Ma."

"Who are you talking to?"

"One of the neighbors. Lost their dog."

"See? You *are* Daniel."

"Don't call me that. What's this about?"

"Mrs. Motorcar!"

"Okay, okay." He opened the door.

I stepped back off the stoop and Motorcar came out. This made him taller than me, which I didn't like. I looked at him. He was stumpy, a little pudgy. He had the look of someone who watched a lot of TV and didn't do much. Hunched into himself. He smelled like wet band-aids.

"You remember me?" I said.

"Like I said—never seen you before in my life." He said it with a real smart-ass tone. "Well?" he sharpened his little eyes at me.

"Summer camp. You were my camp counselor."

"So what?"

"You remember me now?"

"No."

I couldn't believe his attitude. I had expected him to be more remorseful. And no zinger, any zinger, not even a bad one, was anywhere near the vicinity of my brain. It seemed to have swelled shut.

"You know…what you did," I managed to say.

"I didn't do anything."

"Yes, you did."

"Look—I have no idea who you are. I don't know about any camp. And you're the second kid this summer to come here and accuse me of something I don't know anything about. So goodnight."

There was someone else? I wasn't the only victim? Wasn't the only one to confront him? This weird feeling of jealously crawled up into the bottom of my stomach. What the fuck was *that?* I went into a state of mental shock. Corpse shock. I couldn't process. And I couldn't believe he was being such a dismissive little no-account bitch. Which would have been a sufficient zinger. I could think it but I couldn't say it. It was the perfect opportunity for me to lay down a smoking-cold word bomb and I had a metal desk lodged in my mouth.

"I know it's you," I said. "I can tell."

Motorcar waved his hand as if brushing something away. "Well, you made a mistake. Stranger things have happened." Then he folded his arms and looked at me with this smart-ass look. "So, is that all?"

I knew it was him. There wasn't any question. He wasn't even trying that hard to lie. And who was this other dude who came to confront him? Whoever he was, he had probably laid him out with a sweet zinger. Or decked him in the face.

"Look," he said, "I'm going back inside now. I'm going to ask you to remove yourself from my property. Got it?"

Remove myself? I felt like I was hyperventilating, even though I wasn't. My weight was shifting back and forth on my feet. There was a forest fire on the back of my neck.

"Well," I said, "you really. . .you really. . ."

I launched my index finger at him. A world-class power-zinger had to be on its way, rising up from the depths of my wit. I knew it was coming, I just needed a few more seconds. *Pervert sonofabitch* wasn't gonna do it.

Nothing.

"So, goodnight," Motorcar said, and he moved toward the screen door.

"How could you do that to me? I was just a little kid." I couldn't believe how wimpy and desperate it came out.

"*Like I said,*" he snipped. "I didn't do anything and I don't remember you."

"Yes you do, godammit!"

Then I heard someone yell nearby. Motorcar and I both turned and looked. It came from a few houses away on the sidewalk. Then I heard stomping and running. At first I thought it was teenagers letting off steam. But no, it was two dudes. One of them was carrying something. And no fucking way—they came into Motorcar's yard and started running toward us. And it looked like—

Holy fucking shit!

It was Shred and Farns.

They appeared in the yard like insane suicide commandos on a whacked-out hell mission. Shred was shirtless and covered in green greasepaint—chest, face, hair, arms, all—and he was holding a green mannequin of Summer's out in front of him like a psycho death shield. It only had one arm. He looked like a Martian boy from a bad 50's sci-fi movie with his robot Martian wife.

"Pervert motherfucker!" Shred screamed, running across the lawn with Farns a few steps behind him.

My throat filled with raw white panic. I was immediately in a state of cartoon un-reality. I just couldn't believe it.

This is a joke, right? This is a joke, right?

"Oh no!" Motorcar said, jumping for the door. But Farns knocked me out of the way and grabbed him by the shirt and pulled him off the stoop and twisted him out into the yard.

"What the fuck are you doing!" I yelled.

Motorcar lost his footing and fell down on the grass. Then Shred squashed the mannequin into his back. Motorcar went all the way down onto his stomach.

"Hey!" Motorcar yelled. "Stop!"

Shred started ramming the mannequin's handless arm up into Motorcar's crotch from behind, pushing in and letting go.

"Hey! Stop it! Ma!"

"See how you like it," Shred sneered.

I cannot believe it.

No fucking way.

But I had to believe it—green Shred was molesting Motorcar with a green mannequin from behind.

"Get it off me!" Motorcar pleaded.

Farns went over and stuck his big construction boot on the back of Motorcar's neck.

"Ow!"

"What're you doing!" I yelled. I went to push Shred off of Motorcar, but Farns blocked me with his big arm.

"See how it feels, you pervert bitch motherfucker!" Shred screamed with glee.

"Take it, you child m'lester sumbitch," Farns said. Then he stepped up beside Motorcar and pulled out a handgun from under his shirt. He pointed it right at Motorcar's head.

"See this, perv boy?"

"No!" I yelled. "Don't do it!"

Motorcar's face, half-looking up from the ground, turned from pale to pure white. "Please don't kill me," he begged, practically crying. Shred was still faux-violating him with the mannequin's arm.

"Get this fucking thing outta here," Farns yelled, and he kicked the mannequin out of Shred's hands and off of Motorcar's back. She landed near the bushes. Shred tumbled backward and almost hit the ground himself.

Motorcar squirmed over on his back and Farns had his boot on his collar bone.

Farns glared at Motorcar with a real Charles Manson look in his eyes, and then like an ice cold dispenser of frozen justice, said: "All child molesting, scum sucking pervert-ass motherfucker sickos MUST DIE!"

What a *zinger*!

Farns cocked the gun.

"Don't *shoot him*!" I screamed. "Are you crazy!"

"Do it!" Shred yelled.

"No! Please!" Motorcar shielded his face. He was whimpering like a little girl.

I reached in my pocket and put my fingers around the corkscrew and pulled it out. I unfolded the screw and wrapped my fist around the handle so the screw stuck out between my ring and middle fingers and went up to Farns.

"Please," Motorcar cried.

Farns smiled and said: "Prepare for final execu—OW!"

I shoved the corkscrew into Farns's big right shoulder, the arm that was holding the gun. I don't think I did it right, though—it didn't go in very far. Farns flinched and his gun blasted. A dark orange fireball exploded on the ground about two feet from Motorcar's head.

It was just the flare gun. Farns had *Flare Gunned* him.

"What the fuck was that!" Farns yelled, stretching his head around to look at his shoulder.

It felt like someone had reached up inside me and twisted my intestines into a 25 car pile-up and then poured acid on it— the kind of acid that burned *and* the psychedelic kind. What was happening in front of me could not have been real. Motorcar was staring at the smoking spot where the flare exploded next to his head, like he was looking down Satan's throat. Another tiny spot of brown grass by his head was still on fire. This yellow smoke rose up. It smelled like fireworks. Motorcar was still panting. He was holding his stomach.

"Next time you *die*," Farns yelled. "Come on!"

And Shred and Farns took off running.

Motorcar sat up on the ground, shivering, his eyes wide open. The whole thing took about fifteen seconds. I was still in a state of accelerated disbelief. Everything was made out of paper. Science fiction was real. My head felt like it was stuck on the spin cycle of a psychotic washing machine.

"Oh, man," I said. "I am really sorry. I did not mean for—"

"I'm calling the cops!" Motorcar said, his smart-ass voice snapping back, even as he was trying to catch his breath.

I couldn't believe this guy. Here I was apologizing to him for what Shred and Farns had just done—though God only knows why I was apologizing—I had even tried to defend him from getting shot—and why the hell was I doing *that*? Little prick had zero remorse. Just attitude all the way.

"*You're* gonna call the cops on *me*?" I said, and without even thinking about it, I reached down and grabbed him by the shirt. His wet, round cheeks looked like they were filled with butter.

"Fuck *you!*" I screamed. Then it came to me—like the yellow electric flash of the lightning bug—and I knew exactly what to do.

I bitch-slapped him.

Right in his puffy, butter-filled face.

I bitch-slapped Motorcar as hard as I could. It made the perfect slapping sound. His eyes were clenched shut. Then I threw him back to the ground and went over and picked up the mannequin. I didn't want any evidence around if he did call the cops.

"You *suck!*" I shouted as I walked by him. "Pervert sonofabitch." And I headed across the yard toward my car.

Oh my god—that was the worst zinger ever. But it felt awesome. My palm hurt from slapping him. A pain of total joy.

I went to the Hyundai with Shred's green mannequin wife under my arm. I threw her into the backseat. As I drove past, I could see Motorcar brushing himself off. I honked the horn but he didn't seem to notice. "Pervert sonofabitch!" I yelled.

It was all swirling in my head—my crazy cousin and his wild punk-neck bully friend! Shooting off a flare gun? Raping him with a mannequin? What the hell just happened? And why did I defend Motorcar? What was my problem? Was I a pervert too? I was already a stalker. No—I am *not* a stalker. I am *not* a murderer! Those jerks! That was supposed to be *my* confrontation back there. Motorcar was *my* pervert. They had no right to fall up into my deal like that. And I was just about to serve up a titanium-strength hell zinger. Those fuckers ruined everything. And Motorcar—he didn't even apologize!

At a stop sign, I reached back and pushed the mannequin further down so no one could see it.

"They're going to have to burn you, lady," I told her.

For some reason, even though I wasn't really paying attention, I drove right out of the neighborhood without getting lost. I hit the main road and a breeze came shooting through the car, washing my head in cool air.

So I had faced him.

I bitch-slapped him.

I called him a name.

Is that all?

Shred and Farns had way better zingers than I did. Oh my God—they did *not* just show up and ruin my confrontation! I wanted to find Shred and beat him with a claw hammer until Spaghetti-O's came out of his ears.

So I faced Motorcar.

Big damn deal.

I don't feel any better.

I feel exactly the same.

It didn't work.

It wasn't enough.

I should have spit in his face.

I should've grabbed the flare gun from Farns and shot Motorcar in the face. I should have shot all of them. I should have shot all of them with a *real* gun. I wanted a drink. I wanted fifty thousand drinks.

That bitch-slap was pretty satisfying, though. Shit, I dunno.

The bitch-slap is a human act replete with rich and complex meaning. The pain caused by the well-timed, well-placed bitch-slap is more emotional than physical. Injuries sustained from a good bitch-slap are to the slappee's dignity, their pride. While sharp, the pain to the cheek is shallow and relatively swift in dissipation, whereas the pain of bitch-slap humiliation is deep, and the memory of it may last a lifetime or longer.

I should have been happy. I wasn't feeling like the triple deluxe limited-edition super hero I had envisioned for myself. I felt dirty. Empty. Stupid.

Dead inside.

I felt exactly the same as before.

21

MY LANDMARK, THE grocery store. I parked in the lot and started scouring the car for change. I was doing pretty well, had about three dollars collected from the seats and the floor. Then I remembered there was some change in the ashtray. Big score. I felt rich. The a/c in the store was roaring like an arctic tsunami, so I made it quick. I got everything I needed and hurried back up front.

Now I knew the way to Motorcar's house like I'd been there a thousand times. This time though, I parked even further away, over on the next street near some trees at the corner of someone's yard. I popped the rear hatch and laid out my purchases. Then I grabbed a plastic one-gallon gas can I had back there. It was empty. I removed the nozzle and cracked the eggs into the opening, careful to get all of the yoke and white into the hole. I threw the eggshells onto the ground. I added the bleach and screwed the nozzle back on. Then I shook the can and shook it some more. I felt like a mad scientist. I *was* a mad scientist. I closed the hatch and headed for Motorcar's house.

The neighborhood was dead asleep, so I didn't even worry about anyone seeing me traipse across a front lawn carrying a red gas can. If they hadn't noticed the mannequin incident, they weren't going to notice this. And like his neighbors were gonna defend a perv? They were probably all watching from their windows earlier, cheering.

The limousine was parked facing out. He must have been a real talented driver to be able to back such a big car into such a tight space. Prick. I crouched by the front fender and looked around. All clear. I undid the cap on the gas can nozzle and stood up. I slowly poured the egg and bleach mixture into the vent that runs along the hood in front of the windshield. I poured it all the way across for a nice even flow. When the can was nearly empty, I shook what was left onto the driver's door handle. If Farns was right, the bleach and would chemically break down and react with the rotting eggs in a way that would create the a horrific, gut-twisting odor. And its stickiness would make it impossible to clean, forever stuck in the nooks and crannies of the car's metal insides. It was going to stink, a reeking hell stink forever and ever. It'd make skunk spray reminiscent of a jasmine tea party in a rose garden. Talk about a *zinger*. Now Motorcar's motorcar was ruined. Now he'd get fired from his job, just like I got fired from my job. He'd probably have to pay the limo company for the damage. The permanent stink damage. I laughed as I walked back to my car. I tossed the gas can into the trees and wiped my hands on the grass. I drove around the block and pulled up in front of Motorcar's house and stuck my head out the window.

"Pervert piece of human shit!" I yelled. Loud. I honked my horn. "Piece of human shit!" I kept honking. "Piece of human shit! Ha ha!" I headed down the street and proceeded to get lost in the subdivision.

Maybe he won't even notice the stink right off. Maybe tomorrow morning when he heads out for work, he'll think it's just another day. As he's driving down the road, thinking about how he got sexually assaulted by a green mannequin and shot at with a flare gun and bitch-slapped the night before, he'll notice something smells funny. Some type of rancid skank, but he's not sure what. Of course, he doesn't know it's a mixture of putrefied chicken embryos and a toxic chlorine compound, but he knows it stinks, it darkly, darkly stinks.

His hands feel sticky, so he stops somewhere to wash them. But when he gets back in the limo, he smells it again. Did something die in here? he asks himself. He shrugs. He looks under the car. As the morning goes on and it gets hotter and hotter—it's expected to get into the mid-nineties—he notices the smell getting worse and worse.

Hell!—it's coming in through the a/c vent. It's inside the limo and outside. Oh my god! Did a dead animal crawl up inside the motor and die? It doesn't smell quite like a dead animal. It's worse.

He goes to pick up his first customer, a banker in downtown Richmond who's taking a client out to a fancy lunch. The banker comments on the smell right away. "Smells awful in here," he says. Motorcar laughs nervously. He doesn't know what to say. He is sweating. He is sick from smelling the smell all morning. He is beginning to panic.

Within a week he's out of a job. He knows I did it—and he looks at his pervert life and wants to kill himself for the damage he caused me. His mom kicks him out of the house, and he ends up living out of a grocery cart under the on-ramp to the bridge. Talking to himself. That's my cold plate special right there: Daniel Motorcar is now an insane bag lady who foams at the mouth and lives under the on-ramp to the bridge, talking to himself, cussing at the wind. He doesn't have to smell the bleach and eggs smell anymore, but he himself smells. He smells of fear. The fear rises off of him like steam. Anyone who comes anywhere near him can tell he's afraid. He's afraid of the sun. He's afraid of the moon. He's afraid of mannequins. He's so afraid that I'll come back and ruin his life some more that he hides in the shadow of the on-ramp and whimpers for his mommy. This is my everlasting glory.

As I found my way out of his neighborhood, I still felt the same. No catharsis at all yet. Nothing. I stopped at a stop light and closed my eyes and tried.

Zero.

It was Farns' and Shred's fault. It was Motorcar's fault. Mom's fault. Dad's fault. Reinhaus' fault. I wanted to pour stink solution over the entire planet and run.

I told myself it would come eventually. The joy of revenge will grow inside me like a seed sprouting into a wonderful flower. I just had to give it a couple hours. The closer I got to Shred's neighborhood, the more I wanted a drink. I wanted forty-three crystal sharp vodka drinks. I wanted to swim down deep in the vodka ocean, toasting the flying space robots, the waterproof electric death-bots that lived at the center of my night terrors. In the sleepy ocean of electrified vodka where they thrived.

My head felt like it was filling up with industrial adhesive. I am such a stalker psycho freak.

No, I'm not.

Yes, I am.

No, I'm not.

Probably. Am.

Psycho stalker weirdo murderer.

I was at a stop light. I wiped my forehead with my sleeve. I wasn't breathing right. I took in a deep draw of heavy, humid air and exhaled slow. Jealous of Motorcar's other victims? What the hell *was* that? Maybe it was time to just face the truth and kill myself. But what was the truth? It was a mysterious mush that the human eye was prohibited from focusing on. Like a bowl of gray mashed potatoes as viewed from a half an inch away.

No.

Yes.

No.

But I didn't even know exactly what I was saying "No" or "Yes" to. Everything hurt. The blue landmine and adrenaline had all completely worn off and the pain of the ass-kicking was calling at full volume. *I should be in a coffin somewhere. Getting some rest. Yes. No. Maybe. Maybe yes not. A lush, velvet-lined comfortable coffin and some sweet, sweet rest. Now that would be nice.*

Way nice.

22

I CREPT INTO Oregon Kill. I felt like I had been through a war. I was looking for Shred. I was going to make him eat his own stupid green face paint. As I played back the scene in my mind, seeing Motorcar get abused by them did become a bit more enjoyable each time. But I couldn't let Shred get away with interrupting my confrontation. When I got to his house, I somehow found the strength to jump out of the car and bust into the place. I don't know what I was running on at this point—the fumes were long gone.

"Evan Henders!" I yelled, bombarding my way down the hall.

"He ain't here," Kenny said from his roost.

I looked anyway. In the bedrooms, in the studio. I tore through the living room and looked in the kitchen.

"What the fuck's your problem?" Kenny said.

"None of your beez-wax, Gimpington."

"Did Farns shoot that pervert guy with the flare gun?"

"Don't worry about it."

I was headed for the hallway when one of Kenny's aluminum crutches hit my back.

"Ouch!"

"Fuck you."

The crutch didn't really hurt in and of itself, but it hit a bruise. I picked it up off the floor.

"Thanks, Leg-boy."

"Where you going with that? Hey—I *need* that!"

"I thought you gave it to me." And I headed down the hallway.

"That's not cool, man!"

I went out the front door and threw Kenny's crutch into the little front yard. My head was going 10,000 miles per nanosecond. I got in the car and the green mannequin scared the shit out of me. I was really on edge. I needed to name her. How about Mrs. Greenstreet? Done. I figured I'd drop her off on Summer's front porch and then go see Summer at the Ditch. I turned onto her block, and sure enough—there was the gang of Hillites blasting hip-hop on the corner. Close enough to see me carrying the Mrs. Greenstreet up to the house.

I had nothing for them to smell. I was too numb. Besides, my face looked like Frankenstein after falling face-first off a speeding truck—maybe they should fear *my* ass. And I can always swing Mrs. Greenstreet at them and scream like a rabid hyena. I could imagine that working. A mannequin is a dangerous weapon, as I had learned earlier. I'd seen what she could do. I got out of the car and pulled her out of the back seat and took her up to the porch. I set her next to Summer's front door and went back to the Hyundai. All I heard was one "Art fag." No attack. No rocks. I won. And those sons'o'bitches better watch it or I'll beat their heads to putty with a mannequin leg. Yeah.

I got back in the car and it occurred to me that this had been the strangest night of my life.

I made some lights and I was at the Ditch in less than five. Everything in this town was so close together. Like the distance between my face and that iron fence the night before. I looked at it as I drove by.

It looked hard.

I parked and went inside. Summer was behind the bar drawing a beer. The beer taps looked giant in front of her. The Ditch was pretty much empty, only about five or six people. They were all in the other room, where the bands play, but they had tables and chairs in the mosh pit, so I guess there was no band tonight. The place seemed so crisp and sharp—so different from the bourbon aquarium I was swimming in last time I swam through there.

Summer looked up.

"Hi," I said.

"Hey!" she smiled. "Hold on one second."

She took the beer and a mixed drink off the bar and went through the rear passageway of the brick dividing wall. Then she came back through the other archway and right up to me. In spite of everything that had happened, the buzzing energy of her cuteness turned my knees to a buttery liquid.

"So what happened?" she said, grabbing my hand. "You look awful!" She sniffed the air. "Is that bleach?"

"You're not gonna believe this."

"What? What?"

"Well, I went over there, and I was in the guy's front yard, getting ready to chew him a new bunghole for what he—"

The phone behind the bar rang. "One second." She went around and answered it: "Ditch."

I sat down at the end of the bar. Summer finished the call pretty quick and came back.

"Okay, sorry about that. Want something to drink?"

"Do you have coffee?"

"Not right now, but I can make some."

"No, no. I'll have a Coke."

So she got me a Coke.

"So," I continued, "I got the guy to come outside, and I'm getting ready to really give him a piece of my—"

Someone from the lounge area came up to the bar to pay their tab. Fuck!

"Sorry," Summer said.

My neck was getting hot again. I rubbed it with my hand, which just made it made it hotter. When would I learn? Summer finally finished at the cash register and the people left.

She smiled. "Okay."

"So, I'm right in the middle of saying my spiel to the guy, and Shred and Farns show up!"

"No!"

"And Shred was covered in green paint and he attacked Motorcar with one of your mannequins. A green one."

"What!"

"Mrs. Greenstreet. I named her."

"That's a good name."

"The whole thing was totally insane. I'm having trouble, like, believing it happened."

"He said he was borrowing her to use as a prop for his band's show. Mmm."

"He put on a show, all right. He totally ruined my confrontation."

"That is so fucked."

"And after that Farns shot a flare gun at his head."

"Are you kidding me?"

"I thought it was a real gun and I tried to stop him. Shoved the corkscrew into his arm, but it surprised him and he pulled the trigger. The flare went off right by Motorcar's head."

"Unreal." She was taking it all in and looked a little amused. "What did Shred do to him with the mannequin exactly?"

"Motorcar was on the ground and he pushed her into his back, stuck her arm up his crotch from behind, going in-and-out. And he was yelling stuff like: *How do you like it!*"

Summer covered her mouth. "Holy shit." She started to laugh.

"You think that's funny," I said.

"No, no. I know. I'm sorry. It's not funny, it's just very...Shred."

"The whole thing was a waste, anyway. I feel exactly the same. It hasn't changed a damn thing."

"Well, give it some time."

"Time? I've been waiting fifteen years to do this and it got fucking *ruined*!" Then there was a moment of bad silence.

"You didn't get to say *anything* to the guy?"

"No, yeah—I called him a pervert and yelled 'fuck you.' And I bitch-slapped him."

"That's pretty good."

"Yeah, I guess it's not too bad."

She patted me on the arm.

"Then I went back to his house and skunked his car with an eggs and bleach mixture."

"Awesome!" She high-fived me.

"Mrs. Greenstreet is safely back on your porch, by the way."

"Thank you. Is she okay?" She grabbed my wrist. "I mean, seriously, are *you* okay?"

"Yeah, I mean, aside from feeling like a fleet of garbage trucks ran over my face. And then backed up over the rest of me."

Some customers came in. Summer said hey and called one of them by name. She knew everybody. They sat at one of the tables and she went to take their drink order. At that moment, I was hit with a wave of triple déjà vu, something from the night before of getting my ass kicked, something to do with Summer, all mixed with the feeling that somewhere in the big gothic antique mirror they had up behind the bar, I'd been a patron of the Ditch for about eight hundred years. On one hand, the feeling was nice, comforting somehow. But I felt my chest filling up with white hot panic. My ankles were throbbing. I had to get out of there.

Summer got back and started making drinks. She seemed to be ignoring me, even though I knew she was just working. I downed the rest of my Coke and said I gotta go.

"But you just got here."

"I need to go talk to Shred. I'm feeling a little…I'm just gonna go."

"Come by later. I get home about two-thirty."

"Okay."

Wow—I had a date. Maybe this night wasn't turning out so bad. For being the strangest damn night of my life, anyway. I stopped at 7-11 for a big steaming cup of rotten black coffee. It was joy to my lips. As I paid up at the register with the last of my dimes, nickels and pennies, I realized that I never paid Summer for the Coke. She probably wouldn't have charged me, but I should have offered. Or left a tip. I was such a psycho stalker thief wingnut douche. God! No, I'm not.

Am.

Not.

23

I REALLY WANTED to wring Shred's green neck. I burned down Laurel Street and back into Oregon Hill. I thought my little car was going to have a fatal heart attack, if I didn't have one first. This time I crept into the house. Kenny was asleep, thank goodness. I went and got his crutch from the front yard and set it by the sofa. I looked in the rooms and no Shred. I hit my knee on a bicycle wheel leaning up against the wall and it fell over. I heard Kenny.

"Who...uh..." he said, in a sleepy monotone. Then I think he went back to sleep.

I went and sat in the Hyundai to wait for Shred. It seemed like an odd thing to do but I was feeling odd. I figured if the Hillites attacked, I could just drive over them. No, I wouldn't do that.

Yes, I would.

No, I wouldn't.

I drained what was left of my coffee and felt a little better, but not really. I still couldn't believe Shred and Farns had ruined my life. I smelled my bleachy hands. How could I do all that to Motorcar, and still feel totally unsatisfied? Worse, even. Enough time had gone by, I should have felt something by then. Something other than tired.

I sat there. I still wanted to rip Shred's face off, but with each minute that sludged by, I was getting less and less mad at him and Farns. Didn't have the energy. I put the keys in and tried to find a radio station, but I didn't have the energy for that either. Maybe I should just drive around, but I was so freaking tired and I didn't have that much gas. I was coming to the only logical conclusion. There was no denying it anymore so I might as well embrace it. Life *sucks*. After a while, I finally started to cool down. At least I stopped thinking that every car going by was a cop coming to arrest me for attempted murder, assault, stalking, harassment, destruction of property.

The tapping on the windshield sounded like an avalanche. It was Shred. Scared the crap out of me. I wasn't asleep, but I was in some dazed zone between awake and asleep. I kicked the steering column with my kneecap. It was about the third bruise on that same spot, but at that point I was oblivious to pain.

"What're you doing out here, Jar?" He sounded oddly calm and measured.

"Jesus—you scared the shit out of me!" I put my hands on my head and tried to remember who I was.

He had washed most of the green off, but there were still patches of it in his hair and around his forehead. The green and the way he had chopped off chunks of his hair made him look like the victim of an electro-shock therapy session gone wrong. I followed him into the house. He headed down the hallway, but I stopped him by his studio door.

"I want to talk to you in here," I said.

"Okay."

We sat down. He immediately slumped in his chair.

"What's with you?" I said. "Why you got your head down, huh?"

He didn't move. All the hyper-active Shred energy was gone, completely gone. Vaporized. He slumped more.

"What happened to your personal electricity, eh, guy? Get short-circuited?"

It looked like he cracked a tiny smile.

"That was *my* thing, dude!" I said. "You had no right to do that!"

He stared at the floor. "Fuck a buncha perverts."

"What?"

"You heard me. World's a conspiracy of pervs. Fuck 'em."

"I expressly told you guys not to mess with my personal deal—and you pull that shit?"

"You can't honestly say you didn't enjoy seeing me jump him with Greenella. Come on."

"Mrs. Greenstreet."

"Whoever."

"I'm not saying he didn't deserve it."

"Well, then…"

"Dude, for years—for *years*—I've wanted to face that pervert and lay him out with an ice hot death zinger. And right before I was about to, you guys showed up and ruined it."

"What were you gonna say to him?"

"I didn't get a chance to think of anything. I was just putting it together when the 3rd Cavalry from outer hell showed up."

"Didn't get a chance to think of anything? How many years did you say you were planning this?"

I just looked down. "It's a problem I have. And I haven't been *officially* planning it for years, just a couple of weeks. It's been in the back of my mind for years, though."

"Two weeks seems like plenty of time to think up a zinger."

"Like I said, it's a problem I have. I have a lot of problems."

"You seem pretty together to me. I mean, except for getting drunk and becoming the world's biggest a-wipe."

"Yeah, there's that. There's going through four jobs in the last two years. Lost about as many girlfriends in that amount of time. And my nervous stomach problem."

"You keep getting hired though, right? Keep getting the girl. That's saying something."

"I don't need a bunch of positive B.S. right now, okay?"

"What's up with the nervous stomach thing?"

"My guts are a slushy stress pit." I put my hand on my stomach. "Feels like a rancid death swamp down there."

"All the time?"

I nodded.

"Maybe you shouldn't drink so much coffee and tea. You really swill that shit."

"You think that's it?"

"That would rip up anybody's insides, cuz-bro."

"Mmm."

We sat there in a weirdened silence. Shred slumped again. He looked completely drained.

"So was it Farns' idea?" I said.

"What?"

"Duh. The whole revenge plate special thing—it was his idea, wasn't it?"

"I thought it was *your* idea, dude. Come on—we were only trying to enhance your experience."

"Oh, come on."

"We were there to support you, Jarvis."

"No—you guys were there 'cause you're crazy. You just wanted to fuck up a child molester. With a mannequin. God, you're nuts!"

"Mea culpa."

"Can't you find your own damn child molester to confront?"

Shred looked down.

"He's unavailable," he said.

"What do you mean? Who's unavailable?"

"He's dead."

"Who?"

My stomach was churning like a broken food processor filled with raw sewage. Shred took a long time to answer.

"Uncle Pie-rold. Never got a chance to kick his ass."

"What! Uncle Pie-rold? No way!"

"Yep."

"He never tried anything on *me*."

"Count your blessings. He messed with me like ten different times."

That creepy feeling of jealousy rose up again, the one I felt when Motorcar said he'd already been confronted by another victim. *What the fuck was up with that!*

"When did all this happen? How old were you?"

"He even did it once on Thanksgiving. It was like, *thanks a lot.* I guess the first time I was nine and the last time…eleven maybe?"

"I wonder why he never messed with me."

Shred just shrugged.

We sat there. I couldn't believe it. I couldn't be mad at him anymore. I was fully blown away. Didn't think it was possible for the weirdest night of my life to get weirder, but there I was.

"I can't believe it. Is that why you were so happy at his funeral?"

"Yeah."

"Wow."

"I wanted to spit on his coffin, but I never got the chance."

"You know what I did?"

"What?"

"I skunked that dude's car."

"You what?"

"After you guys took off, I went to the store and got some eggs and bleach and mixed 'em together and poured it into the vent on the limo he drives."

"You did?" Shred smiled and perked up. "That is awesome!"

"Yeah—hopefully he'll get fired."

"That is *sweet*, bro." We fist-bumped.

"He acted like such a dick—wasn't apologetic or anything. So I bitch-slapped him and skunked his limo."

"It's called *Washing the Car*, by the way."

"Whatever."

"Man, I can't wait to tell Farns," he laughed.

"That Farns. He's so full of shit. He actually expected me to believe that he welded a giant 'B' on top of Lowe's."

"I have a picture of that somewhere."

"It's *true?*"

Shred started flipping through a stack of artwork and posters on the floor by his work table. It took forever but he finally pulled out an 11" x 17" photo of the *BLOWE'S* sign. The 'B' looked almost exactly like the other letters.

That Farns. What a rascal.

"I guess I stand corrected." I handed the picture back to Shred. "I hope he's not too pissed off about me stabbing him in the arm with a corkscrew."

"No, he's not pissed."

"That's good."

"He felt really bad about last night, anyway."

"What do you mean?"

"Last night at the Ditch."

"I don't remember most of that, which is probably a good thing. I know I got beat up. And some girl kicked me in the face."

"You totally don't remember Farns pounding you like a side of beef? It wasn't pretty."

"*Farns* was?"

"Yeah. He was leading the charge."

"What!"

"I kept telling you to stop calling him 'Farnsworth' and 'Farnzington' and all that."

"Wow."

"He didn't get really pissed until you threw the second drink in his face."

"Damn."

"So I wouldn't worry too much about corkscrewing him in the arm."

"Why'd the girl kick me in the face? Never mind—I actually don't want to know."

"Oh, Lisa Purcell? She always gets into fights."

Shred let his head droop at a funny angle. He looked like a mental patient.

"You okay, man?"

"Yeah, me?" he said, snapping his head back up. "I'm...great."

"I just can't believe that about Uncle Pie-rold."

"Well, believe it."

"Did you ever tell your mom or anybody?"

"You're actually the first person I've ever told."

"Are you kidding me?"

"It's kind of a relief."

"I'm sure it is. You should try therapy."

"Oh, I've had plenty of therapy. That topic just never came up." He started rubbing his eye, like some green greasepaint was stuck in there. "I guess raping that guy with the mannequin was my way of…I dunno…"

"Letting it all hang out?"

We both laughed.

"You know what, Shred?"

"What?"

"Doing that stuff to the guy wasn't all that satisfying. Facing him, calling him out, bitch slapping him, washing his car—I thought it would make me feel so much better about everything. I actually feel more confused and fucked-up now that I did before."

"Dude—chill out. You'll be all right. You gave that sonofabitch a cold plate special he'll never forget."

"I guess so."

"You'll feel better soon," he said, with his head still down.

"Thanks."

We sat there. I let out a big, weighted sigh. Shred was looking glum but I had one burning question for him.

"I hate to ask this, but—what did Uncle Pie-rold do exactly?"

"I don't want to talk about it."

I cleared my throat. "No way, man. That shit ain't gonna fly."

"Nah."

"Come on. You owe me that much."

"All right. He…um…he dinkled with my…" And he gestured around the area of his pants. "That's pretty much it."

"Huh—that's what my pervert did to me."

We sat there as a heavy awkwardness started rising up. Shred started fidgeting. I looked around the room.

"I think I'm gonna go over to Summer's and say goodbye to her," I said. "She told me to come by."

"Cool, I'm gonna hit the sack. Way burnt."

"Later."

"Later."

And I walked out into the yellow, steam-soaked night, keeping a sharp look-out for miscreants. All clear for the moment, so I headed up the street toward Summer's.

24

HER GIANT BOAT of a car was parked out front. Mrs. Greenstreet was still there on the porch. She looked tired. I knocked on the door, but for some reason the dogs didn't go crazy. Maybe they were getting to know my knock.

"Hey. Come on in."

We went down to her living room and sat on the couch.

"This has been the single weirdest night of my life. Ever."

"I'll bet."

"You ready to hear the rest of it?"

"Of course. Tell, tell."

One of the dogs, Vertigo I think, decided to join us. He started sniffing my crotch with great force.

"Verty!" Summer scolded.

"I am completely freaked out right now. Shred just told me something really fucked up about one of our family members." I shook my head. She was so gorgeous in the soft light, I just wanted to forget everything and forget the world and swim in the dream lake of my new punk rock girlfriend. I wanted a sandwich. I wanted coffee and sandwiches real, real bad.

"Is everything okay?"

"No, yeah. Yes. I dunno."

"Do you want to talk about it?"

"Kind of, but…I was pretty pissed at Shred for telling everyone in Richmond about Motorcar. Now the situation is kind of reversed, so I don't really…I shouldn't say anything."

"That's okay. You don't have to."

"But it's like, man…our uncle totally molested him when he was little."

She put her hand over her mouth. "That's horrible."

"Yeah—it's messed up."

"Poor Shreddie!"

"What is wrong with people?"

"They should round up all those pervs and shoot them."

"I guess it explains his whole deal with going nutzo tonight."

"Well, going off his medication didn't help much."

"What? What medication?"

"His bi-polar meds. You didn't know Shred was rabidly bi-polar?"

"No. Jesus."

"I told him not to do it, but he said they were holding him back lately, messing with his personal electricity. So he went off it last week."

"Damn."

"That's fucking horrible about your uncle. Maybe Shred could go have a confrontation too. That would be really healthy for him."

"Too late. He's dead."

"Oh. Well, maybe that's for the best." Then she started sniffing at the air. "I think I smell it."

"Smell what?"

"The bleach and eggs." She popped up and headed down the hall.

I smelled my hands. Nothing. Maybe I was acclimated. Summer came back with some incense sticks.

"Is that bleach'n'eggs flavored incense?"

"No. Gorgonzola and dirty socks."

"Yum."

She lit the stick and let it burn for a minute and blew out the flame. Then she perched it in its stand like an incense pro and sat back down. The room started to smell like a Shanghai opium den, not that I knew what that smelled like. She scooted up right next to me. It was way nice.

"Crazy-ass night," I said.

"Wacky."

"Kooky."

"Outta control."

I thought we were going to kiss, but we just sat there. The moment wasn't right. Then something started to hit me, something I'd never felt before. My body became flooded with an exquisitely painful feeling of complete, raw exhaustion. Deep inner-bone exhaustion. Every bruise, cut and scrape started hurting like a way mad beeyotch. I felt like a bag of rotten groceries that had been dropped down several flights of stairs and then lit on fire. I weighed eight thousand pounds all of a sudden. I was paralyzed.

"Are you okay?"

"Not feeling too good. It's been a rough one."

"You want some orange juice? That might make you feel better."

"That would be awesome."

The juice went down like liquid sunshine. She stroked the back of my head. It was kind of like being in heaven and hell at the same time. I don't remember much after that. I don't even remember if I finished my orange juice.

I woke up on the couch with a blanket over me. It was covered with dinosaurs. A kid's blanket. Light was trying to get in through the purple curtains. I took a deep breath and it hurt. Then I threw the blanket off and sat up. I felt like twelve different kinds of death. Checked my pockets and had a grand total of eleven cents. That wasn't enough for coffee and it *really* wasn't enough for gas to get home. I couldn't wait to leave Richmond in the dust and get home and take a hot shower. The NEWTON CHEESE FARMS shirt smelled more like a pig farm.

Summer must have been down in her room asleep. I felt like I should go in and kiss her goodbye and thank her for all the moral support and orange juice and everything, but for some reason I was afraid to wake her up. I thought maybe I should write a note. Started looking around for a pen and paper. Nothing. She probably had something in her mannequin studio, but I was afraid to go in there as well. I was probably going to be freaked out by mannequins for the rest of my life. Oh well, I guessed there were worse things. I decided to just wake her up. I stood in front of her door and got ready to knock. I raised my fist and then stopped. What if someone was in there with her? What if it was Klavin? If so, he probably still had on his trench coat and boots. I didn't really think anyone was in there but I just felt nervous. Cosmically nervous. Then a voice in my head said: *Jarvis, you've got some getting the fuck out of here to do.* So I did.

It was early. Oregon Hill seemed very peaceful. Innocent even. Except for me. I was a desperate loser and I needed money. At least a twenty to get coffee and gas. I slipped into Shred's like a ghost. Kenny was asleep with his mouth open. His breathing sounded like a broken vacuum cleaner. I scanned the table. There was a dollar bill and some change amidst all the other junk. Not enough. Then I saw Kenny's wallet.

I was already a psycho stalker weirdo freak who sucked, so why not add thief to the list? Besides, I could mail him a check as soon as I got home. So it was really borrowing not thievery. Yeah. His wallet had a twenty, a ten and three ones. I took the twenty and stuck it in my pocket and put the wallet back. All too easy. He'll never notice, I said to myself. He's too high. He'll wonder why he got a check from me for twenty-five dollars. Maybe thirty. You should always pay extra interest when you steal-borrow something. I turned and headed down the hallway and felt like a complete asshole. Fifty. I'll send him a check for fifty. Actually, I should send him cash, that way he won't have to gimp himself to the bank. See? I was thoughtful.

No, I wasn't.

Yes, I was.

Within fifteen minutes I was fueled up and on the highway

with a giant hot coffee. For the first five minutes of the drive, I felt incredibly free. The wind was blowing through the car. The zushing noise the motor was making sounded like music. Then the feeling faded. It dropped to the bottom of my stomach like a load of death bricks. I felt weird about Motorcar, weird about Shred, about not saying goodbye Summer, about stealing twenty bucks from Kenny. I felt embarrassed, compromised somehow, dragged down. This whole thing was supposed to be catharsis but it just made things murkier. The feeling was pulling at me. Each encounter I'd had back there was like a sandbag tied to my ankles. Everything about my life was a sick mistake and I was paying the price.

I dreamed of my hot, soapy, luxurious shower the whole drive home. It kept my mind off of life.

I wondered if Motorcar's limo reeked yet.

I sure as hell hoped so.

PART 3

25

IT FELT LIKE I'd been gone for fifty years. The beige hadn't changed a bit, though. My piles of dirty laundry were still in the same places on the floor. My innards were still a rancid swamp. Made coffee. I was still a loser. I made the coffee extra strong.

I threw the NEWTON CHEESE FARMS shirt onto one of the piles and took the hot shower I had been dreaming about. It hurt. Then I put on some shorts and turned on the TV. Nothing was on, so I threw the remote as hard as I could at the wall. I needed to call the credit card companies and report my lost cards, which I should have done already, but I had no phone. I had to go to DMV and get a new driver's license, but I wasn't feeling it. So I went down to the rental office and used their phone and called Ben. We made plans to meet. Cogbill's. Went back and took a power nap, but when I woke up I wasn't feeling much in the way of power.

I got to Cogbill's first. Everybody was staring at my face. I actually kind of enjoyed the attention. At least somebody around here was living life for once and this time it happened to be me. I went up to the bar and ordered an ice coffee from Craig the bartender dude.

"What the hell happened to you, bro?" he asked.

"Skiing accident."

"In August?"

"Himalayas."

"Seriously?"

"I got on the triple black diamond by mistake."

"In August." He smirked.

I sat there and downed my coffee in relative peace. Ben finally showed. He was dressed up like an astronaut, wearing a light navy jumpsuit with a NASA iron-on patch on the chest. His wispy little mustache was gone and he had a new short haircut. And he was carrying an old motorcycle helmet that had five or six old stove knobs and guitar amp volume knobs glued in a crazy row across the front above the visor.

"Man," he said. "Jesus."

"Let's sit at a booth."

"Damn, dude."

So we sat at a booth, the astronaut and the guy-who-got-his-ass-kicked.

"What happened?"

"Well, I really fell off the wagon hard."

"And landed face first, it looks like."

"Thanks."

"Are you okay? I mean…"

"No. Look at me. Not okay." I shrugged. "So I take it you're done with the cowboy thing? I'm gone for a few days and now you're an astronaut?"

"I fixed the scooter," he said, as if that somehow explained the change in outfits.

"Cool knobs."

"Yeah? I thought you were just gonna give me shit about it."

"No, I like it. Creative. You can use them to regulate your personal electricity."

"My what?"

"Never mind."

"You really got your ass kicked."

"Well aware, thanks."

"What the fuck happened?"

I let out a big black sigh. "I got drunk, acted like a jerk and some people beat me up." I shrugged.

"What people?"

"My cousin's friends."

"He couldn't do anything to stop it?"

"I don't remember. I'm pretty sure that *I* wasn't doing anything to stop it."

"Sorry, dude."

"It was my own stupid fault."

We sat there and drank our respective beverages. I caught a couple of people staring at me, so I smiled and nodded their way.

"So, what all happened with the pervert guy?"

"You mind keeping it down a bit?"

So I told him about going to Motorcar's and all about Shred and Farns showing up, the flare gun and mannequin rape scenario and bitch-slapping him and yelling "fuck you" and calling him a perv SOB and then going back and doing what I did.

"Totally ruins the car," I said. "You just can't get the smell out. And it's his livelihood, so it…it may really fuck his life up."

"That is *sooo* awesome," Ben laughed. "You must feel a lot better now, huh?"

"Not really. I'm just glad the whole thing's over. And I'm not in the hospital. Or in jail. Or in rehab."

"Oh, man."

"Or dead."

"Maybe you should've gone ahead and killed him. That'd be, like, the most awesome redemption ever, dude."

"I'm not even sure I wanted redemption. I think I just wanted the *feeling* of redemption."

"Um…what's the difference?"

"I have no idea. I'm not even sure what redemption even *is*. What are you redeeming, anyway? Coupons at the self-esteem outlet mall?"

Ben looked confused. I felt confused. He started rubbing his hands together and looking around. He started to say something but then he stopped.

"What?" I said.

"Nothing."

We sat there for a while, looking vaguely up toward the ceiling.

"So…um…have you talked to Carly at all?"

"Nope. I've moved on, anyway, man. Met this totally cool girl in Richmond."

"That's good, that's great."

"She's this awesome punker chick. Got tattoos and piercings and everything, but she's actually kinda normal."

"A punker chick is normal? Come on…"

"She's a lot nicer than Carly, I'll tell you that much."

Ben studied my face. "Wow, man. I hate to have to say this, but…I might have to postpone your start-date at the call center."

"Why?"

"Man…" He gestured vaguely at his own face.

"Why do I need a pretty face to talk to people on the phone?"

"Well, it's a…I dunno. We'll see, we'll see."

"*We'll see?* It's not like I'm sitting here flat *broke* or anything, Bucko Rogers." Wow, I thought, that was a pretty sweet zinger.

"I'll see what I can do, I'll see what I can do."

Ben started looking away and fidgeting. He swallowed hard a couple times.

"What's wrong?"

He just looked at me. I could see stress building up in his eyes.

"What?"

"Well," he said, "there is something we kinda need to…talk about. Probably."

"What?"

His voice dropped. "I feel bad."

"Why?"

"She didn't…"

"She who? What the fuck are you talking about?"

He didn't say anything. He looked like he was about to get hit by a bus.

Something was messed up.

"What!" People were looking at us.

"Man, dude, this is so…I dunno." He took a deep a breath and let it out like it hurt.

"What? What?"

He swallowed. "The other night, me and my mom went to Eddie's for dinner, and Carly was there drinking at the bar with some friend of hers. She seemed…pretty wasted."

"And?"

"She said a few people were coming over later to party and she asked me if I wanted to come too. So I said sure, why not? I dropped Mom off and went over there but when I got there Carly was just by herself…"

"No, you did not."

"…acting all crazy and wasted."

"You did!"

His face looked like he'd just chewed up a whole bag of lemons.

"She came on super strong and it just…it happened so fast."

"Dude—I thought we were friends!"

He was barely looking at me. "I'm really fucking sorry, man."

"You're really *fucking* sorry? What kind of lame-ass apology is that?"

He shook his head. "I was hoping you wouldn't take it so bad."

"How the fuck did you expect me to take it?" My personal electricity instantly went nuclear, as in reactor core meltdown stage. "You disloyal fucking tool!" I yelled, slapping my hand down on the table. Then, without even thinking about it, I threw my ice coffee into his face. "Have a nice day, Captain Butt Wipe."

I started to get up when somebody grabbed my shirt collar from behind and started pushing me toward the door.

"What the hell are you doing!" I yelled. "I'm not drunk!"

"Get out and don't ever come back." It was Craig the bartender.

"Who elected you mayor of Cogbill's? Huh, dickface?"

He pushed me out and pulled the door shut. I got into the hot car and sat there baking in unreality. Things were strangely calm. I was pissed and felt completely insane, but somehow calm. I sat there for a minute and breathed. So my best friend stabs me in the back—how fitting for the most fucked-up week of my life. Then I pictured Carly and Ben having sex, but I stopped myself. Then I pictured it again—a straight-up horror movie. The furious death fumes were boiling to a whistle.

By the time I passed the strip mall with the Korean cleaners and Baskin Robins I was cooled off, more or less. I was more mad about getting booted from Cogbill's than anything else. Maybe I was too drained to be mad at Carly and Ben. Or maybe I just didn't give a shit.

26

WHEN I GOT home I made a strong pot of coffee, strong even for me. As in dark black. I did some stretches in the living room. My whole body hurt and my swamp gut was churning. Maybe Shred was right. Maybe coffee *was* destroying my stomach lining. In a flash of revelation I poured my cup out in the sink and then the whole rest of the pot too. It looked like slow-moving tar. This gut-worm thing I had, maybe it wasn't some "nervous stomach syndrome" after all. It could totally be the coffee-and-tea-destroying-my-guts-syndrome! I swilled the stuff like water. What was it with me and liquids? I threw all my coffee beans into the trash and dumped out my iced tea mix. Empowerment was mine. I was going to quit caffeine and the idea was giving me new life.

The headaches started that afternoon. Sledgehammer specials. Über-brutal. But I took it. Took it like the Sheriff of Pain. It really put all my bruises, cuts, scabs, scrapes, ruptures, dents, knots, contusions and other wounds in perspective. Spent a lot of time massaging my temples. Three days of utter hell, during which time I was completely useless. At least it kept my mind off Carly and Ben, Motorcar, space robots and other bad things. Thinking hurt too much. Unless the topic was Summer. Oh, the sweet tattooed punker chick who liked country music and strange movies and kissed me. Crazy sweet little electric Summer! She made my headaches a bit less horrendous. I loved her, godammit! I wanted to share my news with her about quitting coffee. She'd be impressed followed by supportive. I wanted to sit on her couch and feast on lentil salad and take Klavin to an amusement park like we were his parents. I wanted to hold her and kiss her and thank her for all the moral support and the corkscrew. For teaching me that there was more to life than meets the neck. She was the non-beige creamy neon sex blossom wonder girl of my dream shire. But there I was, stuck in the beige suburbs. I didn't even have her number. How could I be such an idiot for not getting her digits? I never felt so isolated. Life was going on in Richmond and I was missing it. Shred and Farns. Those guys were probably having a blast. Who could even guess what wacky new adventures they were already on. In their own sick way they really had my back. Hell, I was *glad* Farns shot Motorcar by his head with a flare gun. If it made Motorcar's nauseating life pass before his eyes, then all the better. I got my bitch slap in. And maybe Farns did play a major role in my beat-down at the Ditch, but I was being an obnoxious drunk.

So I waited for the headaches to dissipate and dreamed about Summer and her luscious blue lips. She didn't really have blue lips, that was just part of the fantasy. One of her mannequins probably had blue lips and that was close enough.

On the fourth day of the no coffee experiment, I got results—my swamp stomach was gone and my headaches were gone. It was unreal. Too good to be real. I had zero desire for coffee or tea. Still felt like I was floating through a sterile beige-hole of dullness and medicine fog, but without the constant stomach worms. I took a walk and breathed in the humid air and the pines. My life was a shit-mess but I felt somewhat awesome. I couldn't tell for sure, but maybe somehow things *were* a bit different. I hadn't fantasized about killing anyone in a while. I had no desire to burn or kill at all. Wasn't bending over sideways trying to think up clever zingers to burn people with. I didn't want to die. Didn't even feel like sticking my head in the freezer. Something was happening. Was all this mentally healthy stuff I'd been trying to do starting to work? No. No fucking way. Nothing had changed. Who did I think I was kidding?

That day at about six, I heard a knock on the door. I knew it was Carly. It was her old after-work visiting time and

I knew that knock. I wasn't surprised. In a weird way, I'd been expecting her.

"Hi!" she said, beaming, her freshly lipsticked smile stretching the sides of her face to their limits.

"Can I help you?"

Her smile plummeted as she scanned my face. "What happened?"

"I got my ass kicked."

"Oh, you poor thing!" She reached toward my face but I waved her off and stepped back.

"Eh, I'm fine."

"Can I come in?"

I shrugged and she came in.

"So, what's up?" I said.

"Oh, just wanted to stop by and say hi." The smile was back.

"Hi."

Then a silence descended on our conversation that was so dense and heavy you could've stabbed it with a machine gun. I held my ground and stared at her.

She finally said: "I'm sorry I didn't return your calls."

"Oh, okay."

"And the texts. Sorry I didn't write back to all the texts." She put her hand on my wrist and I looked down at it. Then I looked back at her.

"Hm. So...how about Ben?"

The smile left again. "What do you mean?"

"I mean, since you're handing out apologies, maybe you'd like to say sorry for *fucking my best friend*."

She shook her head. "That was...we had broken up and I was just...I was feeling..."

"Lonely?"

"Yes."

"Horseshit! Seriously."

"I can't believe he told you."

"You know what, Carly? You know what you are? A loser. Yeah, that's right. You're a superficial, backstabbing loser."

"Wait a second—*you're* calling *me* a loser? That's a good one."

"You're right. It is a good one. Because it's true, *loser*. So why don't you walk out that door, drive home and cook Ben some meats. Oh, wait—you already did that."

"You're disgusting."

"See ya 'round, loser face."

"Fuck you, Jarvis."

"Have a great afternoon!"

"Your face looks like shit!"

I shut the door behind her and locked the dead-bolt. A warm wave of sweet triumph started washing over me, a feeling I'd never felt before. Where the fuck were those ice-hot zingers coming from? I felt purified somehow. I was so energized, I didn't know what to do with myself. So I put on my running shoes and went for a high-speed, invigorating run. All the way to the lake and back. Then I did laundry. I did the fuck out of some laundry.

That night I slept better than I had in weeks. In months. Years. Freaking decades.

I was now officially on a roll. Got a new phone, reported my cards stolen and went to the bank to apply for a new debit card. While I was there I withdrew the majority of my balance, which wasn't much. Then I went to the DMV to get my replacement license. I was kicking ass. Something must have been seriously wrong with me because the DMV wasn't even that bad. I capped it off by going to the Patient First and getting my stitches out. The doctor asked me what happened and I told them I got into a fist fight with a gang of cinder blocks on a renegade escalator. He smirked and said: "Well, stranger things have happened."

"No, they sure have."

When I got home, I got a blank sheet of paper out of the printer and wrote a note:

Kenny –

Before I left I took twenty bucks out of your wallet so I could get gas money for the ride home and some coffee. Sorry, I'm an asshole. Here's sixty. I hope this makes up for my shitty deed. Hope your leg gets better soon. And thanks for letting me stay there.

Peace off,

Jarvis

I had their address but I didn't know Kenny's last name, so I just addressed the envelope to "Kenny," put the twenties in, stuck on a stamp and mailed it. My new phone had seven voicemails and three texts, so I got a nice tall glass of ice water and sat down on the couch to check them out. First voicemail was from Mom. She called while I was still in Richmond but after I'd lost the phone. She wanted to know how "Evan" was. The next three were from Ben, apologizing profusely. Each message was longer and more uncomfortable than the preceding one. At least he didn't say he was *"fucking* sorry" this time. All three texts were from him: 1: *really sorry man,* 2: *let's talk,* and 3: *dude I am soooo sorry bro!* I figured I would forgive him one day, but I wasn't ready yet. The next one was from Carly, but she hung up and didn't say anything. Vindication is sweet. Another one from Ben, sounding like a wounded puppy. I was starting to feel bad for his sorry butt.

The last voicemail was from Shred.

"Hey, cuzzo. It's Shredly. Hope you're doing better. I mean, like, your face. Listen—gimme a call, man. I got something ass-wacky to tell you. Arright, later."

I wondered how Shred could tell me anything *not* ass-wacky. Of all the messages, he was the only one I wanted to call back. So I did.

"Hey, Shred. It's Jarvis."

"Hey man! How the crap are you?"

"Not too crap bad. You?"

"Okay, okay," he said, sounding chipper. "How's your face?"

"It's still here on the front of my head, last I checked. My ribs still hurt. And my shoulder. And my neck. And my face."

"Man, that blows."

"So what's your thing you have to tell me? Farns get arrested or something?"

"Dude, check it out: yesterday Kenny's family came and did an intervention on his ass."

"Seriously?"

"Threw him into fucking *rehab*."

"For the painkillers, I guess?"

"Huh. Painkillers, beer, liquor, bong-hits, skydiving, you name it."

"Skydiving?"

"Adrenaline junkie."

"Ah."

"I was actually getting a little sick of his sitting around moping like a seven-year-old girl who lost her dolly."

It made me feel good to hear Shred criticize him. "Yeah—what's his problem, anyhow?"

"I don't know what his deal is. Leg was crushed pretty bad, but he's always been, what's the word I'm looking for..."

"An asshole?"

"He really needs this break. Not just for the getting sobe. He needs a change, needs to get over Summer and—"

"What! Get over Summer?"

"Oh, yeah. He took that one hard."

"Took what hard?"

"They were together for, I guess about a year. You didn't pick up on that?"

"Jeez." I felt my heart drop to the bottom of my left sock.

"Boy's not afraid to jump out of a moving object and fall a million feet through the sky, but when it comes to women he's just a sack of wet noodles."

"So that's why he hated me."

"He doesn't hate you, Jarvis."

"Yes, he does. He threw his crutches at me."

"He throws his crutches at me all the time. Wow—I'm really not gonna miss that."

I chuckled.

"So, dude, check it," he said. "I wanted to talk to you about something."

"Shoot."

"You got a job up there?"

"No. Remember? I thought I told—"

"How about that girlfriend of yours?"

"We broke up. I *know* I told you about that."

"She was asking about you the other day."

"Who was?"

"Your girlfriend. Summer."

"Are you kidding me?"

"Why's that so surprising? She likes you, cuz-bro."

I didn't say anything.

"A lot."

My heart started making its way back up from my sock and into its rightful place in my throat.

"I like her too. Also a lot."

Then there a long silence. Really long. I got the feeling that he was doing it on purpose.

"What?" I said.

"You gotta move down here, C.B."

"What'd you call me?"

"C.B. For 'cuz-bro.' You can have Kenny's room."

"Naw. No way. I can't do that."

"You totally can. He's moving back in with his folks in Northern Virginia after he gets out of the drunk tank."

"No, I mean I can't just up and move down there. That'd be crazy."

"There are worse things than crazy."

"No. No way." I chuckled, but I had no idea why.

"I thought you liked it here. Aside from all the shit at the Ditch and whatnot."

"I just...I got too much going on up here, you know?"

"Like your great job and awesome girlfriend? Come on, Jarvis. Life's too short. You gotta grab the bull by the nuts or the bull will bite your face off."

"Never quite thought about it in those terms."

"You can get a fresh start. Rent's only four hundred each."

"That's pretty good. I don't know, Shred." I sucked in about a gallon of air through my teeth. "It sounds great, but…"

"But what?"

"Well, don't take this the wrong way, but, um…you're a drinker, a partier. I can't really be around that."

"I'm not drinking at all right now. I'm on new meds and not doing anything. No weed, no nothing."

"For real?"

"A thousand percent for realsies."

"I'm not sure I believe you a thousand percent. It's a tough road. I would know."

"I can't do anything while I'm on these meds. Drinking fucks it up."

"Are you gonna *stay* on the medication?"

"Absolutely. I feel great, man. And we'd be awesome roommates. Someone else who's sober. Someone I can trust."

"You trust me?"

"Of course I do."

"Huh," I laughed.

"What?"

"No, just, all those friends you have down there and you trust *me*. That's just…I'm a little surprised."

"Well, they're not exactly a bunch of super-saints."

"Hey—I got something to tell *you*."

"What's that, C.B.?"

"I took your advice and quit drinking coffee and my stomach thing went away."

"That's turbo, man. Awesome. Told ya."

"I thought it was nerves or like, from stress, but you were right. It was the endless gallons of coffee and tea."

"So what do you think?"

"About what?"

"About moving down here. Jeez!"

"I dunno…I just…I dunno. I appreciate the offer, for sure. I dunno."

"Think it over. I can get you a job. Catering to start. It's good money and good food. I can probably help you get a paralegal gig at one of the law firms if you want."

"Seriously?"

"I know a bunch of the managing partners. I serve them savory cheese breads and yummy crab dip. They love the crap out of me."

"That's actually making me really hungry."

"So, tell me, Jarvis Henders. What is it you want to do with your life, anyway?"

"Not really sure right now. Be a meteorite hunter?"

"Turbo!"

"What about the neighbor kids who smashed my face?"

"Just don't let off any of those fear vibes and they won't bother you at all."

"Really? That's a tough one to get my mind around."

"Just think about it, okay? No pressure. Richmond's a great place to chill out and figure out what you want to do with your life."

"What do you want to do with *your* life, Evan Henders?"

"Uh—never be called 'Evan' again for one thing."

"Sorry, Shred. What else?"

"I'm already doing it."

"You mean the painting and the music and everything?"

"And the serial killing. I've really been getting into being a serial killer lately. It's so sweet."

"You're living the dream."

"I'm actually late for my eight o'clock murder. Look man, you think it over and let me know, cool? You got my number."

"All right, Shred. Thanks. I'll let you know either way."

"Awesome."

"Later."

"Later."

I hung up thinking how good it was to feel wanted for once. But that warm glow started to fade pretty quickly into the sterile beige medicine cloud that was my life. Of course I couldn't move to Richmond. It was out of the question. I just didn't have a reason as to why it was out of the question.

Thus began a game of mind tennis. Why was the idea so crazy? It was. It wasn't. Was. Wasn't. Should. Shouldn't. And what was so bad about crazy? There was good crazy and bad crazy, but I didn't know which category this idea fell under. Maybe both. Maybe neither. Did. Didn't. Shred. Evan. Jarvis. Ceeb. Death. Not death. I smelled cinnamon. Stuck my head in the freezer. Didn't really want to, it was just out of habit. Like living in Beigeburg—a bad habit. My nervous stomach was gone, but now I wanted to puke. Nerves vs. nausea. Badminton tournaments in pink sweaters vs. ultimate fighting on crystal meth. God vs. Satan. Cowboys vs. Redskins. Edgar Allen Poe vs. his grandmother. Napoleon baking cupcakes in a giant shoe house vs. Hitler singing death metal songs in a hot bubble bath.

I was pretty fucking confused.

After about three days of thinking like this, I decided to move.

And it was so easy, the whole thing flowed like butter, velvety rivulets of yes. All I had to do was arrange some crap and roll. The first thing I did was sub-let my apartment to Clint, our buddy from paint-ball. Gave him all my crappy furniture too. He was so happy to finally move out of his parent's basement he even paid the back-rent for all of August. I think his parents gave it to him, just to get him the hell out.

I couldn't wait to see Summer and smell all the exotic smells and live a different life and get my ass kicked by the rumbling of the earth. Go to thrift stores and zany rock shows and the diner. After I had embraced the decision to move, I couldn't even see why I'd had an internal debate. I'd been playing it way too safe. Now it all made perfect sense. I could smell it.

Mom and Aunt Pat were so excited about me and Shred being roommates that I could feel a golden glow of family togetherness being crammed through my cell phone ear hole. So golden that Mom sent me three hundred bucks for moving expenses. This was indeed killer.

I packed my car with as much crap as I could fit and gave everything else to Clint. The whole fresh start thing was really starting to soak in. Should I become a lawyer or a meteorite hunter? Or maybe just a normal person who has some interests. Maybe if I collect tidbits found in alleyways and gutters I'll be inspired to glue them onto a piece of board in an aesthetically composed fashion. Maybe I'll get a skull tattoo on my neck. Perhaps, in time. Baby steps.

I was all ready to go. The car was packed and full of gas, oil checked, tires full. Clint was due to move in tomorrow. Everything was on forward overdrive for busting through the beige and entering the new reality. There was just one thing I had to do before I left.

And that was to make a phone call.

"Reinhaus, Thompkins & Watts."

"Steve Reinhaus, please."

"May I ask who's calling?"

"Jarvis Henders."

"Please hold, Mr. Henderson."

"It's *Henders*."

She put me on hold. Reinhaus finally came on after forever.

"Yep," he said.

"Steve, this is Jarvis Henders."

"I'm aware of that." He had that strain of high-stress professional asshole ripping through his voice.

"Congratulations, Steve-bo. Look—your little warrant-in-debt for the *Citizen Search* bill? Need you to cancel it immediately, or I am going to start informing your clients of the illegal over-billing I witnessed while I was there."

"Are you kidding me?"

"And if that's not enough for you, I'm gonna call your wife and tell her about your schtupping Rhonda in the rolling stacks."

"What the fuck are you talking about?"

"Listen up: I'm prepared to call Voyager, Cerrano-Parkbridge, The Thorson Group, all the big clients, get me?"

"You can't do that. Are you crazy?"

"Yeah—I'm Captain Colonel Fucking Crazy-Pants and I'm calling all of them."

"You wanna got to jail, you little prick? That's illegal."

"*Jail?*"

"Yeah—jail. And I'm recording this phone call."

"A: not afraid of jail. B: you're not getting any money from me either way. And C: calling you a low-life scum sucking weasel would be an insult to weasels."

"That judgment is going on your permanent record. Good luck getting into law school."

"Well, your affair with Rhonda is going on your permanent record with your wife, you fucking fourth-class douche-wipe!"

He had hung up. What a classic, piping cold death zinger! Man—I *nailed* him! I wondered if he heard the whole thing before he hung up, though. Damn. Anyway, fine, I thought: if he doesn't let me off the hook for the dough, I'll work some extra catering shifts in Richmond and pay it back. I wasn't gonna let that jerk-off ruin my credit. Wasn't going to call his clients or wife, either. I only knew for sure that he openly flirted with Rhonda. No evidence of an affair, but flirting on your wife is still pretty trashy. As for the over-billing, I was pretty sure about that but still couldn't prove it. Anyways, I hope I scared him or ruined his lunch or something. Serves him right for firing me. Then again, getting fired from that job was one of the best things that ever happened to me. I should send him a fruit basket.

27

THE DAY I left for Richmond, birds crapped all over my windshield. It was as though they had hovered over the car and coordinated their aimed poops in a dark conspiracy to discourage my ass. Had to be a sign. A sign to give up. Or a sign to not give up. The windshield wipers just smeared it around and I strained to see through the gray smear. At least the zushing sound the car had been making wasn't as bad. The repeated pattern of trees along 95 started passing by in slow motion. I imagined a giant, more heroic version of myself skipping along the treetops in unison with the car. His name was Frank. I don't know why. Everything was going to be awesome and perfect for me and for Frank. I was ninety percent sure of this. Sure with every stitch and thread of my existence, minus that ten percent. My personal electricity was going to bust the voltmeter. Eventually, Frank disappeared. He was taking another route. I figured I'd catch up with him down there. Frank was cool.

Looking out at the slow motion trees, I had this sudden notion that if anyone could see into my deepest, most secret thoughts and feelings, they'd put me in prison. I was jealous of other perv victims. That alone could do it. Having a giant imaginary friend named Frank who's really me was probably just a misdemeanor. Protecting a perv and apologizing to him—who the fuck does that? And fantasizing about killing people, that was bad. I actually hadn't thought about killing people lately, so maybe I would get time off for good behavior. Now when I thought of Motorcar, the picture of him getting sexually assaulted by Mrs. Greenstreet was the vision I saw. Or his face as I bitch-slapped it. I recalled the stink-down I put on his limo and how the putrid aroma of victory was mine. Oh well, I vowed to just forget the whole thing about being jealous of his other victims and how it bothered me that Uncle Pie picked Shred for abuse and not me. I shrugged, in my mind. People are just fucking crazy and I guess I'm one of them. Then again, there's good crazy and there's bad crazy. My tent must have been set up somewhere in the demilitarized zone between the two and I didn't enjoy the benefit of a map. So maybe now that this whole Motorcar thing was settled I could go on another grand quest to figure out why I was fucking nuts. Of course I could simply trace it all back to what Motorcar did to me fifteen years ago, but that seemed so passé at this point. I needed something new to quest after.

I pulled into Oregon Hill at five after six. Shred said he'd be there at six, so I was psyched I had made it, bird crap and all. I was hoping Summer would be there too. Even Klavin and Farns. I wasn't expecting a welcoming party but in the back of my mind I kind of was. Hoping for it, anyway.

The gang of Hillites was spilled out into the street on the corner of Laurel and Spring. Their white tee-shirts and shaved heads seemed a familiar and normal sight. Comforting almost. I had to slow down to edge around them, but I showed no fear, so they had nothing to smell. And now they were my neighbors. Hopefully we would all peace off together. But I'd be carrying my corkscrew around with me just in case.

I parked the car and went up to the front door and it was locked. I knocked and got no answer. Where was Shred and my greeting committee? I decided to go around back and see if the kitchen door was open, but no chance. I peered in through the window and could just see through the kitchen and into the living room.

That's when I saw them.

Beer cans.

On the table.

Pabst Blue Ribbon.

Shred's brand.

A bunch of them.

No Shred here to greet me. His fucking beer cans are inside but I'm not. He wanted someone sober for a roommate, *huh?* Someone he could trust, *huh?* Now he's gonna have to trust me not to shove those beer cans down his throat. I sat down on the back steps and let out a big, nasty sigh. I couldn't live with him if he was drinking. No way. I should have known. But who was I to judge, anyway? He has the same problems I do, the poor bastard.

I decided to stay optimistic. I'd figure something out. No way I'm going back to the beige suburbs.

I had to find Summer. Tell her about the beer cans. Say hi to her. And tell her I loved her. No that would have to wait. Deep breath. I drove by her house but her car was gone. Then I went by the Ditch and then Avalon and then Second Street Diner but she wasn't in any of those places either. Where *was* she? Not with Klavin, I hope. Not with some other guy I don't know about! This wasn't going well so far. I sat at a stop light and rubbed my hands on the steering wheel. Was I being a stalker? I am *not* a stalker! But I just spent the last twenty-five minutes driving around like a mad man looking for a girl. And I stalked Carly. I stalked Motorcar. Sooner or later somebody was going to take out a damn restraining order on my ass.

Maybe I should take one out on myself.

I went back to Shred's and he still wasn't home. I sat on the front porch and looked at the weeds. It was early twilight. The yellow streetlight was flickering, trying to turn on. I felt completely insane. And now here among the crazies, the *artistes*, the freakazoids, the punk-necks, Hillites, the weirdos, I was in good company. I wondered what that perv-bag Motorcar was doing right now. I bet he wouldn't be opening his front door for anyone for a while. Maybe another one of my fellow victims will come by and serve him up a cold plate special with extra gravy. Maybe one day Motorcar will get shot, and not with a flare gun. I actually didn't want him to be killed. Living his own small, gross life was at least some form of punishment. He can get sexually assaulted by a mannequin over and over in his nightmares and that'll be hunky-dory with me.

After a while I walked over to Summer's and saw her car out front. I felt like I'd won the lottery. As I got to her door, I had a terrible thought: what if she hates my guts? What if she has a new boyfriend and he has tattoos and plays in a punk band and sculpts gargoyles out of asphalt chunks and super glue? What if I was just an out-of-town fling but now that I actually live here, I'm just a boring sack of corn meal? This was a lot of terrible thoughts. I stopped on the sidewalk. Maybe I should play it cool and just be friends with her and give this whole stalker thing a rest. Then again, all I really wanted was to take Summer and fold her up and put her in my little pocket and do a spontaneous jig of resounding triumph. The twisted maniacal joy of complete and total possession. I heard a dog bark. Its pure simplicity—a single bar from a single dog—seemed like some kind of cosmic communication: *Chill out, Jarvis. Quit thinking these heavy-ass thoughts and chillax.*

I knocked and all of the dogs barked. A sublime chorus of woofs. My knees were shivering. She opened the door.

"Jarvis!" And I got a big excited hug and kiss on the cheek. It was fucking heaven. "Are you here now? For good?"

"Yep. Just got here."

"Awesome. Well, congratulations." She shook my hand with an exaggerated enthusiasm. She didn't seem to hate me. "You wanna come in?"

"Sure."

The smell of sandalwood incense filled my brain. Everything looked the crazy same except the hamster cage was gone. *Hamsterdammit* was off the map.

"I'm getting ready to take the dogs to the river—wanna join me?"

"Yeah, um—I'm kinda waiting for Shred to show up so I can move my stuff in. I don't know if I should leave it."

"Did you bring a truck?"

"No. It all fit in my Hyundai. I left a lotta crap behind."

"I'm sure it'll be fine. We won't be gone long."

Before I knew it, we were out on the sidewalk with the dogs. It was like old times. It was like new times. I saw a couple members of the white tee-shirt crew down on the corner. I wasn't scared and I even thought about waving to them, but that might've been pushing it.

"Something I've got to tell you, Summer."

"What's that?"

"I don't know about this whole roommate thing with Shred."

"Really? What's up?"

"Well, I got here and I looked through the window and there's all these beer cans sitting around his living room. He promised me he quit drinking. I don't mean to be all uptightie whitey or whatever. If people want to drink that's totally cool. I just can't—I'm not supposed to be around all that, y'know?"

"A few of us were over there last night after the show. I didn't see him drinking at all. No—he didn't drink all night. Pretty sure of that."

"For sure?"

"Yeah—he's really trying. He's so excited to have you move down here. You mean a lot to him."

"Seriously?"

"Absolutely."

"Mmm…then where is he now?"

"I don't know."

"He was supposed to be here to meet me."

"If it doesn't work out I always know someone who's looking for a roommate."

"For real?"

"Yep."

"You always make me feel better about stuff."

I stopped walking. I wanted to kiss her, but she yelled at one of her dogs who had started chasing a kid on a bike. I started walking again and she put her hand on my shoulder. I felt a wild voltage expand through my shoulder and back. She

243

really knew how to get my personal electricity humming. Then another one of her dogs was right in between us, panting at me, so I gave up on the kiss. Too awkward. I like dogs, but this was getting stupid.

We went down behind the giant concrete columns of the Lee bridge and made our way down a steep rocky drop. It was dark and cool underneath the bridge. I saw evidence that the area served as a hobo hotel. Upside down milk crates, empty bottles of rot gut, that sort of thing. We crossed over a little dried up, defunct canal and then around to a pedestrian walk bridge that hung from underneath the big bridge. The sun was getting low and dark orange. Looking west, the James River spread out like something out of a vacation brochure, the giant rocks, the rapids, the thick green trees on its sleepy banks.

"Wow," I said.

"Yeah. It's beautiful, right?"

"This doesn't suck."

The pedestrian bridge ended on a river island called Belle Isle. Summer said it had been a Civil War prison camp for the bluecoats. I said that was wicked. We headed down a wide path that ran close to the edge of the river. The island was covered with trees and I said it was like a forest in the city. She didn't say anything. Maybe she didn't hear me. The rushing water of the rapids was louder than highway traffic at rush hour. Twice as loud. Moosie, Vertigo and Soup were in their canine glory. They had a million smells to sniff and a thousand directions to run. I couldn't believe I lived here. I felt like I was on freaking vacation. In spite of whatever was going on with my cousin, I knew I'd made the right move.

We headed back when it started getting dark. I felt so relaxed, I didn't give a shit about anything. We got back to Summer's and her dogs shuffled inside like good soldiers. She kinda held back on the porch, though, like she wasn't going to invite me in.

"I'm glad you live here now, Jarvis. Let's hang out soon."

"Yeah. Definitely."

That's when it punched me.

With a thousand fists.

The swamp stomach.

The deep center of my guts was instantly visited by sickest, most twisted nuclear winter of squirming hell nerves, a roaring car wreck at the bottom of the death lagoon otherwise known as my intestines. It was back. Full force. Worse than ever. Summer leaned in for a kiss and I jerked back. All I could think about was my bubbling, wormy death stomach. She looked way disappointed. Way.

"I'm sorry," I said. "I don't feel good all of a sudden."

"What's wrong?"

"I've got this...bad stomach condition. I thought it was cured but I guess not."

Her eyes tightened. She looked like she didn't believe me.

A hundred billion desperate thoughts started streaming through my head. *She hates me. I botched this. We should just be friends for a while first anyway. I am such a stalker. I LOVE her! She hates me. Fucking stomach! I'm not a stalker, okay?*

It was too much.

"I gotta go," I said. "See you soon, okay?"

I gave her an awkward peck on the cheek. She still seemed disappointed. Then I stood there feeling like a tub of toxic glue, out of place in the world, every world. She gave me a tiny perfunctory smile and went back inside. I turned and headed down the sidewalk. I decided I would make it up to her somehow. I'll buy her a circa 1872 leather-bound felt-lined Austrian corkscrew case decorated with little skulls. I wanted the Hillites to bash my head in with rocks, but no such luck. So I just got in my car and stared into empty space.

I sat there for about five minutes and it gradually became clear what had to be done. It was the only choice.

I headed for 7-11.

I parked and went in and poured up a big-ass 24-ounce cup of steaming hot brown joe. I carried it like a sacred chalice to my car and sat there in the parking lot, ceremoniously tearing the sip-hole from the plastic lid, the exalted steam rising up in glorious ribbons of yes, the rich hallowed aroma of the roasted bean concoction floating its way into my nostrils and whispering to me: *Welcome home, my dear sweet child.* It had been two whole weeks since I'd had any coffee or caffeine, and as the hot deliciousness reached my lips, I learned that coffee was a forgiving mistress. Even though it was shitty convenience store coffee that had been baking into a black sludge for hours—that was the motherfucking best damn cup of coffee I have ever had. I felt human again. I guess the stomach thing was nerves after all. Oh well, I thought—at least I didn't have to go without coffee now! I took another sip of roasted heaven.

"Ahhh…"

Damn, it was good.

I sat there and savored it. In spite of Shred possibly drinking again and my botching the kiss with Summer, life wasn't too damn bad overall. At least I was on an adventure. Then, at one point, I heard a familiar sound. A throaty, rumbling sound. I looked around and saw Farns's van roaring down Idlewood Avenue. I got out of the car and waved. I waved like an idiot.

"Farns!" I yelled. But he didn't see or hear me. *There goes my buddy Farns. Going to get himself into some Grade-A world class trouble. God Bless America.*

The van turned out onto Jeff Davis Highway and from that angle I could see that it wasn't Farns at all. There were no punk rock stickers on the back. It was some dude with a skinny neck. I got back in the car and laughed.

I was insane but I had this feeling that I was finally home. I felt enormously relieved for some reason. Some strange pressure that I didn't even know was there seemed to have lifted. Maybe it would happen for me and Summer but if not, we could kick it friend-style and let things happen. If they were even going to happen. I felt good about this, free to just let things flow, free in a way I had never felt before. Everything seemed so new-ish. I was finally, *finally* far away from the eggshell off-white light tan of beige. Maybe I could pick up a gig as a roadie for a band or start that meteorite hunting business. Become a genetic eyeball farmer and serve the blind. Or something completely outrageous that I hadn't even thought of yet. Life was indeed a giant tuna salad sandwich and if I wasn't ready to chow the fuck down then I didn't know who was.

Maybe after another coffee, I thought I might go back over to Summer's and give her a proper kiss. I liked that idea. I liked it a lot. What the hell, right? You only live twice.

After an extended stretch of coffee-enhanced pondering there in my parked car in the 7-11 parking lot, I got a text from Shred: *where hell r u?*

I wrote back: *right hell here. b right hell there.*

I slurped in the rest of the joe like a vacuum cleaner and realized it was time for a follow-up. It felt like someone was driving a riding mower across the bottom of my stomach but I didn't care. I was stoked for the deep caffeine super buzz, the rivulets of power and the roasted flavors gliding down the hatch one more time, turning my personal electricity flavor lamp up to screaming turbo level.

For old time's sake.
For new time's sake.
Coffee in the morning, coffee in the evening.
Coffee all the day night long.

Speaking of which, it was now indeed time for that cup number two, so I went into the store and procured she. And I came back and sat there in the car and took my time and drank her down to the fantastic brown end. Down to where the orphan chunks of nasty coffee grounds sat languishing at the bottom of the cup. It was even better than the cup before. And I held it high and I swirled the magnificent dregs around a couple of times and I threw the cup back and downed those too.

And they were good.

•

ACKNOWLEDGMENTS

Many thanks to my editor and publisher J. Boyett, whose tireless efforts turn vague possibilities into tangible realities.

I have been beyond lucky to have studied under some uniquely talented and generous authors such as Sally Doud, Marita Golden, Mary LaChapelle, Joshua Henkin, Victoria Redel, Lucy Rosenthal and Myra Goldberg, and it is with several tractor-trailer loads of gratitude that I say many sincere thanks to you all.

Sometimes when a teacher is also a game changing mentor, a special shout out is in order. Having had two such beacons in William Tester and David Hollander has been crucial to the existence of this novel and has indeed made me feel downright charmed. Thank you much, gents.

ABOUT THE AUTHOR

Rob Widdicombe was born on the Virginia banks of the Potomac River in a military hospital on a typical Wednesday. A former singer, guitar player and songwriter for Richmond-based bands The Wiggins and Flying Shovels, Widdicombe has held a variety of both day and night jobs over the years, including gas station attendant, landscaper, encyclopedia salesman, cab driver, truck driver, maintenance man, cook, dispatcher, catering captain and paralegal. He received an MFA in writing from Sarah Lawrence College and his interests include staring out the kitchen window and falling asleep on the train. COLD PLATE SPECIAL is his first novel.

ALSO FROM SALTIMBANQUE BOOKS:

I'M YOUR MAN, by F. Sykes

It's New York in the 1990's, and every week for years Fred has cruised Port Authority for hustlers, living a double life, dreaming of the one perfect boy that he can really love. When he meets Adam, he wonders if he's found that perfect boy after all ... and even though Adam proves to be very imperfect, and very real, Fred's dream is strengthened to the point that he finds it difficult to awake.

STEWART AND JEAN, by J. Boyett

A blind date between Stewart and Jean explodes into a confrontation from the past when Jean realizes that theirs is not a random meeting at all, but that Stewart is the brother of the man who once tried to rape her.

THE UNKILLABLES, by J. Boyett

Gash-Eye already thought life was hard, as the Neanderthal slave to a band of Cro-Magnons. Then zombies attacked, wiping out nearly everyone she knows and separating her from the Jaw, her half-breed son. Now she fights to keep the last remnants of her former captors alive. Meanwhile, the Jaw and his father try to survive as they maneuver the zombie-infested landscape alongside time-travelers from thirty thousand years in the future.... Destined to become a classic in the literature of Zombies vs. Cavemen.

THE LITTLE MERMAID: A HORROR STORY, by J. Boyett

Brenna has an idyllic life with her heroic, dashing, lifeguard boyfriend Mark. She knows it's only natural that other girls should have crushes on the guy. But there's something different about the young girl he's rescued, who seemed to appear in the sea out of nowhere—a young girl with strange powers, and who will stop at nothing to have Mark for herself.

BENJAMIN GOLDEN DEVILHORNS, by Doug Shields

A collection of stories set in a bizarre, almost believable universe: the lord of cockroaches breathes the same air as a genius teenage girl with a thing for criminals, a ruthless meat tycoon who hasn't figured out that secret gay affairs are best conducted out of town, and a telepathic bowling ball. Yes, the bowling ball breathes.

RICKY, by J. Boyett

Ricky's hoping to begin a new life upon his release from prison; but on his second day out, someone murders his sister. Determined to find her killer, but with no idea how to go about it, Ricky follows a dangerous path, led by clues that may only be in his mind.

BROTHEL, by J. Boyett

What to do for kicks if you live in a sleepy college town, and all you need to pass your courses is basic literacy? Well, you could keep up with all the popular TV shows. Or see how much alcohol you can drink without dying. Or spice things up with the occasional hump behind the bushes. And if that's not enough you could start a business....

THE VICTIM (AND OTHER SHORT PLAYS), by J. Boyett

In *The Victim*, April wants Grace to help her prosecute the guys who raped them years before. The only problem is, Grace doesn't remember things that way.... Also included:

A young man picks up a strange woman in a bar, only to realize she's no stranger after all;

An uptight socialite learns some outrageous truths about her family;

A sister stumbles upon her brother's bizarre sexual rite;

A first date ends in grotesque revelations;

A love potion proves all too effective;

A lesbian wedding is complicated when it turns out one bride's brother used to date the other bride.